PRAISE FOR
THE NOVELS OF THE MIST-TORN WITCHES

Witches in Red

"Terrific . . . a smooth-flowing narrative that results in re-markable readability. . . . Fantasy readers should enjoy this entertaining novel." —Bitten by Books

"Complex characters, relationships, and interesting sto-ries . . . plenty of suspense, danger, intrigue, and a bit of romance. Barb Hendee's novels are not to be missed." —SciFiChick.com

"A great page-turner." —Open Book Society

The Mist-Torn Witches

"[An] engaging fantasy novel. . . . Clues as to the sisters' magical heritage, hints of romance, threats both super-natural and human, and courtly intrigue combine for a fun fantasy mystery." —*Locus*

"A well-constructed fantasy with two likable and inter-esting main characters . . . a fun read." —A Book Obsession

"The murder mystery at the core of this book . . . will hold readers spellbound." —*RT Book Reviews*

continued . . .

"Hendee knows how to hook her readers with beautiful detailed settings." —Seeing Night Book Reviews

"Incredibly vivid . . . a must read, full of suspense, drama, and magic." —SciFiChick.com

PRAISE FOR
THE NOBLE DEAD SAGA

"A mix of *The Lord of the Rings* and *Buffy the Vampire Slayer*."
—*New York Times* bestselling author
Kevin J. Anderson

"Don't miss this exciting series of magic, mythical creatures, and incredible lore." —SciFiChick.com

"The Hendees excel at delivering action and intrigue."
—*Romantic Times* (4 stars)

"A combined fantasy masterwork that will surely stand on the highest pinnacles of literary fantasy lore."
—BookSpot Central

"A nicely nuanced tale. . . . The authors use a deft touch to keep the pacing even and set the stage for future adventures in this endlessly intriguing horror-fantasy mix."
—Monsters and Critics

"Readers who love vampire novels will appreciate the full works of Barb and J. C. Hendee, as they consistently provide some of the genre's best. . . . The audience will want to read this novel in one sitting."
—*Midwest Book Review*

WITCHES WITH THE ENEMY

A NOVEL OF THE MIST-TORN WITCHES

BARB HENDEE

A ROC BOOK

ROC
Published by the Penguin Group
Penguin Group (USA) LLC, 375 Hudson Street,
New York, New York 10014

USA | Canada | UK | Ireland | Australia | New Zealand | India | South Africa | China
penguin. com
A Penguin Random House Company

First published by Roc, an imprint of New American Library,
a division of Penguin Group (USA) LLC

First Printing, May 2015

 REGISTERED TRADEMARK — MARCA REGISTRADA

ISBN 978-0-451-47133-8

Printed in the United States of America
10 9 8 7 6 5 4 3 2 1

For my mother,
who has read every book I've published.

PROLOGUE

I was in the dining hall when Carlotta died.

Although I had done everything possible to bring about her death, my success still surprised me. Until that moment, I'd not been entirely certain my efforts would work.

There were seven people sitting around the long, solid oak table, including Prince Damek—who sat at the head with an almost civilized expression on his normally feral face. The meal was a celebration of his own impending wedding . . . with the bride's entire family in attendance.

His bride-to-be, the pretty Rochelle, sat with her eyes downcast, for all practical purposes looking the part of the sacrificial lamb.

Her mother, the Lady Helena, and her uncle, Lord Hamish, sat one on each side of her, and her elder sister, Carlotta, had been seated as far from Damek as possible. This came as no surprise—as Carlotta lacked both beauty and charm. Her coarse hair was pulled into a bun at the nape of her neck, and her tight, angry mouth always appeared pursed as if she existed in a state of perpetual judgment over everyone else.

I had no pity for her. She was the main orchestrator behind this impending wedding, and she had to die.

So far, no food had been served, only dark red wine.

Almost as if on cue, Carlotta took a sip from her goblet. I'd been hoping she would do that. Then she tried to swallow.

My eyes locked on to her in a kind of fascination.

"Is the wine to your taste?" Prince Damek asked Rochelle, as if he cared for her feelings.

I paid no mind to Rochelle's politely murmured answer and kept my attention on Carlotta's face . . . waiting.

She attempted to swallow again, and her eyes began to widen as she struggled to breathe. Triumph flooded through me.

"Are you well, my dear?" Lady Helena asked, looking more embarrassed than concerned.

Then Carlotta turned red and half stood, with one large sinewy hand grasping her throat and the other gripping the table. In all my life, I'd never felt such satisfaction, such power. I hoped she would not die too quickly. I wanted her to feel fear, to feel pain.

Her eyes bulged as several people around the table finally realized she was in genuine distress, and they jumped to their feet, moving to help her.

It would do no good.

"Is she choking?" Lord Hamish asked.

"No!" Rochelle cried. "None of us have eaten anything. She only took a sip of her wine." Her hand reached out toward her sister. "Carlotta!"

Ugly sounds came from Carlotta as her face twisted

and she fell backward. Lord Hamish caught her, and Lady Helena gasped.

Prince Damek strode toward them, and the sight of his alarm brought waves of pleasure flowing through me. He didn't care two bits of straw for the life of Carlotta, but it certainly wouldn't look well for him to have his impending bride's sister die at the dinner table.

Carlotta made one final struggle to breathe, and then she went rigid in her uncle's arms—with her eyes still bulging.

"She's dead," Lord Hamish said in stunned disbelief. He raised his gaze to Damek and then lowered it to Carlotta's wine goblet.

I fought not to smile.

CHAPTER ONE

Céline Fawe almost couldn't believe it when old Master Colby half limped through the front door of her apothecary shop, the Betony and Beech . . . again.

He'd come here every other day for the past three weeks.

"Master Colby," she said, trying to hide her mild exasperation, "I thought I told you to give the juniper elixir more time to work."

He glanced around and seemed pleased. "Your sister isn't here?"

That was obvious, but Master Colby did not care for Céline's younger sister, Amelie.

"No, she's at the market buying bread. She should be back by now. How can I help you?"

"The pain is terrible," he answered, and then lowered his voice. "And it's . . . moved." He placed his hand on his left side.

Really, he was a harmless aging man with too much

money and no family. He was short and walked with a pronounced stoop that made him appear even shorter. His hair was thick and gray, and his nose was reddened from an overfondness of strong spirits. Most of all, he was lonely for company other than his own.

At the moment, however, Céline stood behind her work counter, and she was wrist deep in goose fat—working on a salve for burns made from purple opine flowers. Her large orange cat, Oliver, sat on top of the counter, stealing a paw full of goose grease now and then when he thought she wasn't watching.

Céline was busy.

She was well aware that the front room of the shop was a welcoming and cheery place and that people did like to visit. There was the sturdy counter running half the length of the room, and the walls were lined with shelves of clay pots and jars. The wooden table was covered in a variety of accoutrements such as a pestle and mortar, brass scales, small wooden bowls, and an open box of tinder and flint. A large hearth composed the center of the south wall. A set of swinging doors in the east wall led through to a storage area and bedroom.

Master Colby gazed across the front room and over the top of the counter with a kind of pathetic hope.

"Let me wipe my hands. I'll come and look," Céline said, summoning some pity.

Gratitude washed over his face. His eyes focused on her hair, and she suppressed a sigh. She knew most men found her pretty, but in addition to working as an apothecary, she also made some of her living as a "seer," and it was necessary to look the part.

She was small and slender. She wore a red velvet gown, which fit her body snuggly, a good deal of the time.

Her overly abundant mass of dark blond hair hung in waves to the small of her back, and both she and her sister, Amelie, had inherited their mother's lavender eyes.

Until last spring, Céline and Amelie had been living in a grubby little village, running a much smaller shop, often taking skinny chickens and turnips as payment. But fate and mixed fortune had landed them in the prosperous village of Sèone, living in this fine shop, with the protection and patronage of Prince Anton of the house of Pählen.

All in all, their lives were much improved.

And yet . . . there had been a few surprises, such as patrons like Master Colby. Céline couldn't help expressing kindness for those who suffered, and more than a few people in Sèone had money to spare.

Unfortunately, a few of them had absolutely nothing better to do than visit her several times a week, to tell her about their pains and aches and troubles with various foods and difficulties sleeping. She could always be found here and had become somewhat of a target. These customers paid her well, but in several cases, she was beginning to feel as if she was being paid for her company rather than her skills as an apothecary, and she wasn't quite sure what to do about it.

Perhaps she needed to be a little less sympathetic and a little more businesslike? The prospect seemed unkind.

Master Colby shuffled closer. "And my bowels are loose," he whispered in conspiratorial tones.

Céline steeled herself. This could not continue.

Though she was now close enough to touch him, she did not.

"Did you eat cheese and drink spirits with your dinner last night?" she asked.

He blinked in surprise. Although she had counseled him on various things not to eat or drink, she'd never approached the subject so bluntly before.

"Well . . . ," he stammered, thrown off balance by her lack of pity.

On the inside, she felt awful for doing this, but it was necessary if anything was going to change. Summer was over, autumn was upon them, and Céline would need to spend a good deal of time harvesting herbs and rose petals to prepare medicinal supplies for the village for the coming winter. Soon, she'd be tending people with coughs and fevers.

Before Master Colby could continue, she said, "Your bowels can no long properly digest cheese, rich butter, and strong spirits. If you stick to vegetables, bread, and baked meat or fish, I promise you will feel better soon. If you must drink something besides water or tea, take a little wine with meals . . . perhaps just half a goblet. Continue with a few spoonfuls of the juniper oil I sent home with you—to protect your stomach."

He blinked again. "But the pain is fierce, right here." He lifted the left side of his shirt.

"Master Colby," she said, not looking down at his exposed side. "I have given you the best counsel possible. It is up to you to follow my advice. Try my suggestions for at least four days, and if you are not feeling better, come back to see me." She stepped away. "Now, if you will excuse me, I do need to finish making this ointment."

Her tone was final, and he now looked at her as if she'd somehow betrayed him. "I don't pay for advice on what I should eat," he snapped.

"Of course not. Good day." She walked to the door and opened it.

Angry—and possibly hurt—he turned and shuffled out of the shop.

Céline sighed, still feeling regretful over having treated him so coldly, but without hesitation, she closed the door and went back to work on the ointment. People tended to burn themselves far more often in the winter than in the summer—from building more fires—and she needed to be prepared.

Amelie Fawe had been returning from the market, carrying fresh bread and a sack of autumn pears. She'd almost reached her home, the Betony and Beech apothecary shop, when she saw who was entering the front door—old Master Colby—and she froze.

"Not again," she muttered, looking around for a place to hide.

She wasn't going in there until he left. Why Céline put up with some of these people was a mystery. Well . . . a few of them paid well, but it wasn't as if the sisters needed the money *that* badly.

Instead of hiding, Amelie decided to continue on down the street, sauntering as if she'd never paused. She would walk around a little while and then go back. In truth, she liked being outdoors in the colorful streets of Sèone.

But she did wish Céline would learn to be a bit more firm with some of the people who took advantage of her kindness. It seemed that no matter what, Céline could always at least pretend to be sympathetic.

How did she do it?

Amelie and Céline had depended upon each other almost entirely since they were orphaned when Céline was fifteen and Amelie was twelve. But they were nothing alike in either temperament or appearance.

They both had their mother's lavender eyes, but that was all.

Having recently observed her eighteenth birthday, Amelie was even shorter than Céline. But where Céline was slight, Amelie's build showed a hint of strength and muscle. She despised dresses and always wore breeches, a man's shirt, a canvas jacket, and boots. She'd inherited their father's straight black hair, which she'd cropped into a bob that hung almost to her shoulders. She wore a sheathed dagger on her left hip—which she knew how to use—and she kept a short sword back at the shop, but she normally didn't wear it out in the village, as there was no need.

Most people found her a bit peculiar, but she didn't care.

Last spring, she and Céline had come to live here when they proved themselves useful to Prince Anton—who ruled Castle Sèone and its six surrounding fifes. Both sisters possessed a unique "gift." Céline could read a person's future—just by touching him—and Amelie could read a person's past.

More than once, Prince Anton had leaned upon these abilities in order to search out murderers or anyone who might be a threat to his people.

However . . . late summer and early autumn had been rather quiet, offering the sisters a reprieve, and after their last adventure for Prince Anton, Amelie was glad for Céline to have a little peace. Most of the things they were asked to solve involved blood and death and madness.

Céline often needed time to recover afterward.

Swinging the bag of pears, Amelie came back around the corner and peered down the street toward the shop.

To her relief, Céline opened the front door and held it as Master Colby shuffled out.

He didn't look happy.

Still, Amelie waited until he was well out of sight before walking to the shop and heading through the front door herself. Inside, Céline was back behind her work counter with her hands in goose grease and purple opine. Oliver watched the pail of goose grease with great interest. He would do better to go and catch mice. Wasn't that his job here?

"Bought some pears," Amelie said, lifting the sack.

"Mmm?" Céline answered absently. She seemed troubled.

"What's wrong?"

"Nothing . . . I . . . Master Colby was just here again, and I had to . . ." She trailed off and shook her head. "Nothing."

Amelie frowned slightly, wondering what had happened. Maybe Céline had taken a firmer hand with the old boy after all. It was about time.

"I'll make tea. Do we still have butter?" Amelie asked. "I forgot to check before I left."

She didn't care for bread without butter.

Céline looked up from her work, but before she could answer, the front door burst open so hard that it slammed against the wall.

"And I'm telling you!" a female voice bellowed. "I never touched your hammer!"

"Then who did?" a deep voice bellowed back. "It didn't just walk off by itself!"

Amelie whirled, her mouth falling partway open at the sight of Bernard, Sèone's massive blacksmith, and his diminutive wife, Abigail, both striding into the shop.

Amelie had never seen either of them so angry, and both were well-known for their tempers.

To make matters worse, their daughter, Erin, was a good friend of Céline's—and had even given her Oliver as a gift—so Amelie felt she could not comment on what she considered Bernard and Abigail's very poor manners.

Céline, however, came around the side of the counter, wiping her hands on cloth. "What in the world is wrong?" she asked. "Abigail, if that door just damaged the wall, you're paying to have it fixed."

Amelie was surprised by her tone. Céline was indeed in a strange mood today.

"What?" Abigail nearly shouted at Céline, and then she seemed to come back to herself and glanced at the still-open door. "Oh, I'm sorry, my dear," she apologized, "but I'm in such a state." She motioned toward Bernard with one hand. "This . . . this madman is accusing me of taking his good hammer and hiding it! As if I have nothing better to do than sneak into his smithy and hide his tools just to vex him."

"She did!" Bernard cut in. His long, dark hair and beard swung as he turned to Céline. "I was out playing cards last night, and I lost a bit . . . just a bit, mind you, of coin, and she didn't want me to go in the first place. She hid my good hammer so I'd be forced to use my old one and take twice as much time for the same work. She's punishing me."

Abigail threw both hands in the air. "Do you hear him? As if I'd be so petty."

Actually . . . from what Amelie had seen of Abigail, it seemed more than possible that she could be so petty, but Amelie didn't say this.

Céline stepped closer. "Why exactly did you come to us?"

"So you can tell him I didn't take it," Abigail said, crossing her arms. "Do a reading and tell him where it is."

Céline shook her head. "Abigail . . . my gift doesn't work that way. I cannot see Bernard's hammer by looking into his future and—"

"No, not you," Bernard interrupted. "Amelie. She can read this she-devil's past and tell me where my hammer's been hidden!"

Céline's expression was growing more flummoxed by the moment—and Amelie could certainly see why. Indeed, there had never been such a scene inside the shop.

"Two silver pennies," Amelie said from where she stood near the hearth.

The room fell silent, and all three other occupants turned to look at her.

"Oh, Amelie," Céline said in some embarrassment. "I don't think we should charge Abigail and Bernard for our services."

This was another of Céline's weakness: hesitance at taking money from those she considered friends. But Amelie didn't do readings for free—or at least not for anyone but Prince Anton, who'd given them this shop.

"Of course you should be paid," Abigail said, reaching into the pocket of her apron. "I'd pay double to see this great oaf proven wrong."

"And I'd pay triple to see this harpy admit her guilt!" Bernard shouted.

"Please," Céline said, her expression shifting from flummoxed to flustered. "Lower your voices. People can hear you in the street."

Amelie had no objections to a good dispute and had

been known on occasion to raise her own voice, so she stood with her left hand out as Abigail dropped the two silver pennies into her palm.

"Who should I read?" Amelie asked.

"Her," Bernard answered instantly, "and tell me where my hammer is."

Abigail went red in the face. "Fine."

Amelie reached out and grasped Abigail's small, roughened hand and closed her eyes. She focused her thoughts first on the spark of Abigail's spirit, and then she pictured Bernard's hammer—which she had seen at the forge more than once—in her mind, holding the image firm. If Abigail had anything to show her, Amelie would soon be caught up in the mists and see a clear image of the past.

Nothing happened.

After a moment, she said, "Bernard, I'm not seeing anything."

"Then you're not looking hard enough," the blacksmith answered.

"Read him," Abigail challenged. "See if he has anything to show you."

With a shrug, Amelie walked over to Bernard and grasped one of his enormous fingers. He didn't object, but he frowned. Amelie closed her eyes and focused on the spark of his spirit and then on an image of the hammer.

The first jolt hit her almost instantly, and she braced herself.

When the second jolt hit, she experienced a now familiar sensation, as if her body were being swept along a tunnel of mist. For a moment she forgot everything but speeding backward through the mists all around her as they swirled in tones of grays and whites.

The mists vanished and an image flashed before her. She found herself standing inside a small house. Bernard was there, along with young Hugh, one of Sèone's thatchers. Amelie knew him slightly. Inside the memory, they would not see her. She was only an observer. Her body was still back in the shop.

"Oh, Bernard, those are quite fine," Hugh said. "Thank you."

Outside the window, the sun was setting as evening approached.

"Let me just make sure they're the right size," Bernard answered. He stood in front of an open doorway, lacking an actual door, and he held up a new hinged iron bracket where the back of a door would be hung. In his left hand . . . was his good hammer. "Yes, these will do nicely. Do you want me to attach them for you?"

"No, I can do that myself. But come have an ale for your trouble."

Looking pleased, Bernard leaned his hammer against the wall and went to the table to join Hugh. A moment later, both men were chatting and enjoying large cups of ale.

The room vanished, and Amelie was once again sailing through the mists, this time moving forward.

Opening her eyes, she found herself back in the apothecary shop looking up at Bernard. "Um . . . did you visit Hugh the Thatcher yesterday before you went to play cards?"

Bernard stared at her for the span of a few breaths, and then he went pale.

"I think you'll find your hammer is still at Hugh's," Amelie finished.

"Ha!" Abigail said. "I told you I didn't take it. Don't you ever go accusing me of sneaking into your smith and hiding your tools again." Her hands were firmly on her hips. "And you owe me an apology."

Bernard's face was still pale, but he managed to draw himself up to his full height and resume some semblance of dignity. "Well . . . I was mistaken this time."

"Mistaken indeed." Abigail swept past him toward the front door, glancing back over her shoulder at Amelie. "Thank you, my dear. Money well spent."

Bernard opened his mouth to say something, closed it again, and followed his wife outside.

Once the sisters were alone, Céline leaned back against the counter. "That was awkward."

"Really?" Amelie tossed the two coins in the air. "I rather enjoyed it."

Lieutenant Kirell Jaromir sat at a table in his private office inside the barracks for the guards of Castle Sèone. Corporal Luka Pavel sat directly across from him, and the two men were busy discussing possible changes in the rotation of the watch. They both wore wool shirts, chain armor, and the tan tabards of Prince Anton of the house of Pählen.

"You've had Guardsman Rurik on night duty for too long," Pavel said. "I'd change him out for Voulter."

Jaromir nodded, glad that he and Pavel had reached a stage of easy camaraderie again. Over the summer, there had been some . . . unpleasantness between them, but they'd managed to put it in the past. While Jaromir believed in unwavering discipline, he didn't care for tension on a personal level and much preferred what he thought of as "smooth sailing." It was in his nature.

For most of his life, something about him had put other people at ease.

In his early thirties, he knew he wasn't exactly hand-some, but he wore a small goatee around his mouth and kept his light brown hair tied back at the nape of his neck. From his weathered skin to the scars on his hands, most elements of his appearance gave him away as a hardened soldier, but he could live with that. After all, he was a hardened soldier. He liked to view himself as tough but fair, and he was comfortable inside his own skin.

He also held almost absolute power over the law in Sèone, second only to Prince Anton himself.

"All right," he answered Pavel. "Rotate Voulter with Rurik. And we should probably pull Sergeant Bazin off the front gate and give him another assignment. He's been down there too long as well."

Pavel had a long stick of charcoal in his right hand and a piece of paper on the table in front of him. He made a note. "Anyone else?"

"No, I think that's it." Jaromir studied the young corporal briefly.

Pavel was a younger man with cropped dark hair and a long, lanky build. He was good in a fight, able to take on two or three men at the same time, and he was steady and dependable . . . with one exception.

His behavior toward Céline Fawe.

For reasons Jaromir didn't fully understand, Corporal Pavel had become obsessed with Céline to the point of using physical strength to keep her from walking away from him, and he'd once pinned her against a tree to try to force her to speak to him.

Jaromir had put a stop to that.

He was not only fond of Céline as a friend; he had great respect for her abilities as a healer and a seer, and it was his job to protect her. Pavel had resented his interference last summer, but he seemed to have gotten over it and had stayed away from Céline.

Hopefully, the problem was gone.

Jaromir stood. His sheathed long sword was leaning against the table. He picked it up and strapped it on. Then he reached out for a set of crutches, also leaning against the table, and passed them over to Pavel.

That was another unfortunate occurrence over the summer. Pavel's horse had fallen while crossing a river. When the horse jumped back up, Pavel's foot had been in the stirrup, and his shin had snapped. Thankfully, Céline had been able to set the bone and splint the leg quickly. It was nearly healed now. The splints were off, but he still needed crutches.

Céline had assured Jaromir that within another moon or so, Pavel would be running again.

Jaromir was grateful for this even though Pavel had been managing his duties in the castle and village quite well on crutches.

"I'm going to head for the main hall and see if supper is laid out yet," Pavel said. "I'm starving."

Jaromir hid a smile. "I'll come with you."

Pavel was always starving. Where did he put all the food he ate?

Just as Pavel had both crutches positioned under his arms, the sound of trotting footsteps echoed from the passage outside, followed by a quick knock on the door.

"Sir?" someone called.

"Come," Jaromir called back.

The door opened, and Guardsman Rimoux peered in, panting and appearing somewhat unsettled.

"What's wrong?" Jaromir asked.

After a short hesitation, Rimoux answered, "Sir, there's a messenger down at the outer gate."

Puzzled, possibly annoyed, Jaromir frowned. "Well, let him in and bring him up."

Rimoux shifted his weight between his feet. "I . . . he's wearing a black tabard."

Jaromir stiffened

In this part of Droevinka, solid black tabards were worn only by soldiers who served Prince Damek, who was Prince Anton's older brother . . . and his enemy.

Not long past dusk, Céline and Amelie found themselves hurrying through the streets of the village, making their way up to the castle.

They had been summoned—via a delivered message at the shop.

"Anton's never called us this late before," Amelie said, sounding worried. "Maybe someone is ill, and he needs your skills?"

"Then why didn't he say so in his message? If that was the case, he'd have asked me to bring my box of medicines."

Amelie didn't answer her.

Céline had a bad feeling their peaceful reprieve had come to an end and that Anton was about to make another . . . request.

The two sisters pressed onward and upward through the people and the shops and the dwellings of the village as the castle loomed large above them. Finally, they reached a short bridge leading across a gap to a huge doorway at the front of the castle. Céline glanced at the pulley system on the other side that would allow the bridge to be raised, thus cutting off access to the castle—if ever necessary.

They crossed the bridge and entered the great walled courtyard. Inside, soldiers and horses came into view, and a few men nodded a greeting at the sisters, who were well-known here, as they walked past.

After crossing the courtyard, Céline and Amelie passed through a large entryway inside the castle itself. They walked down a stone passage and emerged into the great common hall. An enormous, burning hearth had been built in the wall directly across from the arched entrance. Servants and more soldiers in tan tabards were milling around. The hall seemed alive with dogs as well, spaniels, bloodhounds, and wolfhounds.

Céline looked around for either Jaromir or Prince Anton, but saw neither.

As she scanned the hall, her gaze stopped and her stomach tightened when she spotted Corporal Pavel standing near a table, leaning on his crutches, staring at her.

Immediately, she looked away.

I am safe here, she told herself.

To the right of her was a closed door—which led to a small side chamber. Céline was familiar with the interior of that chamber, as Anton often used it for private discussions, so she wasn't surprised when the door opened and Lieutenant Jaromir stepped out.

He paused in his tracks at the sight of Céline and Amelie and then motioned with his hand. They went to him.

"Good, you're here," he said, stating the obvious. His expression was tense, and Céline's trepidation began to grow.

As the delivered message had sounded urgent, simply saying, "Come at once," neither sister had bothered to change or even check her personal appearance before leaving the shop and hurrying up to the castle. Amelie's hair was uncombed, her pants were dusty, and her face was smudged with goose grease, as she'd been helping to fill small jars with the burn ointment. Normally, had she appeared for a castle audience in such a state, Jaromir would have teased her without mercy.

Céline knew the relationship between Jaromir and Amelie was . . . complicated, and he often compensated by making jokes at her expense until she grew angry and shot back a retort. This *seemed* to relieve a little tension for them both.

But now he didn't even notice the smears of goose grease.

"Come in," he said, stepping back inside the room. Perhaps he had only come out to see if they'd arrived.

Again, Céline was not surprised to see Prince Anton waiting inside. His brown eyes moved to her face, and, as always, she felt unsettled but not uncomfortable in his presence.

Approaching his mid-twenties, Anton was of medium height with a slender build. When she first came to Sèone, he'd been ill, but he was now fully recovered and his frame had filled out with tight muscles that showed through the sleeves of his shirt. His face was pale with narrow, even features, and he kept his straight brown hair tucked behind his ears.

From behind, Céline heard Jaromir close the door.

The room was small, with a single table, two chairs, and no window. Several candles glowed from the table. No one sat down.

"Something has happened?" she asked Anton.

His gaze moved from her to Amelie and back to her

again, lingering on her red velvet dress. She realized he hadn't seen it in quite some time, as she always dressed carefully before coming up to the castle, normally in silk or dyed wool.

Anton was a difficult—almost impossible—person to know, but whenever he looked at her, his expression wavered between overly guarded and lonely.

"I disturbed you at work," he said.

Goodness. She and Amelie both must look a sight for Anton to make such a comment.

"Yes, we came as soon as your message arrived."

"What's wrong?" Amelie asked him, sounding worried and impatient.

Jaromir stepped over beside Anton, but neither man spoke for a moment, and Céline's trepidation turned to anxiety.

"My lord," she said, looking at Anton, "please say something or I will imagine the worst. Has your father died without naming an heir? Is the village somehow at risk?"

Her words startled him, and a flash of guilt crossed his face. "No ... forgive me. It's nothing like that." There was a sheet of paper on the table, and he picked it up. "I've had a letter ... from my brother."

"Damek?" Amelie asked in alarm. "Why would he be writing to you?"

Jaromir cast a look of warning her way—as he often felt that she didn't show Anton proper respect.

However, Anton didn't appear to notice Amelie's lack of manners, and he walked closer, holding out the letter. "It seems our father has arranged a marriage for Damek to a young noblewoman from the line of Quillette on her father's side, but whose mother is sister to Prince Rodêk's mother."

Céline went still at this news.

Droevinka had no hereditary king. Instead, it was a land of many princes, each one heading his own noble house and overseeing multiple fiefdoms. But ... they all served a single grand prince, and a new grand prince was elected every nine years by the gathered heads of the noble houses. At present, Prince Rodêk of the house of Äntes was in rule.

"A marriage for Damek?" Céline repeated. "To a first cousin of Prince Rodêk."

Her mind raced over the ramifications of this. Within two years, a new grand prince would be voted in.

Anton and Damek were sons of the house of Pählen. Their father, Prince Lieven, controlled a large province in the western region. He'd given Damek, who was the elder brother, a castle and seven large fiefs to oversee. He'd given Anton a better castle but six smaller fiefs. These assignments were a chance for each young man to prove himself. But Prince Lieven had been aging rapidly in recent days, and it was rumored he would soon be naming a successor as leader of the house of Pählen. It was his right to choose between his sons, and should a victor be chosen within the next two years, then he would have the right to place his name on the voting list for the position of grand prince.

Both brothers wanted this honor.

The ugly result was that it pitted them against each other—and Damek had proven himself not above at- tempted assassination.

"What does this mean?" Amelie broke in. "That your father is preferring Damek to you?"

"I don't know," Anton responded. "I think it's more likely that my father is trying to shore up our family's funds and connections. Though Prince Rodêk's mother comes from a noble family, it's not a royal one . . . but they are very wealthy. Via her marriage, she's been part of the royal family for many years, and so this new bride, her niece, brings both royal connections and money."

"And you're worried?" Amelie asked, less alarmed now, but clearly puzzled.

"No, I have no interest in whomever Damek marries." He held out the letter. "But something . . . unfortunate has happened, and Damek has asked for my help."

"Your help?" Amelie asked, incredulous.

Indeed, Céline could hardly believe she'd heard correctly herself, and Jaromir's expression darkened until her anxiety began to grow again.

"Yes," Anton continued, with his eyes focused on the wall now. "The bride's name is Rochelle Quillette. Damek invited her and her entire family to Castle Kimovesk for an extended visit . . . I'm still not certain why. It's possible they requested it before approving the marriage. Several nights ago, at a small banquet in the dining hall, Rochelle's elder sister, Carlotta, took a sip of wine at the table and then died, apparently murdered by something in her goblet."

"Murdered?" Céline gasped.

"Of course Rochelle's family immediately began packing to leave," he continued. "Damek stopped them by promising he would root out whoever was responsible and see the killer executed. For now, he's convinced them to stay, but the betrothal is in jeopardy." Anton paused. "Damek knows something of you and Amelie, or at least that I have two seers at my court who have been solving such difficulties for me. He requests your assistance."

"Us . . . go to Castle Kimovesk?" Céline tried to absorb this. "My lord, you can't mean it."

She and Amelie had grown up in the village of Shetâna under Damek's rule. They both knew the extent of his savagery.

Anton's eyes flew to her face. "I would never ask you to *go* to that place on your own. I will take you myself."

"It's a trap," Amelie stated. "He's just trying to lure you out of here."

"Possibly," Anton agreed, "but I can't refuse."

Moving even closer to Céline, he showed her the letter and pointed to the last line.

> *Our father is anxious that this marriage should take place.*

Céline fought not to wince as she read those words. Once again, the wishes of Anton's father would rule the outcome of a dilemma. Anton couldn't refuse to assist in anything his father requested, even if it meant placing himself under the power of his brother.

She looked at Amelie. "We have to go."

Amelie breathed out through her nose and paced across the room. "At least we know it could be a trap." She glanced at Jaromir. "And there's no one better at security than you. I assume you've already begun to choose a contingent from your men?"

The open compliment surprised Céline. Amelie might think well of Jaromir—very well—but she never said it.

The lieutenant nodded. "Yes, of course, and I was thinking I might take—"

"Jaromir?" Anton said, shaking his head. "No, you're

not coming with us. You're staying to guard the castle and the village."

Whirling on one foot, Jaromir stared at Anton.

Amelie froze at Jaromir's expression as she tried to take in what Anton saying.

"My lord!" Jaromir exploded. "You cannot walk into Castle Kimovesk alone!"

Céline dropped her gaze. Jaromir never openly disagreed with Anton. Never.

Amelie, however, did not drop her gaze, and instead, she watched Anton's face tighten in anger. He was a good prince, a fair one, but he ruled here, and he was accustomed to being obeyed.

Jaromir suddenly remembered himself and put one hand to his forehead in agitation. "Forgive me," he breathed. "But you know I'm right. My place is at your side."

Anton's face softened. "As we have all agreed that this could be a trap set for me, it could just as easily be a ploy to lure us both away from Sèone. I would put nothing past my brother." He motioned to the sword strapped to Jaromir's side. "And you often forget that I am nearly as skilled with a blade as you. I can protect Céline and Amelie."

"And who will protect you?" Céline asked. "If Jaromir is not to go, then who will lead your contingent and act as bodyguard?"

Everyone fell silent for a moment, as if this was a difficult question—which it was. Most princes of the noble houses had captains and lieutenants to spare. Because of the odd history of the creation of Castle Sèone's current forces, Jaromir, as a lieutenant, was the highest-ranking officer, and for reasons he would not explain to Amelie, he refused to let Anton promote him to captain. This did not mean he was viewed as weak. The princes of the other houses respected—even feared—Jaromir, but it *did* make the state of affairs unusual.

"Who is your most trusted second?" Anton asked Jaromir.

"Corporal Pavel." Jaromir glanced at Céline, who had gone still, and he rushed to add, "But he's recovering from a broken leg and cannot yet ride."

Amelie felt a rush of gratitude toward Jaromir. Injured leg or not, Pavel could not be chosen to lead their contingent.

"What about Guardsman Rurik?" Céline suggested. "I found him most reliable on our last journey."

"Guardsman?" Jaromir echoed. "*Guardsman* Rurik?"

"You object to the man's low rank?" Anton asked.

"Of course I do," Jaromir sputtered.

"He is both even-tempered and brave," Céline went on. "Up in Ryazan, when we faced those wolf-beasts, he rushed one of them with nothing but a spear and impaled it."

"Truly?" Anton said, and then turned to Jaromir. "Promote him, and then you handpick the rest of our contingent. This is a family visit, so I don't want a large show of force. Choose twenty men." He turned back to Céline. "We leave tomorrow. I want you and Amelie to sleep in a room here at the castle tonight. We have preparations to make. If you need anything from home, give Jaromir a list, and he'll have it brought up."

He did not bother to address Amelie, but she didn't care. She cast a quick look at Jaromir, who almost appeared to be in pain. He met her gaze, and she'd never seen him so exposed, so helpless. He hated this.

Still, Prince Anton had spoken.

Jaromir would remain behind, while Céline and Amelie and the prince would ride into Kimovesk . . . to solve another murder.

CHAPTER TWO

Not long after, Céline and Amelie followed a familiar route into the stairwell of the north tower of the castle. At the third landing, they stepped off and made their way down a passage to the room they always shared when staying here—which was not often.

Upon opening the door, Céline looked in to see the room readied and pristine as if they'd been expected.

The four-poster mahogany bed had been made up and covered in a sunflower yellow quilt. Interior shutters over the long window were open, letting misty light filter inside.

A full-length mirror with a pewter frame stood in one corner and a mahogany wardrobe stood in the other. Dainty damask-covered chairs had been placed in front of a dressing table that sported a porcelain washbasin. A three-tiered dressing screen offered privacy for changing clothes. Best of all, the room contained its own small hearth.

Céline went to the window and looked down. They were on the inner side of the tower and had a view of the courtyard below.

She turned back to watch Amelie enter and close the door. The sisters were alone.

Amelie's face was as tense as Céline felt inside, but Céline had no idea what to say.

"I know . . . ," Amelie began slowly. "I know we owe Anton our lives and our livelihood. I know we agreed to use our abilities whenever he called us, but this is different."

Céline couldn't argue.

Last spring, Anton had saved their lives. The problem was that he'd saved them from Prince Damek. The sisters had never actually met Damek, but he ruled over Shetâna Village, and they had gone against his wishes once, and he ordered their shop to be burned and for them to be put to death.

Anton had given them refuge.

"I don't see how we can refuse," Céline said.

"So no matter what he asks, we're obligated to do it? I'm grateful for everything he's done, but shouldn't there be a limit on gratitude? I think him asking us to walk into Prince Damek's castle crosses a line." Amelie glanced away. "The price for safety and comfort here might be growing too high."

In part, Céline agreed, but this situation was not of Anton's making. Kimovesk was the last place he'd wish to go as well. And more . . . Céline liked her life here. She had no desire to live anywhere else. For her, the price for remaining in Sèone might never be too high.

She didn't say this aloud.

Instead, she sat down at the dressing table and opened a drawer that she knew contained paper, ink, and a quill. She wrote two notes, and just as she finished the second one, the bedroom door banged open and another familiar face came in, belonging to old Helga. She carried an armload of wool gowns, white cotton shifts, and fine cloaks.

"Good gods," she exclaimed, shifting the burdens in her arms. "His Lord Majesty Lieutenant is in a mood! Nearly chewed my ear off, he did."

Céline stood up. "Oh, I am sorry. I'd have sent you a warning if I could."

"Can't blame him, I can't," Helga babbled on as if Céline hadn't spoken. "Don't know what that fool of a prince thinks he's doing, hauling you girls off on his own."

Even Amelie appeared shocked at the old woman's use of "fool" in reference to Anton, but Helga was . . . unusual.

Though quick on her feet, she was at least in her seventies, with thick white hair up in a bun that was partially covered by an orange kerchief—nearly always askew. Her wrinkled face had a dusky tone, and she wore a faded homespun dress that might once have been purple.

Though she was officially a servant here in the castle, Céline had long suspected she was more. For one, everyone else treated Jaromir with deference and respect—even fear on occasion—but Helga often referred to him sarcastically as "His Lord Majesty Lieutenant" and had a tendency to boss him around . . . and for some reason, he let her.

Even more, Helga had been responsible for helping Céline and Amelie understand at least the roots of who they were and where their mother had come from: the Móndyalítko or "the world's little children," traveling gypsies.

Before arriving in Sèone, Céline and Amelie had known little of their origins.

Their father had been a village hunter for Shetâna, and one year, he'd been off on a long-distance hunt, traveling for days. He'd come back with their mother and married her. Then the couple had built an apothecary shop in Shetâna and started a small family. Once Céline and Amelie were old enough, their mother taught them to read. She taught Céline herb lore and the ways of healing—while saying nothing of her own past.

Neither of the sisters had ever heard the term "Mist-Torn," before Helga explained it to them, that they were not only born of a Móndyalítko mother, but were of a special line called the Mist-Torn, who each possessed a natural power. As sisters, Céline and Amelie were two sides of the same coin, one able to read the future and one able to read the past.

The full comprehension of this knowledge had changed their lives.

At the moment, however, Amelie was looking warily at the gowns in Helga's arms.

"What are those for?" she asked.

"For you, girlie," Helga grunted, dropping her entire armload on the bed. "Prince's orders . . . through His Lord Majesty Lieutenant. If you're going to Prince Damek's castle to meet some hoity-toity noble family, you've got to play at being women of court again. I've got brushed wool dresses here for the journey and at least eight dinner gowns packed."

Céline closed her eyes briefly, opened them again, and tried not to groan at what was coming. On their last mission for Anton, for their own safety, they'd had to pretend to be highborn ladies . . . which meant Amelie had to forgo her pants and wear dresses the entire time.

Beforehand, she'd put up quite a fight.

"Oh, I am not!" Amelie squared off with Helga. "Not again."

Céline was well aware that Amelie was fast approaching her breaking point, first being asked to put herself in close reach of Damek, and now being told she'd have to wear skirts again.

"Amelie," Céline began, "as before, I'm sure Anton is only doing this for our safety. Damek's soldiers would never abuse women of Anton's court, and . . . if we're to investigate Rochelle's family, we must be seen as near equals."

"I don't care!" Amelie exploded. "And I can protect us better as myself. If I was dressed as myself, I could wear my sword and my dagger openly. Didn't I always protect us in Shetâna?" She paused and drew a deep breath. "It won't work anyway. Captain Kochè knows us too well. He'll recognize us on sight and give us away."

This thought had occurred to Céline as well, but she hadn't mentioned it. Captain Kochè was Prince Damek's chief bullyboy and tax collector—and he was the one who had burned their old shop. He knew they'd both grown up as peasants scraping out a living via Céline's herbal medicines and her ruse of playing the "seer" before her true powers manifested.

"Don't matter," Helga said, straightening a blue wool dress on the bed. "Anton's orders. He may be a fool for leaving Jaromir behind, but he's always got a plan or two in his back pocket. If he wants you dressed as women of court, then that's how you're going." She looked up and smiled. "Oh, and I'm going, too. I'm to be your maid."

Amelie froze. "What?"

"Yup. Can't have two ladies dressing for dinner at Damek's table without a lady's maid."

"Oh, this is just . . ." Amelie ran a hand over her face. She glanced toward the door. "Céline, I need some air."

Without waiting for an answer, she strode out, leaving Céline staring after her.

Then Céline took a few steps to follow.

"Leave her be," Helga said, and when Céline turned back, she could see genuine pity on the old woman's face. "Poor mite. This isn't going to be easy on any of you. Let her have a few minutes tonight."

Céline sighed. Perhaps that was best. "I'm glad you're coming with us," she said, and she was.

Helga nodded. "Jaromir said you might need some things from home?"

"I do." Céline walked to the dressing table and picked up both notes, handing one over for Helga to read. "The main thing is this first item, my box of medicinal supplies. Make sure that gets packed. I'd also like my own lavender wool gown brought up tonight, if possible." The second note was folded in half. "Then have this message run down to Erin, the blacksmith's daughter. She's always kind enough to look after Oliver when I'm called away, and she knows how to care for him."

For the most part, Oliver could take care of himself. Céline always left one window open at the back of the shop so that he could go out to hunt as he pleased. But it was important to her that he know he'd not been abandoned, and Erin was good about going to the shop every day to leave him bowls of fresh water and milk — and pet him if he wished for attention.

"Easy enough," Helga said, and looked toward the door. "You're handling this a lot better than your sister, the prospect of walking into Damek's territory, I mean."

Was she handling it better? Perhaps she was, but she didn't like to admit why. In the back of her mind, she couldn't stop thinking that this time . . . this time Anton wasn't sending them off to do a service for him.

This time, he would be riding at their side.

After leaving the bedroom, Amelie stood out in the passage, trying to breathe evenly for a few moments, wondering where she should even go. She needed time to herself.

Everyone else, including Céline, seemed to be simply *accepting* whatever Anton ordered here. Amelie felt as if she'd been dropped into a river and was now being carried along on a current she couldn't fight.

Of course she couldn't refuse to go to Kimovesk. That wouldn't keep Céline from going, and Amelie had no intention of letting Céline go with no one but Anton, Rurik, and a few guards for protection. Yet the prospect of putting herself and her sister in the hands of Damek seemed too much.

Too much.

She looked down the passage toward the stairs and considered going for a walk in the courtyard. But that would mean greeting some of Sèone's soldiers and probably being invited to join card games. Tonight, she had no wish for company.

Instead, she turned, walked to the other end of the passage, and entered a stairwell leading up.

The stairwell wound in a few circles, and it was darker than she remembered, as she'd never gone up here at night. But soon enough, she saw dim light at the top and she stepped out into a much wider passage, almost a hall. There were tall, narrow windows to her left—possibly slots for archers—and some light from the great braziers out in the courtyard came through.

Amelie now occupied an almost-forgotten portrait hall. She and Céline had learned of its existence during their first stay at the castle.

The wall to her right was covered in enormous portraits, some larger than herself, in ornate frames wider than her hand.

Even in the dim light, she could see that dusty spiderwebs covered the ceiling and some of the paintings. A few corners of the frames had teeth marks, as if rats had chewed on them.

None of the servants ever visited this hall.

Walking slowly, she looked up at the first portrait. The background was dark, but it depicted a proud-looking middle-aged man with a close-trimmed silver beard. He wore a sword on his hip and had a cream-colored dog standing at his side.

Amelie did not continue to view the paintings. She was in no mood tonight. This place offered her some much-needed solitude and that was all. Walking a short ways in, she sat down and leaned up against the wall with her knees to her chest.

Tomorrow, she would have to put on a dress and climb into a sidesaddle and leave Sèone on another dangerous task for Anton.

"Amelie," a deep voice said.

Jumping slightly, she whipped her head back toward the stairs to see a tall, familiar outline: Jaromir. He stepped into full view. Though she'd wanted to be alone, his was probably the only company she could stand right now. He looked as miserable as she felt.

"How did you know I'd be here?" she asked.

After walking over, he crouched down. He had a small, wrapped bundle in his hands. "Céline said you'd gone out for air. I went to the courtyard first, and this was the only other place I could think to look." He glanced around. "You and I . . . we've both come here before."

Yes, they had.

"Anton's wrong," she said bluntly. "Leaving you here."

"It's his decision."

He said no more on that subject.

Amelie should have known that was the closest he would ever get to criticizing Anton. Jaromir was fiercely loyal to his prince. He would kill for Anton . . . had killed for Anton. Amelie had once seen a body lying at her own feet.

This situation must be torture for him.

But when she met his eyes, she saw a different kind of fear. He stared at her in open worry. He feared for her.

She'd stopped trying to deny the connection, the fire, between herself and him, but anything beyond their current friendship was impossible. Jaromir would not allow himself to love any woman. He was married to his job.

He also had a long series of women in his past—and he was well-known for having a "type." That type was certainly not Amelie.

His last mistress had been a lovely, haughty, wealthy young woman named Bridgette. Amelie had learned through the other soldiers that Bridgette was never allowed to visit Jaromir's apartments until she was sent for—which was always the arrangement with Jaromir's mistresses. For about six months, Bridgette had slept in his bed whenever he sent for her, and when he got tired of her, he'd cast her aside like baggage and never once looked back.

Amelie was not about to become another one of his obedient mistresses until he got bored with her.

And yet right now he seemed almost ill with worry.

"I can't stand the thought of you in Damek's castle without me," he said, lowering the cloth bundle to the floor and opening it. "All I can do is try to protect you from a distance."

Inside the cloth lay two sheaths with protruding hilts. Both were small, with leather ties. One sheath was slightly wider than the other.

"Even in a dress, I keep my own dagger in my boot," she said.

"I know you do, but these can be hidden inside the sleeves of a gown and can be drawn much faster." He picked up the slightly wider sheath and drew the blade. Silver metal glinted in the light from the braziers coming through the windows. "This is razor-sharp. Strap it to your left wrist so you can pull it with your right hand."

Wordlessly, she took it from him, and he picked up the other sheath, but he didn't draw the blade.

"Strap this to your other wrist, but don't pull it unless you intend to kill," he said, "and don't tell anyone you have it, not even Céline. It's a stiletto . . . and the blade is poisoned, so whatever you do, don't scratch yourself. If you even nick someone with this, he'll be dead in moments."

"Poisoned?"

That wasn't like Jaromir.

As if reading her thoughts, he said, "No one inside Castle Kimovesk cares about honor or anything besides themselves. You have to think like them. Now strap those on and don't hesitate to use either."

Her eyes lifted to his face. On their last journey, she'd bristled against his arrogance and his penchant for giving orders, but now . . . and it hit her that tomorrow, he wasn't going with them.

"Oh, Jaromir," she whispered.

He looked away. "I know."

The next morning, Anton stood in the courtyard. He was dressed simply, in dark pants, a wool shirt, and riding boots, but he also wore a heavy cloak over his shoulders and a sword on his hip. The gray sky above him drizzled with a slow rain, as was typical in autumn, but he left his hood down and allowed the drops to soak into his hair.

Activity buzzed all around him.

Twenty-four horses had been saddled and two more were harnessed to a wagon of luggage and supplies. Twenty guards, along with the newly promoted Corporal Rurik, were almost ready to leave. Jaromir walked around giving orders and making certain the wagon bed was properly covered.

Corporal Rurik still appeared somewhat stunned at having been given this assignment, but he was busy checking saddles and talking to the men. Anton watched him for a moment. Rurik had a wiry build and curly light brown hair he wore to the tops of his shoulders. He was known as the swiftest rider in Sèone, and until recently, he had served in the position of messenger between Anton and his father.

Last summer, it was discovered he'd been providing Prince Lieven with more information than simple dispatches, and under normal circumstances, this would have resulted in his dismissal from the guards, or worse. But apparently, Rurik had been attempting to bolster Prince Lieven's opinion of Anton by sharing news of his successes as a leader—which Anton had not authorized him to share. Still . . . Jaromir was convinced of Rurik's innocence of anything other than overzealous loyalty. Jaromir had assigned a new messenger, but kept Rurik in the guards.

For Anton, this was good enough. Jaromir was the most suspicious man he knew, and if he trusted Rurik, then so did Anton. In addition, Céline had suggested that Rurik head up the guards for this journey, and Anton had come to rely on her judgment when it came to people.

Once the wagon was tied down, Jaromir strode toward Anton but wouldn't meet his eyes.

"All is ready, my lord," he said, his face drawn. "Céline and Amelie should be down directly."

"Good," Anton answered.

He longed to tell Jaromir that he hated this arrangement as well, and that a part of him knew it was foolish to go to Kimovesk without his lieutenant. Jaromir was much more than a bodyguard and the leader of Sèone's soldiers. He was Anton's best friend . . . his only friend really.

No matter how quick-witted Jaromir might be, he did *not* understand Damek. How could he? Only someone who had grown up with Damek could possibly comprehend how his twisted mind worked. The letter he'd sent had been almost brotherly, with a hint of warmth, pleading for Anton's help.

When Damek showed a hint of warmth, he was at his most dangerous.

One of Anton's most vivid memories came from a boyhood experience when their father had bought each brother a fine spaniel puppy so they might train the dogs to hunt birds. As a lonely child, Anton had loved his dog excessively and named him Arrow because he ran so straight. He slept with Arrow and spent many hours training him. As a result, his dog became a much better hunter than the dog given to Damek, and one day, their father commented on this.

That night, Damek came to Anton's room to praise Arrow and give the dog a treat of raw chunks of beef. Damek's rare display of brotherly warmth made Anton happy. A few hours later, Arrow began to whine in pain. He died before morning, poisoned.

This wasn't the first or last time Damek managed to leave Anton rocking in sorrow, but it was one of the most painful experiences in Anton's memory.

Jaromir had to remain here to protect Sèone.

Right now Damek could be plotting anything. He could be setting a trap for Anton. He could be attempting to lure both Anton and Jaromir away at the same time. He could truly need help catching a murderer. He could be up to something completely different. There was no way to know.

But Anton's father wanted this impending marriage to take place, and even Damek wouldn't lie about that— for fear such a ploy might get back to Prince Lieven. So Anton couldn't refuse to help. That meant he had to anticipate as many outcomes as possible and plan accordingly.

Still, a prince of Droevinka did not explain his decisions, not even to someone as close as Jaromir. He needed to maintain absolute authority at all times. Anton's father had taught him that, and in his heart, he knew it to be right.

"Here come the sisters and Helga," Jaromir said, looking toward the doors of the castle.

Anton turned. Céline was walking toward him across the courtyard. With her hood up, he couldn't see her hair, only her pretty face. Even in a thick cloak, she looked so small to him, so fragile. Yet she was one of the bravest women he'd ever known. She seemed brave to him because she always faced the things she feared. He admired this.

He admired her.

Amelie and Helga came behind her, both covered in cloaks as well. Those two left him more ill at ease. Amelie struck him as more fierce than brave, and she had no understanding of how her coarse behavior affected other people. She would have to be watched closely on this trip.

Helga . . . well, Anton had no idea why Jaromir put such stock in the old woman. She struck Anton as half-mad, but Jaromir had nearly insisted that she accompany the sisters, and this was at least something to which Anton could agree.

Céline came up to him and then looked over to the readied wagon and horses. "Are we late, my lord?" When she turned back, her eyes moved to his wet hair, but she did not suggest he draw up his hood.

"Not at all," he answered.

Jaromir studied Amelie for a moment, and then he strode over to Corporal Rurik, leaned down, and began speaking in a voice so low it could not be heard. Rurik flinched and his eyes widened.

"Poor Rurik," Amelie said. "Jaromir must be threatening with everything from beheading to being burned alive if anything should happen to us."

She was probably right.

Anton turned his attention to other matters. "I've arranged for the same horses you rode on your last journey," he said to Céline and Amelie. "I trust they proved satisfactory?"

He'd handpicked both horses before, a quick-footed black gelding for Amelie, and a gentle gray mare named Sable for Céline.

"Oh yes," Céline answered quickly. "I grew fond of Sable."

"And what will I be riding, my lord?" Helga asked, both hands on her hips.

"I thought you might prefer to ride up on the wagon bench with Sergeant Bazin," he answered stiffly. It felt awkward to be conversing like this with an aging servant. "If that is acceptable."

Helga snorted and started toward the wagon. "Of course it's acceptable," she called over her shoulder. "And don't you take that tone with me. I'm old enough to be your grandmother."

Watching her walk away, Anton wondered if there was still time to change his mind about her inclusion.

Jaromir came back leading the small black gelding. "Hop up," he said to Amelie. "I'll hold him." He sounded miserable.

For once, Amelie didn't fire back some retort at being ordered about, and she climbed up into the sidesaddle. Anton reached out for Sable, who had been standing close by, and he helped Céline settle into her saddle as well.

All around them, men were mounting their horses, and Sergeant Bazin was up on the wagon bench, reins in his hand, with Helga beside him.

Feeling even more awkward, Anton turned to Jaromir. "I hope not to be away long. Perhaps the sisters will solve this quickly." He paused, not certain what else to say. "I'll send messages and keep you informed."

Jaromir nodded but didn't speak.

With nothing left to say or do, Anton grasped the reins of his own horse—a tall bay stallion named Whisper because of his low, almost inaudible whinny. Anton swung up. "Lead us out, Corporal Rurik."

With a nod, the young corporal urged his own mount toward the exit from the courtyard. The entire contingent followed. Anton rode directly behind Céline and Amelie, and he could feel Jaromir's eyes watching.

Even so, he didn't look back.

CHAPTER THREE

Droevinka was a land of dense, wet forests. Moss hung down from the trees, fungus grew outward from their trunks, and the damp air was often laden with the scent of loam. The dirt roads grew muddy when it rained.

Céline kept her hood up for most of the morning as she rode beside Amelie, traveling north on a road barely wide enough for two horses. The supply wagon rolled ahead of them, and Anton rode directly behind. But this small group was rather boxed in by soldiers, as Rurik led the contingent with ten men at the front, and he'd ordered the other ten to bring up the rear.

The house of Pählen controlled a good deal of the southwest provinces. Sèone was in the southernmost sector of their lands. Kimovesk was to the north and slightly west, almost to the border between Droevinka and Belaski.

The morning passed quietly, as no one seemed inclined to speak much ... with the possible exception of Helga, who sometimes barked criticisms at poor Sergeant Bazin regarding her opinions of his driving skills. He accepted this with a hard-set jaw and fairly good grace.

Near midday, the drizzling rain stopped, and Céline pushed her hood back, looking up at the gray skies above. She was cold and damp and her back hurt from having ridden for several hours straight now, but she'd known this was coming and didn't complain.

The narrow road they traveled emptied into a much wider one, and Rurik turned west. He appeared to know where he was going, so Céline asked no questions. Though she'd grown up in this country, she'd never traveled until last spring and was embarrassed by her lack of knowledge of Droevinkan geography.

Slightly quickened hoofbeats sounded behind her, and she looked back to see Anton positioning his horse between hers and Amelie's. Céline drew Sable to the left to make room for him, and his mount, Whisper, trotted up in between them before slowing to a walk again. On this wider road, three riders could easily travel side by side. Water dripped from Anton's hair, running down his cloak. He didn't seem to notice.

"How long to Kimovesk?" Céline asked.

"A day and a half," Anton answered.

Amelie turned to look at him. "Jaromir took us from Shetâna to Sèone in a single night."

Anton nodded. "Yes, but Shetâna is closer ... and from what I understand, Jaromir took a shortcut through the forests that night. We'll stick to the roads and spend tonight in a town called Rékausi. We should reach Kimovesk by midday tomorrow."

Céline couldn't help wondering what "spend tonight in a town" meant. Would some of the local people put them up? On their last journey, with Jaromir, they'd made camp every night and slept outdoors among the trees.

Anton's expression was troubled, though, as if he

wished to speak of other matters, so she asked him no more questions and simply waited.

"Do you feel up to speaking of the task ahead of us?" he finally asked.

This was a polite formality, as it would probably never occur to him they might refuse, but even tired and damp, Céline had no wish to refuse. She wondered what he was about to say.

He remained quiet for a long moment.

"I won't be able to pass you off as nobles this time," he finally began. "The Lady Helena, who is the bride-to-be's mother, knows every noble family in Droevinka, at least by reputation. So I'm going to say you are the daughters of a wealthy wool merchant, Miss Céline and Miss Amelie. Helena will respect that. She married a baron who was also a merchant."

Céline found the title of "Miss" to be wisely ambiguous. The wives of wealthy merchants were often called "Mistress," and daughters were called "Miss." This distinguished them as somewhere above the common peasants and yet beneath the nobility.

Amelie exhaled loudly through her nose. "I don't see the need for this ruse at all. Why can't you just tell them we're your seers, we're there to do a job for you, and they need to let us start reading them?"

He shook his head. "That won't work. You don't know what most nobles are like. They need to agree . . . to almost believe that your reading of them was their own idea."

"Well, some of Damek's soldiers, the ones who worked in Shetâna, will give us away on sight," Amelie pressed.

"You let me handle that," he answered, almost dismissively, as if the issue was not worth discussing. "But *you* need to know more about the family with whom you'll be dealing."

Céline turned her head. "Have you met them?"

"Some of them." He paused again as if wondering where to start this next part of the conversation. "Prince Rodêk's father fell in love with a woman somewhat beneath himself, the Lady Clarisse, and he married her. Her family was titled but not royal. But back then, the house of Äntes didn't enjoy the power it does now, so the marriage gained little attention and neither did the birth of Rodêk. It was Rodêk who later increased the influence of the Äntes, and when his father died, he was named leader of the house, and then he was voted in as grand prince. So the status of his mother and thereby his mother's family rose substantially. Do you follow me?"

Céline blinked. "Of course."

"Long before Rodêk was elected grand prince, his mother's sister, the Lady Helena, married a minor Baron, Alexis Quillette, who was also a wealthy wine merchant. They had four children. Carlotta came first, then a set of twins, Heath and Rochelle, and then a younger daughter, Lizbeth. Heath is the only son. Two years ago, the baron died, and Heath took his title and took over the business, but Helena's brother, Lord Hamish, came to live with them, and from what I've heard, he's taken charge of the family. Their fortunes have only continued to increase."

"How do you know so much about them?"

"It's part of my duty as a prince of Pählen to know as much as possible about the other houses . . . especially anyone connected to the house of Äntes." He hesitated again. "And I've met the Lady Helena and Carlotta. They attended a gathering of the royal houses in Kéonsk when I was a youth and—"

"You've met the murder victim?" Amelie cut in.

Anton frowned ever so slightly at the interruption. "Yes, but I don't remember her well. I'm telling you this so you'll have a better idea what to expect. These people were not born with royal connections. They were elevated via marriage. That means they will be constantly defensive of their status, to the point of being insulting. Just be prepared. Also, you can see why this impending marriage of Damek's is so important to my father?"

Céline nodded. "In addition to allying your house with the house of Äntes, Rochelle's dowry must be large."

"Yes, it must be." Anton almost sounded bitter.

"So . . . ," Amelie said. "We're helping to elevate both the treasure chest and the political status of Damek?"

Céline threw her a warning glance. There was no need to state the obvious. Anton was well aware what they'd been asked to do.

"There is one more thing," Anton said, shifting uncomfortably in his saddle. "While you are in Kimovesk, you must be mindful of your manners inside Damek's court. You'll need to show him proper respect at all times."

He kept his eyes forward, but Céline knew this short speech was intended for Amelie's benefit and not hers. Amelie's face darkened, and she seemed on the verge of spitting out something unpleasant when Anton rushed on.

"I say this for your safety. Damek will brook nothing but deference that borders on the sycophantic from anyone he considers beneath him—which is almost everyone. I've seen him cut down servants he found insolent."

The anger faded from Amelie's face. Céline wondered if her sister knew the word "sycophantic," but it didn't matter. Anton's meaning had been clear.

All three fell silent, and they listened to the clop of their horses' hooves.

As Céline mulled over everything Anton had told them, she hoped Amelie would take his words to heart.

At midday, they stopped briefly for a short rest, but by then, although Céline was desperate to get off her horse, she felt almost too sore to climb down—and she knew Amelie wasn't faring much better. The sisters had never ridden horses before coming to Sèone last spring, and had only taken one lengthy journey since ... several months ago. Their bodies were not conditioned to riding for hours on end.

Already on the ground, Anton looked up at her. "Are you all right?"

"Of course."

Without asking, he reached up and lifted her down. Her legs trembled upon touching the ground, but she managed to stay on her feet. At the sight of this, Amelie managed to climb off her black gelding and put both hands to her back. Everyone ate an apple and a biscuit and drank shared cupfuls of water.

Anton had his own cup.

There was a stream nearby and Rurik had all the horses watered. Then, somewhat reluctantly, Céline climbed back on Sable.

Thankfully, the afternoon passed quickly, and as the sun was dipping in the sky, Rurik turned and called, "Rékausi up ahead," over his shoulder.

"Are we still in your territory?" Amelie asked Anton.

"Yes," he answered, "right on the edge. I thought it best. We cross into Damek's lands first thing in the morning."

As the town came into sight, Céline squinted at what

appeared to be a sea of movement in the streets. "What is that?"

Almost absently, Anton responded, "Our greeting."

Rurik's horse entered the town . . . as the contingent came after. Hundreds of people lined the streets, some holding late-autumn flowers or early holly berries, and they began to cheer at the sight of Anton—who still rode between the sisters.

He raised one hand and waved to the people as they cheered, and some began throwing flowers and branches of holly into his path.

Céline had no idea what to make of this. She turned her head and looked past him to Amelie, who appeared equally taken aback.

"Smile and wave," Anton said quietly. "The people expect it."

Attempting to recover herself, Céline smiled and raised a hand in greeting.

"Prince Anton!" the people cheered.

Although he very seldom left Sèone, he was loved, even here on the edge of his lands.

"How did they know you were coming?" she asked through her carefully set smile.

"I sent a rider last night. I had to have an inn made ready for us. The innkeeper must have spread the word."

Céline tried to get her head around this. He'd sent a rider to have an inn prepared? Anton left very little to chance.

The people remained at a respectful distance, allowing the contingent to pass. Again, Rurik seemed to know exactly where he was going, and led the way through town, stopping his mount in front of a whitewashed, three-story building with numerous windows.

Some soldiers began to dismount, and other horses pressed up from behind. Sable was jostled a bit, and Céline found herself separated from Amelie and Anton.

"Céline," someone said.

Looking down, she saw Rurik standing on the ground beside her.

He reached up with both arms. "Put your hands on my shoulders."

Wordlessly, exhausted, she did as he said, and he lifted her down. When her feet touched solid earth, she expected him to let go, but he held on to her. Still, his grip was light, as if he wanted her to know she could pull away if she wished.

"I wanted to thank you," he whispered.

"Thank me?"

"Yes . . . not long ago, I thought . . . I thought I might be finished as a guard of Sèone, but you spoke up for me. And then yesterday, Jaromir told me that you'd named me as head of the prince's guard on this journey." He looked around at the flowers and holly in the street. "This was the best day of my life, and I have you to thank."

"Oh, Rurik, no. I only told the truth about your courage in Ryazan. You won this on your own merit."

He shook his head. "Not entirely." His gaze was intense, but she saw only gratitude and friendship in his green eyes. "I would die for you . . . or Amelie. You know that?"

"Corporal?" said a low voice.

Céline turned her head to see Anton watching them. His expression was unreadable.

Rurik stepped back. "My prince?"

"Have someone see the horses stabled and then see

the innkeeper yourself about our rooms. We'll need to have tonight's baggage brought in."

"Yes, my lord."

Rurik barked a few orders to Sergeant Bazin about the horses and then hurried inside.

Anton's gaze was still on Céline, but he motioned toward the front door. "Shall we?"

Amelie followed Céline and Anton inside, feeling somewhat ill at ease. She'd never admit it, but it was Anton who made her feel unsettled.

He always had.

He was simply so . . . guarded. Even after living under his protection for nearly half a year, she knew nothing about him and could never tell what he was thinking. Yet here she was, trusting both her and Céline's life to his judgment. Jaromir might be overbearing, but at least she understood him. She could have a conversation or play a hand of cards with him—or even fight with him once in a while. Anton was unknowable. Untouchable.

Inside, she looked around.

The common room of the inn had been polished until every table and chair shone. The aroma of roasting meat and fresh bread wafted on the air. A warm fire burned in the hearth. A stout man in an apron strode toward them with an eager expression, but Rurik intercepted him before he got anywhere near Anton.

"We will sleep here?" Céline asked Anton.

"A room has been prepared for the both of you," he answered. "With a palette on the floor for Helga. I apologize for the cramped conditions, but we have all the guards to house as well."

"No, that will be fine. I like the idea of Helga staying with us."

Amelie did, too. There was safety in numbers.

As if on cue in a play, Helga stomped through the front door and sniffed the air. Several strands of gray hair had escaped her crooked orange scarf. "When do we eat? I'm starving. That so-called lunch we ate wouldn't keep a rat alive."

Anton's jaw twitched. "Dinner will be served directly."

Amelie thought perhaps they would get settled in their rooms first, but that wasn't the case. All the soldiers in their tan tabards and chain armor began coming through the door and finding a seat at one of the tables. She didn't mind the prospect of eating right away. She'd had tea for breakfast and only an apple and biscuit for lunch. Her stomach was close to rumbling.

It was warm inside, and she took off her cloak, revealing the light blue dress beneath it. Though she hated being forced back into a dress again, she had her own dagger stored in its sheath in her right boot, and Jaromir's weapons strapped to her wrists, covered by her long sleeves.

Céline removed her cloak as well, showing the lavender wool dress she'd worn. It fit her slender form well, and it matched her eyes.

A Sèone soldier Amelie didn't recognize came through the door carrying several bags up on his shoulders, and Helga strode over to meet him. "You know which room is Miss Amelie and Miss Céline's?"

"Yes, ma'am. I was just informed."

"Good. Then take those up and mind you be careful!"

"Yes, ma'am," he said good-naturedly, and headed for a stairway at the back of the room.

Amelie raised an eyebrow at Céline. "It appears we have porter service."

Helga plopped down on a bench at a table. "You girls come sit down."

Amelie's backside still hurt, but she was hungry enough to risk sitting on a wooden bench, and she took a place beside Helga. So did Céline.

However, Anton stood uncomfortably, with his jaw still tight, looking down at Helga, as if uncertain what to do.

"Here, my lord," Rurik called.

The young corporal appeared to be preparing a small, single table—with one chair—by a window. In visible relief, Anton said, "Please excuse me," and he walked over to sit by himself. The instant he was seated, Rurik joined another table populated by some of his men.

"Anton's too good to eat with Helga?" Amelie whispered in Céline's ear.

"I don't think he has a choice. We're on uncertain . . . social ground here."

And *that* was another thing that bothered Amelie. No matter what Anton did, Céline always defended him. Amelie dropped the subject. Young women in white aprons began coming through a door behind the bar, carrying trays full of tankards of ale and plates of roast beef.

After that, for a while Amelie forgot everything but the food.

In addition to tender beef, they were served potatoes, warm bread, and apple compote. After dishing up once, she devoured everything on her plate and looked around for more.

Céline smiled. "Not so bad after all, traveling with the prince? Do you remember our camp rations with Jaromir?"

Although Céline had clearly meant this as a joke, it only gave Amelie a fresh jolt of anxiety. Honestly, she'd rather they were eating camp rations and drinking water from a bucket with Jaromir than trusting their lives to Anton.

During dinner, darkness fell and candles were lit. A few of their guards lit pipes, and more ale was served. Amelie glanced over at Prince Anton. Once his dinner dishes were removed, he stood up and took a step toward the stairs.

Just then, Rurik called out, "Céline, will you entertain us like you did before?"

On the dark road to Ryazan, Céline had considerably lightened the mood at night by the campfire. Amelie was exhausted, and she knew Céline was probably more so. But her sister stood up.

"What would you prefer," she asked, "fortune-telling? A story? A song?"

Four men—who had all been on the previous trip—rang out together, "A story!"

This didn't surprise Amelie. The men loved stories, and Céline was gifted at the art of "telling."

Céline walked toward the hearth. "An adventure? A romance? A comedy?"

"What about something darker?" Rurik asked, flashing her a grin from across the room. "We aren't in the northern forests now. Tell something to give us a shiver."

"A ghost story?" Céline smiled in return, and her face lit up.

Amelie then noticed that Anton had frozen in place by his table, watching this exchange.

The innkeeper and the serving girls gathered by the bar, watching Céline expectantly. Her face glowed by the candlelight from the tabletops, and firelight glinted off her blond hair.

"My own sister and I are close, and we hold each other dear," she began, "but not all sisters are so fortunate, and some are divided by jealousy." She lifted her hands to her sides, palms upward. "And between siblings, jealously is the most dangerous emotion of all, more than hatred, more than fear."

With that, she lowered her head briefly, and when she raised it again, any and all traces of her previous smile were gone.

"Years ago, up in the north, there lived a man with two daughters, both beautiful. The elder had rich brown hair and the younger had hair of copper gold. But while the elder sister's nature was cold and reserved, the younger was more open with her love and affection, and people were drawn to her."

Céline moved away from the hearth, slipping easily through the tables and chairs as she spoke. Everyone watched her.

"There was a handsome and prosperous young farmer who lived not far from them. They didn't know him well, but one day, he came to visit, and after that, he came more often. In this province, it would be considered poor manners for him to pay attention to a younger sister if the elder were not yet married. So the young man did his due by speaking mainly to the father and to the elder sister."

Céline's voice dropped lower.

"But . . . at every chance, his eyes strayed to the younger sister."

She stopped on the other side of the room and slowly began walking back toward the hearth. "The father organized horseback rides and dances for entertainment, and soon, the young man could be seen riding at the younger sister's side and dancing with her in the village common hall, laughing and enjoying her company. The elder sister watched all this without a word, waiting and biding her time."

Anton still remained frozen where he stood, staring at Céline.

"Then one afternoon, the sisters went walking by the great river that flowed through their father's land, and the elder sister called the younger closer to the edge. When the younger sister willingly came, perhaps thinking to see something in the water, the elder sister pushed her into the deep river. The poor young woman struggled in the cold water, crying, 'Help! Help me, sister. Grab my hands!' But the elder sister stepped back and watched. The younger sister's head went down beneath the surface, came up, and went down again as water flowed into her mouth and nose . . . and then she came up no more. The current carried her dead body downstream."

A serving girl by the bar gasped.

"The elder sister ran home, telling a tale of how the younger had fallen into the river and could not be saved. Their father and the handsome farmer both wept. The young farmer was bereft, and somehow the elder sister managed to overcome her cold nature and offer him comfort. Before long, the two were betrothed, with him in ignorance that he would soon wed a murderess."

She paused. The common room was silent but for a soft crackling from the hearth.

"Then . . . ," Céline began again, "a band of traveling minstrels were walking along the river, and one of them saw something on the shore. They went to investigate and found the body of the younger sister. Even in death, her beauty moved them. Their singer, who was a woman, knelt by the younger sister's side and touched her dead face and said, 'I wish with all my heart that I could tell your kin what happened to you and where you were laid to rest.' But as they had no idea who the dead girl was or who her family might be, the best they could do was to bury her."

Amelie couldn't help looking in Anton's direction. He stood rooted to the same spot with his eyes locked on Céline.

"Several nights later, the father, the young farmer, and the elder daughter went into town to the large common hall to hear the minstrels play. Entertainment of this sort was rare in their part of the land, and the father thought that perhaps some fine music might ease their sorrow. They took their place among a small crowd as the minstrels made ready. The singer stepped out to begin her first song, and to everyone's astonishment, her face began to alter, growing rounder and lovelier, and her hair turned thick and copper gold . . . until she had taken the form of the younger sister, and she began to sing in sorrow-laden strains. 'I weep. I weep for my lost father. I weep for my lost love, and I weep for my sister, who pushed me into the river and watched me drown.'"

Several of the soldiers drew in sharp breaths.

"Then the singer looked exactly as she had before. But the handsome farmer turned and looked in horror at the elder sister, who had guilt all over her face." Céline was nearly whispering now, but her voice carried across the room. "She would soon be punished for her crime of jealousy . . . exposed by a singing ghost."

Céline dropped her head. The story was done.

The room remained silent for a long moment, and then applause burst out, filling the large space.

Amelie took a final glance toward the front window.

Anton was gone.

The following morning, they got a late start. Though somewhat frustrated, Anton realized he should have expected this. It was the first time Corporal Rurik had ever been charged with packing up twenty-five people, their horses, their wagon, and then getting everyone back on the road.

Finally, though, the large party pulled out of Rékausi and crossed over into Damek's territory. The road they traveled was once again lined with thick, dark trees while a drizzle of rain fell from the sky. Anton rode behind Céline and Amelie, keeping himself as isolated as possible.

For the most part, his mind had been so occupied he'd barely noticed the delay.

Every step closer to Kimovesk filled him with further dread.

Worse, he could not stop picturing the sight of Céline from the night before ... and the sound of her voice as she'd told that story. He wanted to push the image from his thoughts, and he couldn't.

In all his life, he had only fallen in love with one woman. After the lonely, pain-filled years of his childhood and youth, at the age of eighteen, he'd met Jocelyn Chevrier. She was sweet, sheltered, and shy, with a gift for small kindnesses. With her, for the first time, he didn't feel alone.

Though from a noble family, she was not royal and

she was not rich. Prince Lieven had forbidden a marriage. This was the only time Anton defied his father, and he didn't care about the repercussions. As Anton was already ruling over Sèone, his father couldn't afford to disinherit him. Anton dealt with the initial anger without flinching—though it troubled him more than he cared to admit, as he had no wish to hurt his father. But almost immediately following the marriage, Jocelyn became pregnant, and then all was forgiven.

Prince Lieven wanted a grandson.

Jocelyn died in childbirth, along with the baby, and Anton had wished to die with them. It took him a long time to recover, and he'd never even looked at another woman . . . until now.

In most ways, Céline was nothing like Jocelyn. She was certainly not sheltered or shy. She had suffered more than her share of hardships and exhibited a poorly hidden caution of most men. She was a consummate liar and showed no compunction against using this talent when necessary.

But . . . she was also warm and sympathetic and generous with small kindnesses. She was beautiful and intelligent and took pride in supporting herself and Amelie with her noted skills as an apothecary.

He had not thought to ever feel so drawn to a woman again, and yet he couldn't act upon his feelings or even tell her.

Marriage was out of the question. She would be viewed by everyone who mattered as a gypsy peasant, and given the current political situation, even Anton wouldn't go that far outside social convention. Nor would Céline wish him to. She cared about her country, and she wanted to see him named as grand prince. That left him with the prospect of making her his mistress, and he'd never allow such a thing for someone so fine as Céline. On several occasions, he had wanted her to touch him so badly that he almost forgot himself, but one or both of them had pulled back at the last moment.

Thankfully.

No, it was his fate to remain isolated, and he understood that. Unlike Damek, he would not marry for money or connections, and love was rare for him. Yet self-awareness was a strength—or at least his father had always said so.

His tall stallion walked easily along the muddy road, and again, he fought to push the image of Céline last night standing in front of the hearth, telling that story, from his mind.

He was so focused on his thoughts that his horse almost collided with the back of hers before he realized the entire contingent had stopped.

"What is it?" he called.

Before anyone answered, he looked ahead, up past Corporal Rurik, to see a large but shabby wagon blocking the road. A wheel had come off on the rear left side, and that corner had fallen into the thin top layer of mud on the ground. A half-starved mule was harnessed out front. Perhaps twelve peasants—men, women, and children, all bone-thin—were gathered around the back of the wagon, as if assessing the damage.

Several of them turned to see the contingent about the same time Anton saw them, and terror flooded their faces.

"Run!" one of them shouted.

Instantly, the small crowd began to flee for the trees.

To Anton's surprise, Céline urged her horse around the side of the guards in front of her.

"Please stop!" she called. "We won't hurt you. Please!"

Before he could move, she was cantering her gray mare down the edge of the road, still calling to the peasants. Some of them began to slow down and look back at her.

With a jolt of realization that she might be in danger, he kicked Whisper in the sides, urging him forward. He heard Amelie coming after him.

By the time he reached the front of the contingent, Céline's horse was beside Rurik's, and she was leaning down from the saddle, speaking to one of the peasant women.

"I promise no one will hurt you. These are Prince Anton's men," she said.

The woman was filthy, in tattered clothing, and her eyes were frightened as they turned up to him. He had no idea what to do and was indeed rather embarrassed by Céline's display. He would simply have had his men ride around the broken wagon and leave these people to return from hiding once all the soldiers had passed.

"What has happened?" Céline asked the woman . . . and then she climbed off her horse!

"Céline!" he called, more harshly than intended.

She looked back at him. "My lord, these people require our assistance. The wheel to their wagon has come off."

Biting the inside of his cheek, he jumped down and walked to her swiftly. In some alarm, Rurik jumped off his mount as well. Without thinking, Anton grasped Céline's wrist and pulled her a few steps away.

Suddenly, Amelie was on the ground beside them, looking at his hand. He let go.

"These are Damek's people," he explained quietly, "and there is nothing we can do for them. The kindest thing we can do is to be on our way."

Céline's eyes clouded in confusion. "No, they need help, and ... what do you mean by 'Damek's people'? If you are elected grand prince, all the people will be your people."

He stared at her. Her hood had fallen, and the drizzling rain was darkening her hair.

"Can you not show them what sort of grand prince you would be?" she asked.

Anton glanced at the fallen wheel and lopsided wagon. Then he turned to Sergeant Bazin, who was still up on their own wagon's bench. "Can that be repaired?"

"Yes, my lord, with a few strong men to lift it."

Although stopping to help Damek's suffering peasants had not occurred to Anton, the prospect no longer seemed so strange. "See to it," he told Rurik.

Céline turned back to the frightened woman. "Gather your women and children at the back of our wagon. We have apples and biscuits to spare, and I can hear some of the children coughing. I have a syrup that will help."

And with that, Anton stood on a muddy road of his brother's province, in the rain, and watched the activity around him. Tattered peasants began melting from the trees, coming back to join them. Rurik and Bazin called some of their men down to help with the fallen wheel. Amelie and Helga were at the back of the wagon, giving away the remainder of their supplies, while Céline attempted to dig out something among the luggage. She looked over to him.

"My lord, I need my box of medicines, and I cannot pull it from beneath this luggage. Can you help?"

To his astonishment, he wanted to help. He could have ordered a guard, but he didn't.

He climbed up into the back of the wagon, pulled out a large wooden box, and handed it down to her. He watched as she opened it and began to administer cough syrup to the children, giving a large bottle to one of the women to take home.

As she was dabbing some sort of astringent on the arm of a boy with a festered insect bite, she lifted her head and looked back toward the guards repairing the wagon. "My lord, do you see that old man limping? I think he suffers from sore knee joints. Can you bring him over? I have a liniment."

This was indeed one of the most unusual experiences in Anton's memory, but he went over and helped the old man to Céline. A moment later, she had the old man pull up his pant legs and she began to rub a dark liniment into his knees.

"I'll send some of this with you," she said to him, "but you must be careful to wash every drop from your hands after using it. It's very good for sore joints, but dangerous if swallowed."

Anton continued to watch her work.

Before long, the wagon was repaired, the sick had been tended, and food had been passed out.

"Give them some grain for that mule," Anton ordered Sergeant Bazin.

"How much, my lord?"

"At least half a bag. We're almost to Kimovesk, and we can resupply."

Putting her hands to her back, Céline straightened. "Is their wagon ready," she asked.

"I think so," Anton answered, and then he was at a loss again. He was glad they had stopped. He was glad they'd done what they could to help some of Damek's people. But he couldn't say that.

Céline smiled at him and raised her hood to cover her head. "Then shall we get back on the road?"

This all seemed so cut-and-dried to her, as if their actions here had been commonplace. They weren't commonplace to him.

"Yes," he said.

Everyone mounted up, and once again, Anton took his position behind the sisters, riding alone. In his mind, the image of Céline telling her story last night was now replaced by one of her urging her horse around his soldiers to stop a band of fleeing peasants.

Several hours passed, and he was still lost in thought when Rurik called out, "Kimovesk Village ahead."

They would need to ride through the village and travel a league beyond it before reaching the castle. Anton had been through here only a few times, but as his remembrance of the place was suddenly jogged, he rode up beside Céline.

"Prepare yourself," he said. "The people here might be . . . worse than what we saw earlier."

She turned her head toward him. "I know exactly what we'll find. You forget I grew up in Shetâna."

Yes, she had grown up in Shetâna, and sometimes he did forget it.

CHAPTER FOUR

In spite of Céline's calm response to Anton, as he let his horse drop back behind hers again, she dreaded the prospect of riding directly through one of Damek's villages. For much of the day's journey, they had passed roads that led to villages, but they had not been exposed to many tragic sights regarding the overtaxed and oppressed people who lived in this part of the country. Unlike the soldiers in Anton's province—who were hired and trained to protect the people—Damek's soldiers had free rein to abuse almost anyone they wished.

Céline feared being forced to remember too much that she'd managed to successfully push to the back of her mind. Although she and Amelie had lived in Sèone less than a year, their previous life sometimes seemed distant.

She was now Prince Anton's seer and his people's apothecary.

She liked this new life, this new self, and although she felt no shame regarding her former self, neither did she care to be reminded of the years when she had barely scraped by while living in fear of Damek's soldiers.

"You all right?" Amelie asked, riding beside her.

The edge of the village was only a few horses' length away.

"Yes, I'm just ... too many memories."

"I know. Me, too."

Céline wanted to reach over and grasp Amelie's hand. She wanted to glance back at Anton, but she did neither of these things. Instead, she gripped her reins and followed the guards ahead of her into Kimovesk Village.

It was as shabby, dirty, and depressing as she'd anticipated, consisting mainly of wattle and daub huts with thatched roofs. As soon as Rurik passed the first dwelling, people began running out of sight. Céline saw no one's face clearly. She only saw thin villagers in tattered clothing fleeing for doorways.

The contingent rode on, and the passing proved to be not as difficult as she'd expected. Within moments, the main street was empty, and she saw nothing but decaying dwellings and a few shops—with closed doors. Before she knew it, they were out the other side. She wished she could feel some relief, but their next stop was the castle.

They pressed onward until she realized the road had begun to both narrow and incline upward. Soon, they were forced to ride single file, and Céline found herself following Amelie.

The road continued to narrow until the branches of trees were close enough to touch, and Sergeant Bazin began having difficulty getting the wagon through without getting himself or Helga hit by a branch. Helga was not polite about this.

Trees overhead blocked out nearly all light from the sky, and the world around them grew dim.

"We're almost to the gate," Anton said from behind. "You and Amelie keep your hoods well over your heads and around your faces. You cannot be seen just yet. Do you understand?"

"Yes." But she did not understand the urgency for this, as they were both going to be seen soon enough. "Did you hear him, Amelie?" she asked, leaning forward.

"I heard him."

Céline expected a break in the trees, but this didn't happen. Instead, she looked ahead, through the branches, over the top of Rurik and the front guards, and she saw a dark tower stretching into the sky.

"Halt," Anton called out.

Rurik halted.

Anton ducked low, steered his horse around the side of Céline's, and trotted toward the front of the contingent. Even passing beneath low branches on the side of the narrow road, he managed to do this gracefully, and he took the lead as they headed onward.

Almost immediately, Céline saw the gatehouse and part of a high stone wall.

Moments later they reached a portcullis with thick crisscrossed bars. Several hard-looking men in black tabards peered out. Céline looked left and right to see the stone wall stretching in both directions as far as she could see. Soldiers in black tabards walked the top of the wall. The break between the thick forest and the wall was only about twenty paces—far enough that the wall could not be breached by anyone climbing a tree and yet close enough that a gathering of any sort of forces out here would be nearly impossible.

Anton rode directly to the portcullis, making certain the guards inside could see him clearly.

"Raise the gate," he ordered.

Without argument, one of the men behind the bars looked upward and called, "Raise it!"

A creaking and grinding sounded, followed by the portcullis opening. Anton led the way, and as Céline passed through, she found herself traveling down an enclosed gatehouse tunnel. There was a second portcullis at the far end, but that one was already up. Although the defenses here were not as sophisticated as they were at Sèone, they were certainly sufficient. The castle would be difficult to breach.

However . . . the double walls around Sèone protected all the people of the main village. Here, Damek left his castle's namesake villagers to fend for themselves.

Once out of the gatehouse tunnel, the contingent rode into the courtyard, to the sight of dozens more men in black tabards, and Céline got her first full look at the castle. It was constructed of dark stone, and it was both older and smaller than Anton's home.

It was also of an unusual design. On the east end, a single tall tower stretched at least five stories into the air. The center section of the castle was a long, two-story, rectangular block. On the west end stood a shorter, four-story tower, connected to what appeared to be a half-width tower that connected to another four-story tower. The half-width tower also contained the main doors to the castle.

The layout produced a rather lopsided effect. Still . . . lopsided or not, it was forbidding—which probably pleased Damek.

Anton rode directly toward the main doors, and someone stood there, waiting.

When Céline saw who it was, her stomached tightened: Captain Kochè. He looked exactly as she remembered him. Kochè was tall but with a protruding belly and a stringy mustache that stretched down past his chin.

Anton rode right up to him and looked down. "Have someone see to stabling our horses and arranging proper bunks for my men." His tone was arrogant, as if he resented even having to speak to one of Damek's underlings. "I want a private audience with my brother *now*."

Kochè stared back at him in undisguised contempt.

As of yet, no one had even looked at the heavily cloaked Céline and Amelie, but Céline pulled her hood closer to her face.

Kochè barked out a few grudging orders to his own men, and Anton's men began to dismount. Rurik was on the ground by now, and he hurried over to lift Céline down first and then Amelie. Thankfully, Amelie didn't cause a fuss, and she let him.

Anton turned toward them. "The three of you, with me."

Captain Kochè opened the doors, and with that, Céline followed behind Anton, leaving the activity in the courtyard behind. She hoped their guards and horses would be well looked after, but that was out of her hands.

The pace Kochè set was quick. Upon entering the castle, he turned right and headed into a stairwell that curved up through one of the west-end towers. Why had Anton insisted on an immediate private audience with Damek? Their small group was wet and mud-spattered from the road. Would he not prefer to face his brother after bathing and dressing? She felt as if she was being swept along into something she didn't understand and had no power to stop.

In being so focused on keeping up, she wasn't even certain how far up they'd traveled when Kochè stepped out into a passage, walked all the way to the end, and knocked on a door.

"My lord, your brother is demanding to see you."

Silence followed at first, and then the door opened.

A very small man, shorter than Amelie, stood on the other side, peering past Kochè to Anton. The man was dressed in fine black pants and a quilted tunic. A red birthmark covered nearly half his face. He looked back into the room and nodded.

"All right. Get out," said a voice from inside.

Lowering his head, the small man scurried past everyone waiting in the passage. Céline thought he must be one of Damek's attendants. Anton didn't care much to have personal attendants fussing over him, but most princes did.

Kochè entered first, followed by Anton, Céline, Amelie, and then Rurik.

The room they entered was warm, with a fire burning in the hearth. The walls were covered in tapestries that depicted designs of color rather than pictures or clear images. Stuffed chairs and low couches with velvet upholstery were carefully arranged. An open door led into a bedroom, and a man stood in that doorway.

Although Céline had lived under his rule, this was the first time she'd ever seen him in person. She had, however, seen him while conducting readings of people involved with him—and seeing images of their future.

He appeared to be in his late twenties, with narrow, even features. His hair was long and dark. His skin was pale, and he wore a sleeveless silk dressing gown loosely tied at his waist. Like Anton's, his build was slender, with tight, defined muscles in his arms. For the most part, he looked like Anton, except for his eyes. Anton's eyes were haunted. Damek's were cruel.

"Dear brother," he said sarcastically. "You look positively muddy. Did you just climb off your horse?"

He yawned and stretched like a lazy cat, and Céline realized that even though it was early afternoon, they had woken him.

Anton didn't respond to the question. He turned and nodded to Céline, who understood what he wanted, and she pulled her hood down. So did Amelie.

"May I present my seers?" Anton said. "As requested." He motioned with his hand. "This is Amelie and this is . . . Céline."

Before speaking her name, he'd hesitated, and as he said it, his voice altered ever so slightly. Damek's eyes lit up, and he no longer appeared sleepy or lazy. He focused intently first on Anton, then Céline, and then back to Anton.

Anton's already pale face went white.

Céline had no idea what this was about, but she didn't have time to wonder. For in the same moment, Captain Kochè sucked in a loud breath and pointed at her.

"My lord! That is the charlatan who crushed your betrothal plans to the Lady Rhiannon."

Céline tensed. She and Amelie had warned Anton about this. Last spring, Damek had sent someone to Shetâna to pay Céline in advance to do a private reading for a wealthy young woman . . . on the understanding that Céline would counsel the skittish would-be bride to marry Damek. Yet, when Céline had done the reading, she saw a future image of Damek falsely accusing his new wife of adultery and having her strangled. He'd wanted her dowry . . . but not her. In good conscience, Céline couldn't fulfill the bargain she'd made, and she'd tried to send the money back. As a result, Damek had ordered their shop burned and the sisters killed. While escaping the flames of the shop, Céline and Amelie had encountered the unexpected intervention of Jaromir, who had put down several of Damek's guards and then secretly taken the sisters to Anton.

However, in response to Kochè's outburst, Prince Damek's expression grew mildly puzzled and dangerously annoyed. Céline guessed that his guards did not normally interrupt such discussions.

Kochè seemed to realize this and rushed on. "Do you not remember, my lord? The seer from Shetâna who was paid to counsel Lady Rhiannon to accept your offer?" He pointed at Céline. "That is her! She is one of your own peasants."

Some realization dawned on Damek's face, but before he could speak, Anton stepped in front of Céline, speaking directly to his brother. "None of that matters. She lives in Sèone now, and she serves me, and you've asked for my help."

From behind, Céline heard Rurik move close enough to her that she could have reached back and touched him. He might not be Jaromir, but his presence was comforting.

No one spoke for a moment, and Damek appeared to be absorbing and considering things. He walked farther into the sitting room and moved to where he could see Céline standing behind Anton.

"You're the seer from Shetâna who scared off Rhiannon?" Damek asked, but he might as well have been speaking to himself. "Yes, I *was* put out about that. I remember now." He paused and looked to Anton. "How did she end up with you?"

"Doesn't matter," Anton answered. "I'm assuming Father told you about her and her sister now working for me? Whatever he told you about their abilities is the truth. If you want their help, we'll stay. If you don't, say so now, and we'll be back on the road."

With a sigh, Damek put one hand in the air. "Calm down, little brother. I've no quarrel with your seer. In fact, she might have done me a favor, as I've a much bigger prize on the hook now."

Anton's body relaxed slightly. "All right. Then if the sisters are going to seek out whoever killed Carlotta, they'll need to mingle at length with your bride's family. I'm going to introduce them as Miss Céline and Miss Amelie, the daughters of a rich wool merchant who often dines at the court of Sèone. The Lady Helena has to accept them socially before anything can be uncovered. Do you see?"

Suddenly, Céline began to understand the reason for this quick meeting upon their arrival.

"Yes, of course, I see," Damek answered, sounding annoyed again.

"Then you'll need to order Captain Kochè to keep quiet," Anton went on, "as well as any guards who ever visited Shetâna to collect taxes . . . or amuse themselves by preying on the people there. All your guards must treat *Miss* Céline and *Miss* Amelie as honored guests."

"My lord!" Kochè began to object.

Damek turned on him, and he fell silent.

"Captain," Damek said, "you will do as my brother asks. Be clear with your men. Anyone who even hints of the identity of these women will be . . . reprimanded."

Céline could only imagine what that meant.

Kochè's face darkened. "Yes, my lord."

And so, Anton had effectively solved the problem of Captain Kochè—at least to a point—and all the guards would be ordered to show Céline and Amelie proper respect. She could not help being somewhat impressed by how quickly Anton had headed off several of their initial problems.

But now the hard part began.

Damek studied her, glanced at Amelie, and then back to her. "And how did you plan to catch this murderer?"

Céline instinctively knew that showing him an ounce of uncertainty would be a mistake.

"Do you still have Carlotta's body, my lord?" she asked.

He smiled. The sight made Céline feel chilled, even in the warm room. "Yes," he answered. "It's in the cellars. I thought her family would wish to bring it home for burial."

"May we examine it?" she asked.

If he found the request macabre, he didn't show it, and instead looked to Anton, who nodded.

"By all means," Damek said. "Allow me to get dressed."

At some point along the walk down into the cellars— Céline didn't notice exactly when—the small man with the birthmark rejoined them, carrying a lantern. When they all emerged into a dark room below the main floor of the castle, the party felt rather large, but Céline supposed there was no help for it. She and Amelie were necessary. Both princes wanted to witness the examination, and both princes also had their own personal bodyguards present, so Rurik and Kochè brought up the rear.

And Céline was grateful for the small attendant carrying the lantern.

All such thoughts vanished from her mind, though, when she saw the body laid out on a long wooden table. Stores of wine casks and wheels of cheese and barrels of oats filled the back half of the room. It unsettled Céline that Carlotta's body had the appearance of being "stored" here with the food.

Amelie stepped up to the table first, and Céline moved to join her. Since arriving, Amelie hadn't said a word, but that wasn't unusual. She normally let Céline take the lead at the beginning of an investigation.

"What exactly do you wish to see?" Prince Damek asked, sounding genuinely curious.

"Signs of poison, my lord," Céline answered. "Some are easy to obtain, and others are more difficult. If we know what was used, it could help in our search." She looked over at the small man with the lantern. "Could you . . . would you mind bringing the light closer?"

Instantly, he was at her side, holding the light over Carlotta's face. "I am Lionel," he said politely. His voice was almost musical when he spoke. "Please inform me of anything you require."

"Thank you," she answered. "I am Miss Céline. Just continue holding the light there for now."

First, Céline took a visual impression. The body was several days old, and stiffening had set in. Carlotta had been a large-boned woman in life, and her age was difficult to determine. Her dark hair was coarse with strands of gray, but her face seemed younger. Her mouth was downturned, and her hands were large and sinewy. Her dress was black with white trim, and it covered her entire form with a high neckline and long sleeves. Even in death, something about her gave Céline the impression that she'd been an unhappy woman.

Anton stepped up to the table. "Anything?" he asked quietly.

Céline moved around him and pushed up one of Carlotta's sleeves, examining her skin. Then she continued to the end of the table and did a check of the legs. "No red rash, so it wasn't Belladonna." Circling back to Anton, she whispered, "Could you ask your brother to describe exactly when Carlotta . . . when she died?"

"You can ask me such things yourself," Damek interrupted. "I don't bite."

Céline wasn't sure she believed that, but she looked over at him.

He shrugged. "She took a drink from her goblet and then she couldn't breathe. She died."

"Was she choking?" Céline asked, and then remembered to add, "My lord."

"None of us had eaten anything, so it had to be the wine," Damek answered. "She made choking sounds, but it was more like someone attempting to draw air and failing."

Céline leaned down over Carlotta's head.

"What do you think?" Amelie whispered to her.

"I don't know."

Reaching down, Céline put her fingers in Carlotta's mouth and pried her teeth apart.

"What are you doing?" Anton asked in what sounded like revulsion.

Without answering, Céline leaned close to examine Carlotta's tongue and throat. She looked up to Damek. "My lord . . . her tongue isn't swollen, and her throat isn't red. Her windpipe is clear. I'm not . . . I'm not certain that she was poisoned. Did the family mention any history of illness? Perhaps a weak heart?"

A mix of pleasure and hope washed over Damek's face. "They mentioned nothing to me, but are you saying she might simply have died on her own? That would be welcome news were it true. It would certainly ease the way for my betrothal to Rochelle."

Although Céline was mildly sickened by his callous attitude toward Carlotta's death, she understood what he was saying.

"When will Céline have a chance to speak to the family?" Anton asked. He sounded hopeful as well. If this were to turn out to be a tragic but natural death, it would leave him free to take his people here and go home.

"You'll meet them at dinner tonight in the great hall," Damek answered. "I know everyone is supposed to be in mourning, but we all must eat." He tilted his head. "If Céline is so sure this wasn't murder, is there any need for you to continue?"

"I am not sure," Céline put in quickly. "I am just telling you what I see here. In order to be sure, we must press onward."

"I agree," Anton said reluctantly. "I hope you're right, but we can't leave until we're certain. Father would not be pleased otherwise."

Damek stretched his arms. "As you wish. I will see you at dinner." He yawned again. "Lionel will see to you from here." Without another word, he turned and walked out of the cellar room. Captain Kochè followed him.

Anton glanced at Céline and then down to Carlotta. "You really think she may have died from an illness or a weak heart?"

"I don't know, but I don't see any evidence that she was poisoned."

Lionel bowed his head once and asked, "May I see you up to your rooms? I can have hot water for washing and tea brought in for you."

Suddenly, a mug of hot tea sounded very good.

Anton nodded to the small man. "Yes."

"I have rooms prepared for all of you on the second floor of the east tower," Lionel continued. "Miss Céline and Miss Amelie's maid has already begun unpacking in their rooms."

"Rooms?" Rurik broke in. "You have the women in separate rooms?"

Lionel's expression turned offended. "Of course."

Rurik shook his head. "No." He looked to Anton. "My lord, Céline and Amelie should stay in the same room, with Helga on a palette on the floor. You should have a room nearby, with me sleeping on a palette. I'm in charge of your safety, and Lieutenant Jaromir would have my head if I agreed to anything less."

The offense on Lionel's face increased—as this was a clear insult—but Céline understood Rurik's insistence. Céline had no wish to sleep alone in this castle. Nor did she want Amelie alone . . . or Helga. More, she was relieved by the idea of Anton and Rurik sleeping in a nearby room.

Anton must have understood as well, because he turned to Lionel. "See to it."

Lionel's mouth tightened. "Yes, my lord."

Not long after, Anton was finally in his assigned room, with some privacy. He'd sent Corporal Rurik down to check on their men and horses.

Anton leaned against the wall, feeling sick.

A servant had delivered hot water in a pitcher and a steaming cup of tea. He'd ignored both.

He barely noticed the room's furnishings, which were sparse: a bed, a wardrobe, a small table with a basin and pitcher. He didn't care. He would have given almost anything to go back in time to the moment he'd introduced Amelie and Céline to Damek.

Closing his eyes, he relived the horrible moment in his mind again, cursing himself.

He'd given himself away, given his feelings for Céline away.

Damek *knew*. He'd heard the slight shift in Anton's voice. And Damek would now focus upon her as a target. Since childhood, Damek could always manage to learn what Anton loved, what he cared about . . . in order that it might be made to suffer.

Damek couldn't love anything or anyone, so he needed to torture whatever Anton loved.

Before coming here, Anton had promised himself he'd give nothing away, that Damek would read nothing on his face, nor hear anything in his voice. Fool that he'd been, Anton believed he could keep this up for the duration of the visit.

He hadn't lasted through the first hour.

He realized he'd spent too long away from his family. For nearly six years, he'd been prince of Castle Sèone, and he'd begun to view the world as a sane place populated by sane people. He had even begun to respect himself, no longer the terrified favorite victim of a mad older brother.

He'd pictured himself arriving at Kimovesk as the man he had become: an authority figure with pride in his province and his own rule. Now . . . he was wavering. He was reverting into what Damek had once made him.

Biting down on the inside of his mouth, he pictured Céline in his mind. She saw him as he had always wanted to be seen. He had to hold on to that. He could *not* revert.

Walking over to the bed, he sank down. He still had time before he'd have to dress for dinner, and he planned to spend every minute of it inside himself, shoring himself up, preparing himself for what was to come. For the remainder of this visit, he would not give away a single emotion for Damek to use against him.

Not one.

"You get out of that mud-spattered dress and get over to the wardrobe and pick out a gown for this evening," Helga said with a hint of threat in her voice. "Or I'll pick one for you."

Amelie stood near the bed with her arms at her sides, glaring back at Helga. After choosing this room, out of the three that had been prepared for them, all three women had had time for tea and to rest in the late afternoon. Though Céline had taken off her travel dress and napped in her white shift, Amelie had insisted on remaining fully clothed.

She had two sheathed blades strapped to her forearms, and she'd promised Jaromir she'd keep them a secret. Normally, she never kept secrets from Céline, but . . . Céline was the type to worry most about maintaining the ruse, and she might try to talk Amelie into leaving the blades behind at dinner, in case someone saw them up her sleeves and began to wonder why the wealthy daughter of a wool merchant chose to wear weapons at the dinner table.

"Helga's right," Céline said. "You must pick a gown. I

suggest that dark burgundy silk. It will complement your dark hair."

"I couldn't care less what complements my hair," Amelie retorted.

The doors to the wardrobe were open, exposing a ridiculous number of velvet, silk, and satin gowns. How had Helga managed to pack so many? And why?

Céline walked over and took out a silk burgundy gown with a voluminous skirt. "Please put it on?"

At least it was long-sleeved.

Helga strode over, took the gown from Céline, and turned back around, waving one hand at Amelie. "You heard her! Now get that muddy thing off."

Thankfully, Céline turned her attention back to the wardrobe, probably deciding on a gown for herself, and Amelie used the moment to unlace the front of her sky blue travel dress—which was indeed mud-spattered—and pulled it off quickly.

She held it over her forearms and said, "Helga, just lay the gown on the bed. I'll put it on myself."

Helga caught her off guard by grabbing the travel dress, jerking it away, and dropping it. "Don't you start that. I'll need to hold that gown while you step in or it will wrinkle, and then I'll need to . . ." She stopped speaking upon seeing the sheathed blades.

Céline's back was still to them, and Amelie shook her head, just once, at Helga.

A flicker of something unreadable passed through Helga's eyes, and then, instantly, she went on as if nothing had happened. Picking up the silk gown, she lowered it almost to the floor. "Now you step into this, and get your arms in so I can pull it up."

Moving as fast as she could, Amelie nearly jumped

into the gown and shoved her hands into the long sleeves. With one swift movement, Helga had the garment up and over Amelie's shoulders—while still barking orders.

"Now, you turn around and I'll lace you in."

The idea of wearing anything that required a second person to "lace her in" struck Amelie as beyond absurd. She disliked the wool travel dress, but at least it laced up the front. In the end, though, she only cared that her weapons were now covered and that Helga hadn't given her away.

As the cranky old woman pulled and prodded at the back of the gown, Amelie glanced about herself. Their room here was not as nice as the one back at Castle Sèone. The furnishings were adequate: a large bed with several comforters, a wardrobe, and a vanity table with a chair and mirror. But there was no fireplace and no window.

Thankfully, it wasn't cold. Perhaps heat from the lower hearths was coming up, and the lack of a window helped keep it in.

Helga handed Amelie a pair of flat silk shoes. Normally, the idea of leaving her boots behind would have panicked her—as it meant leaving her dagger behind. But tonight, she was well armed, so she put the shoes on without comment.

"Helga, what gown would you choose for me?" Céline asked. "I want Lady Helena to think us quite privileged."

Her comment brought Amelie a pang of guilt. Céline didn't enjoy playing at "dress up," either. For her, these gowns were costumes they needed in order to fulfill a part. Amelie realized she herself would do well to remember that.

"The amber velvet," Helga answered. "That should take anyone's nose out of the air."

"All right." Céline drew out a fine gown with a V neckline, and she held it up to herself while turning toward the mirror. "My hair up or down?"

"Depends on what you're after. You look more fetching with it down, but you look more the proper young lady with it up."

"Up, then," Céline said.

She stepped into the gown herself. Perhaps velvet didn't wrinkle? Helga went over to lace her in. Amelie had to admit Céline looked quite prosperous. The rich-toned amber velvet seemed to almost magically draw Amelie's eyes.

Sitting at the vanity table, Céline kept still while Helga twisted the majority of her hair, piled it on top of her head, and pinned it. Several strands were left to curl down past her cheekbones.

"Perfect," Céline said as if assessing a properly baked pie. "And we'll have to put Amelie's up as well. It's long enough to pin now."

"Oh for the gods' sake!" Amelie exclaimed, forgetting her resolution from a moment ago. "Nobody is pinning up my hair."

"Yes, we are, dear," Céline answered sweetly.

Amelie drew in a long breath and was about to protest with greater ferocity when an almost inaudible knock sounded on the door.

All three women froze, and a soft, female voice called, "May I enter? I am alone."

Raising one eyebrow, Céline answered, "Come in."

The door opened hesitantly, and a face peered inside. Amelie was startled when she saw the face.

A beautiful young woman stepped into the room with her hands pressed together. Her hair was black and silky straight. The top of it was held back by a thin silver band. Her dress was simply cut, but of good quality, brushed wool in a shade of light peach. Her dark eyes were slanted, giving her a hint of the exotic. Her nose was small, and her mouth was heart-shaped.

"Forgive me," she said, looking at the floor. "I didn't mean to interrupt. Master Lionel sent me up to see if you might need anything to help you prepare for dinner."

"*Master* Lionel?" Amelie asked. She'd assumed the odd little man was Damek's personal attendant.

"Yes, my lady. He manages the household, and he wishes to make certain you have all that you require. He sent me."

The young woman spoke quietly, with a frightened, almost defeated tone.

Céline walked over to her. "Please assure him that we have everything necessary. And I thank you . . . ?"

"Johanna, my lady."

"You needn't call us that," Céline said. "I am Miss Céline, and this is Miss Amelie, and this is our faithful maid, Helga." She said this last part with humor in her voice, and Helga grunted.

"Very good, miss," Johanna whispered. "When the gong sounds, you must go down to dinner. Master Lionel is very particular about the gong. Make sure you come down directly."

With that, the young woman fled the room, closing the door behind her.

Céline turned around with a puzzled expression. "What do you think of . . . ? Was she a servant? And what did you make of the whole 'Master Lionel' deference? He may be higher placed than we thought."

Helga grunted again. "I wouldn't try and make sense of anything just yet."

Amelie shrugged at Céline. Helga was probably right, and they'd have a better idea of the hierarchy here after dinner tonight.

"All right, then," Helga said, pushing Amelie forward. "You sit yourself down at that table and let me pin up your hair."

Céline gave Amelie a stern look of warning, and with a loud exhale, Amelie gave up. She plopped down at the dressing table and sat there stewing as Helga brushed out her shoulder-length hair and then deftly pinned it up, again, with a few loose strands at her temples. When it was all done, Amelie looked into the mirror in surprise, barely recognizing herself. The burgundy gown did suit her pale skin . . . and Helga had arranged her hair so effectively that no one would even be able to tell it only reached her shoulders.

"Lovely," Céline said approvingly. "We should be able to play our parts well."

From somewhere below, a gong sounded.

Before going to his own room, Anton had explained that as the Kimovesk guards would now be under orders to treat Amelie and Céline as honored guests, they were safe to walk the common areas of the castle on their own—such as between their room and the great hall. He did stress that he preferred they walk together.

Further, he'd told them that most of the Sèone guards in their party had been assigned for protection along the roads, but it was considered bad manners for any visiting guest, even a prince, to have too many guards inside a castle. So apparently, there would only be a few Sèone men in the hall and the rest would remain in the barracks. Anton, of course, was free to do as he liked, but for much of the time here, Rurik would be with him playing bodyguard, as would be expected by everyone else.

Before coming here, Anton had promised he would protect the sisters, and Amelie couldn't help noting that while Jaromir's idea of protection was constant vigilance and a sword, Anton's idea was to look ahead for any possible threat and cut it off before it happened.

So . . . it was now time to head down for dinner.

Amelie could see Céline in the mirror, and Céline met her eyes.

"You ready for this?" Amelie asked.

After a few breaths, Céline nodded.

Chapter Five

Locating the great hall took little effort. At the bottom of the stairs of the east tower, the sisters entered a passage that ran down the backside of the middle portion of the castle, and it emptied directly into the hall itself.

Still, as Céline walked into the hall through an archway, she feared that she and Amelie might be late, and she was surprised to see only Anton, Damek, several servants, and fifteen guards in the hall. The number of guards didn't surprise her, but one color in the mix of tabards did. In addition to the five black tabards of the Kimovesk men and the five tan tabards of Sèone men, there were five guards wearing the bright red tabards of the house of Väränj . . . and the Väränj were always assigned to protect whichever of the houses had a leader serving as grand prince at the time. They must be here in temporary service to the family of Quillette, and their very presence spoke strongly of the importance of Damek's future bride.

Corporal Rurik and Captain Kochè both stood a respectful yet close distance from their lords. Among the Sèone guards who were present, Céline recognized

Guardsman Voulter, Guardsman Rimoux, and Sergeant Bazin, who all stood at attention at various positions around the hall.

However, none of the other dinner guests had arrived yet.

Céline took in her surroundings.

The vast chamber was rectangular, with a long table and high-backed chairs positioned at the far end. A blazing fire burned in the hearth.

There were no dogs.

Directly across the hall was another archway, on the west side, which led to the first of the double towers on that end of the castle.

Both Anton and Damek turned as the sisters entered, and as they were standing side by side, Céline couldn't helping noting how alike they were in appearance, even in their choice of clothing tonight. While Anton wore a sleeveless midnight blue tunic over a white shirt, Damek wore a red sleeveless tunic over a white shirt. Both men wore black pants and boots. Anton wore his long sword, while Damek wore a sheathed dagger at his left hip. Damek's hair was longer and a little darker, but their faces were almost identical. The effect was somewhat eerie considering how different they were in temperament.

As the sisters approached, Damek glanced at Amelie — who was beautiful tonight — and then smiled at Céline.

"Ah, *Miss* Céline," he said. "What a vision you are."

His attention unnerved her. Why did he focus on her? The emphasis he'd placed on the word "Miss" dripped with sarcasm, as if reminding her that he knew exactly who she was: a peasant from one of his own villages.

She shot a quick look at Anton, worried that he might

take offense. But his expression didn't change, almost as if he hadn't heard the slight.

"Are we early?" Céline asked him. "I thought we heard the gong."

"No, you're precisely on time," Damek answered. "All of Rochelle's family enjoy making . . . an entrance, and who am I to object?"

Anton's gaze swept over her gown and hair, and then he took in the transformation of Amelie.

"You both look lovely," he said politely, but his voice held no emotion at all.

Céline wasn't sure how to respond.

Several large casks of wine had been stacked against the wall across from the hearth, and the striking black-haired woman, Johanna, was drawing a pitcher.

"A precaution," Damek explained. "After Carlotta's death, I ordered several casks that had been locked in the deep cellars to be brought up here and guarded. No one but Johanna has been allowed to touch them."

"You trust Johanna above anyone else, my lord?" Amelie asked, speaking directly to Damek for the first time.

He glanced at her absently. "Johanna can be trusted."

As Céline mulled that over, movement from the archway caught her attention. Two middle-aged, finely dressed people walked into the hall: a man and a woman.

Damek offered them both a bow, and then said, with some ceremony, "The Lady Helena and Lord Hamish."

Céline took in as many details as possible in the next breath. Lady Helena's hair must have once been reddish blond, but was now fading, leaving only hints of its past color. It was elaborately arranged on top of her head in a fashion that must have taken a maid at least an hour. She was statuesque, with her waist just beginning to thicken and her generous bosom beginning to sag—even though she was tightly laced into a satin gown of sapphire blue. Her expression caught Céline's attention the most: haughtiness mixed with a hint of desperation.

Lord Hamish was well over six feet tall and broad-shouldered. His hair was thinning, and this made his overly broad features look even broader. He had the appearance of once having been quite fit, but was now going to fat. The only thing Céline could read in his expression was privileged arrogance.

However, the instant he spotted Céline and Amelie, his eyes raked over them both with a glint of lecherous interest, and Céline fought not to shudder.

This was going to be a long night.

Lady Helena paused at the sight of Anton.

"My lady," Damek continued. "May I present my brother, Prince Anton, Miss Céline and Miss Amelie of Castle Sèone?"

Helena ignored the sisters as her eyes locked on to Anton. Céline had no idea how this would play out, as by all reckoning, Lady Helena should be in a state of mourning.

"My lord," Helena said, with a curtsey to Anton. "It is an honor. I remember meeting you once when you were but a youth."

Anton stepped forward, took her hand, and kissed the back of it.

"Forgive my intrusion at this time, and I offer my condolences," he said. "My father sent me to assist you." He motioned toward Céline and Amelie with one hand. "And he asked me to bring my two seers."

Lord Hamish frowned. "Seers?"

"Yes, they have proven invaluable to my family," Anton answered. "My father himself recently sought their help to resolve a difficult matter."

"Indeed," Damek put in with some bravado. "And our father would do anything to offer you all the resources of the house of Pählen."

As Lord Hamish was about to speak again, voices came from the archway, and Céline looked over to three much younger people who swept into the hall, side by side. From Anton's earlier descriptions of the family, it was not difficult for Céline to know who was who.

Rochelle was on the left. The first word that came to mind was "exquisite." She looked to be about eighteen years old. She was tall for a woman, probably reaching Damek's nose, with a slight, willowy figure. Her hair was red-gold and hung to the small of her back. Her eyes were so light brown they seemed to glow. Her complexion was creamy and flawless, and she wore a light green gown of crushed velvet, similar in cut to Céline's, with a V neck that exposed her slender throat and collarbones. Her walk was so graceful she might have been gliding on ice.

To the right of the trio was a much shorter girl of perhaps fifteen. This would be Lizbeth. Although she shared her elder sister's coloring, there the resemblance ended. A few spots—commonly suffered by those her age—marked her cheeks. She was of a healthy, slightly stocky build. Her hair had been carelessly woven into a loose braid, and she walked with both arms swinging at her sides. The skirt of her satin gown was already wrinkled. She exuded a youthful energy and struck Céline as one of those people who showed every emotion on her face.

Finally, in the center was a young man ... Rochelle's twin brother, Heath, already a baron, wearing a sleeveless cream tunic over a black wool shirt. He was only an inch or two taller than Rochelle, with her same willowy build, coloring, and delicate features.

On her the effect was ethereal. On him ... it was something else. It gave him an aura that was borderline effeminate. While Anton and Damek were both slender of build, the bones in their wrists, arms, and shoulders looked solid, as if neither would put much effort into swinging a sword, hurling a spear, or handling an unruly warhorse.

The young baron could be described as fragile and almost pretty.

Directly behind these three young people came a tall, armed man, most likely their bodyguard. However, he wore the pale yellow tabard of the house of Äntes.

All of them stopped only a few paces into the hall.

"Who are they?" Lizbeth asked bluntly, looking at Anton, Céline, and Amelie.

"My dear," Lady Helena said, her voice rising in reprimand. "Please remember yourself." She gestured somewhat regally to Anton. "This is Prince Damek's brother."

Damek strode to Rochelle and took her hand. "Anton, I introduce my bride-to-be, Rochelle Quillette."

Rochelle dropped her head and blushed prettily, but the pride in Damek's voice was clear. Perhaps he truly valued her?

Or ... was he just throwing his good fortune in Anton's face?

Further introductions were made, along with the background that Anton had created for the sisters—as the daughters of a wealthy wool merchant—and Céline found herself caught up in a current of polite nods and responses.

The young baron was barely able to make eye contact with the new arrivals, and as a result, Céline felt an unwanted rush of pity. He seemed even shyer than his twin sister.

Lizbeth, however, did not labor under any form of shyness, and as Céline was further assessing Rochelle, she heard Anton use the word "seers" again.

"Seers?" Lizbeth asked. "Why would your father want you to bring them?"

Anton's expression flickered, as if he wasn't certain how to broach this topic with a fifteen-year-old girl, and so Céline stepped in.

"As it has been feared that your sister might have been poisoned, the princes' father hoped my sister and I could uncover whoever was responsible."

"She was poisoned," Lizbeth returned. "That's not in doubt."

Céline found herself thrown somewhat off-kilter by this straightforward girl.

Before she could respond, Amelie broke in. "Why would anyone want to poison Carlotta?"

"Why, to put a stop to this marriage, of course," Lizbeth answered derisively, as if the question were foolish. "She'd been negotiating the match for weeks."

Lady Helena's face tightened with undisguised anger. "That has nothing to do with why some mad person would poison her wine, and you will keep your ignorant assumptions to yourself." She turned back to Céline. "Forgive my youngest daughter. I fear she has not the years or the sense to be out in polite society. Whoever committed this horrible act most likely has a grudge against those better than him or herself and wished to do my family harm."

Lizbeth's face tinged red, but she kept silent, and Céline's mind raced. Carlotta had been the one negotiating the betrothal? That was a worthwhile piece of news.

An awkward moment followed until Damek said, "Miss Céline presented me with another possibility today."

Céline's eyes flew to him, and he gave her a hard, almost threatening look. He wanted her to repeat what she'd told him in the cellar.

With little choice, she turned to Helena. "My lady, I am not certain your eldest daughter was killed intentionally. In addition to serving as Prince Anton's seer, I am also his court healer and apothecary." She hesitated at the next part, wondering how it would be received. "Prince Damek allowed me to examine Carlotta's body . . . and although it was a difficult task for me to conduct, I saw no signs of death by poison. Almost every form leaves some telltale mark, and your daughter bore none. It is possible she died of a natural cause . . . perhaps a weak heart."

Both Lady Helena and Lord Hamish suddenly stared at Céline as if she were their savior. Helena even grabbed her hand. "Oh, my dear, is this true? If so, you are the bearer of good news." Then, perhaps mindful of how *that* might have sounded, she quickly added, "Of course we are in pain over the loss of Carlotta, but the thought of her being murdered has been too terrible to bear. If indeed her sad death was natural and unavoidable, it would give me some peace."

Helena glanced at Damek with a gleam in her eye,

and Hamish looked as if he'd just been granted a great boon.

With a jolt, Céline realized that they wanted the marriage to take place just as badly as Damek and Prince Lieven. An ugly murder at the dinner table was hardly conducive to negotiations, but if Carlotta had simply died ... things could move forward with much greater ease.

"Perhaps you and I could speak later in private?" Céline asked Helena. "It would be helpful for me to know the history of Carlotta's health. I may be able to shed more light."

"Of course, my dear," Helena answered readily, "as soon as you like."

Johanna approached silently, carrying a tray laden with goblets and a large pitcher.

People began taking goblets from the tray as Johanna moved between them, pouring dark red wine. All talk of Carlotta's death ceased, as it would be unseemly for her mother to discuss her health history in such a setting.

"Let us have wine and conversation before dinner is served," Damek said, playing the gracious host. "We are still missing the Lady Saorise. I've tried to speak to her about listening for the gong, but I fear it is a losing battle."

At the mention of that name, Amelie's eyes went wide, and she froze in place. Thankfully, no one but Céline noticed.

What was wrong?

Further movement in the archway caused Céline to half turn, and as if she had been called by Damek's comment, a woman walked into the hall. She was middle-aged and slight of build with long silver-blond hair. Her face showed signs of fading beauty. She wore rings on all her fingers, and as opposed to a gown she wore a long robe of purple silk, like that of a scholar or a priestess.

"Ah, there you are," Damek said. He turned back to Anton, "I don't believe you have met my counselor, the Lady Saorise."

Amelie was taking in quick breaths, and Céline moved to her side. "Whatever is wrong, do not show it now," she whispered. "Tell me later."

As Amelie recovered her composure, Lady Saorise entered the group. Céline smiled and nodded again, but she was beginning to grow slightly overwhelmed at having to take stock of so many people at once.

Several guests took sips of wine, and Rochelle broke her shy silence by asking Anton, "Was your journey pleasant, my lord? I hope it did not rain."

"I fear it did," he answered, "but the distance is not too far, and we spent a comfortable night in Rékausi."

Céline again nodded politely in agreement as she silently tried to get a read on everyone. Although she'd seen no evidence yet that Carlotta had been murdered, something about Lizbeth's absolute certainty was troubling.

Lady Helena and Lord Hamish both seemed beyond eager to have a natural death proven to be the case. But how could it be proven? And if there was a killer here, and Anton took his own people and left, and then the killer struck again, Anton would look negligent to Prince Lieven. No, they couldn't leave Castle Kimovesk . . . and yet, because Damek had forced her to share her initial thoughts on this matter, she was now uncertain how to continue with a murder investigation.

Her mind rolled over other possibilities.

What if Carlotta had been murdered after all? Céline tried to think of any poison she'd ever heard of that might leave no trace. She'd heard rumors of a few from distant lands, but how could such be obtained, and by whom?

Her gaze moved to the tall bodyguard who had come in with the trio of siblings. He was handsome in a rugged way, with a weathered complexion. His chin was solid and his nose was aquiline. His dark hair curled down the nape of his neck, and his build suggested great strength. He wore chain armor over a wool shirt, covered by his pale yellow tabard. Céline couldn't help noticing how his eyes constantly followed Rochelle whenever she moved, with a hint of hunger.

As she continued her scan, she stopped on Captain Kochè. He, too, stared at Rochelle, but with an entirely different expression. His eyes were narrow . . . as if he hated her.

What possible reason could he have? Prince Damek's marriage wouldn't affect him.

"What exactly does Prince Anton mean when he says that you're a seer?" Lizbeth asked Céline suddenly.

Céline turned to the girl. "Pardon?"

"What does a seer do?"

Lady Helena pursed her mouth as if again displeased with her youngest daughter's manners.

But Céline saw a possible opening. "I can read a person's future, and my sister, Miss Amelie, can read the past."

Lizbeth raised an eyebrow. "Prove it."

"Oh, Lizbeth," Heath said quietly. "Can't you just leave off for once?" His tone was not harsh or scolding. He sounded more embarrassed than anything else.

"Why?" Lizbeth challenged him. "I want to see this. She says Carlotta may not have been murdered, and our mother can't wait to believe her. Let her prove who she is."

Although the girl had a penchant for stirring up trouble, there was something refreshing about her . . . something that reminded Céline of Amelie.

"Shall I read you?" Céline answered the girl. "Tell you your future?"

Lizbeth's gaze grew sharp. She shared the same light brown eyes of her siblings. "No . . . ," she answered slowly, "not me." Looking around, she pointed at Johanna. "Her. And have your sister read her past. That way, Johanna can verify if the reading is true."

A penchant for stirring up trouble indeed.

Startled by this quick change of events, Amelie glanced at Anton. What should she do? To his credit, Anton turned casually to Damek and asked, "What say you? It could provide some entertainment before dinner."

Amelie knew well that Anton had no interest in providing entertainment, but a successful show here could be useful if he had to press the family later—and try to convince them that their guards, their servants, or they themselves must agree to a reading. Or, if someone vehemently refused after seeing what Amelie could do . . . well, that could be just as telling.

Prince Damek, however, seemed uncertain, and he smiled at Lizbeth. "Must it be Johanna? She so dislikes attention. Could you not choose someone else?"

"No," Lizbeth answered firmly. "Her."

Damek's eyes glinted in warning at Lizbeth, but the girl was not daunted. Amelie began to suspect that there was something behind Lizbeth's choice.

When Damek did not argue further, his silence appeared to imply assent.

"Good, then," Lizbeth said, turning to Amelie. "How do you start?"

This posed the next dilemma for Amelie, as Céline always took the lead in situations like this one. Céline knew how to play the game, how to put on a show . . . how to smile and put people at ease.

Thankfully, Céline was well aware of Amelie's shortcomings in this regard.

"Over here," Céline said, pointing to the table. "They'll both need to sit down." She smiled reassuringly at Johanna, who, as a servant of Damek, had no choice in this. "Amelie only needs to touch your hand."

Before she knew what was happening, Amelie found herself seated in a high-back chair, facing Johanna—who was seated so close their knees almost touched. Hoping that she sounded reassuring, Amelie said, "Just give me your hand."

Hesitantly, Johanna reached out, and Amelie grasped her fingers.

As Amelie had no set question in mind to be answered, she closed her eyes and focused on the spark of Johanna's spirit and then on Johanna's past. Amelie's gift as one of the Mist-Torn often showed her scenes that were important for one reason or another.

She focused more intently on the spark of Johanna's spirit.

When the first jolt hit, Amelie braced for another. The second jolt hit, and she found herself rushing through the gray and white mists, moving backward in time.

Her ability was slightly different from Céline's in several ways. While Céline could only see someone else's future as an observer, if Amelie wished, she could bond with her target and see the past through his or her eyes. In these cases, the people Amelie read could be just as conscious as she was of the scenes being replayed, and afterward they were aware of exactly what she'd seen. The people Céline read never had any idea what she was seeing. The two sisters had discussed these differences, and Céline guessed they might be due to the fact that the past was set in stone, and the future could still be changed—that she was just seeing one possible line unless something was done to alter it.

This time, Amelie did not bond with Johanna. She wished to be only an observer. When the reading was over, Johanna would have no idea what images from the past Amelie might have seen.

The mists rushed around her, and when they cleared, Amelie found herself in a familiar room with low velvet-covered couches . . . Damek's private chambers.

Looking toward the hearth, she saw Damek holding Johanna in an embrace. It didn't appear to be forced, as Johanna wasn't struggling, but her face was turned away from him.

"Nothing has changed," he whispered in her ear.

"Everything's changed. You're to be married. She and her family arrive tomorrow. What would you have me do? I swear I will leave and not return."

His expression shifted to anger, and he shoved her away. "You have no place to go and we both know it. But I'll not have sulking women about me, and you know that, too." His tone was cruel as he asked. "Do you love me?"

Tears streamed down her face. "I love you."

He reached out, slowly pushing the top of her gown over the edge of her shoulder. "Show me."

The image vanished, and Amelie was once again in the mists, this time rushing forward. Then she was back in the great hall trying to control her expression—wishing she were as skilled at this as Céline. Johanna had not been concerned before, but now she looked anxious as she took in Amelie's expression. Perhaps she had not believed Amelie would see anything.

Everyone around them waited expectantly.

Damek stood by, tense and wary.

Johanna could certainly not be exposed as Damek's lover in front of Rochelle and her entire family. That would only cause embarrassment and further hinder the marriage negotiations. Panic flooded Amelie. What could she say? Céline would be able to tell the perfect lie here, but Amelie had never been skilled at the art of lying.

"What did you see?" Lizbeth asked.

Somehow Amelie managed to imitate her sister and she smiled, saying the first thing that came into her mind. "The mists took me back to Johanna's youth. Her brother bet her a moon's worth of chores that she could not ride a new horse purchased by their father. She accepted . . . and was promptly thrown into the mud . . . and did her brother's chores for an entire moon."

Relief flickered across Johanna's face, and Damek relaxed.

Only Lizbeth frowned as she studied Johanna. "Is that true?"

Johanna nodded. She must be more quick-witted than she looked, because she lied. "Yes, it's true. I've never forgotten that day."

Lord Hamish stepped forward and held his hand out to Amelie. She didn't care for the interested glint in his eye. "How charming," he said. "You must read me after dinner."

Amelie bit the inside of her cheek and allowed him to help her up from the chair. "Of course."

Anton knew Amelie well enough to see that she'd lied, but he also knew she must have a good reason, so he kept silent and stood close in case she needed any help extracting herself from Lord Hamish's grip.

She did not, and she deftly moved away from Lord Hamish to stand near Céline.

The entire evening had been torture so far, and he longed to be away from this place. He did not know how long he could keep this polite mask on his face. It might help if he could stand with Céline for a little while. Her close presence sometimes helped him gather himself. But he didn't dare. If he showed her any notice at all, Damek would see it.

The sound of light, clicking heels echoed through the hall as the diminutive figure of Lionel came through the archway and went directly to Damek.

Damek leaned down as Lionel spoke in his ear and then Damek nodded and addressed his guests. "I am informed that dinner will be served. Could we take our places at the table?"

"Do you have a preferred seating arrangement, my lord?" Rochelle asked quietly.

"Tonight?" Damek said as if mulling this over. "I think not."

To Anton's surprise, Amelie walked over to Heath. "Would you sit with me, Baron? You can tell me about the wine business."

The young man stared at her. "Oh, my uncle is the one

who runs the . . . I'm not allowed to . . ." He trailed off and then gathered himself, looking pleased at her invitation. "It would be my honor. And please call me Heath. No one here will notice."

Anton experienced a moment of relief, followed by guilt, that he wouldn't have to converse with the young baron at dinner. Heath seemed so shy that conversation would be difficult and require effort, and Anton would rather keep his attention focused on everything transpiring around him.

Lord Hamish hurried toward Céline, and held his arm out for her to grasp. "Shall we?"

Without hesitation, Céline took his arm. Anton ground his teeth but didn't move. Rochelle took Damek's arm. Remembering his manners, Anton turned to look around for Lady Helena, but she was already drifting over toward the table with the Lady Saorise, and Anton found himself facing Lizbeth.

Though he found her somewhat brusque, he held his arm out politely. To do less would be unthinkable.

She blinked and blushed, and for a brief moment, she lost all her bravado and turned into an uncertain teenage girl right before his eyes. Pity washed through him.

"Please join me for dinner," he said.

Quickly, she took his arm, and he decided he would not mind her company so much. She was certainly preferable to attempting small talk with Damek . . . and Céline could handle Lord Hamish, so he need not worry too much.

The main thing was just to get through the evening and then see what Céline wanted to do next regarding this "investigation." He fervently hoped she'd be able to prove Carlotta had died a natural death.

Then they could go home.

As people took their seats, Céline sipped from her goblet. "This is a good wine, at least to my palette." She turned to Heath, who sat across from her with Amelie. "Baron, what do you think? Is this a good vintage?"

Lord Hamish snorted in disgust. "The young fool wouldn't know a white grape from a red. He knows nothing about wine."

Heath kept his eyes on his plate, but Lizbeth glared at her uncle. "At least he doesn't drink up half our stores."

Lady Helena stiffened and another awkward silence followed, but Anton's assessment of Lizbeth was rising. Brusque or not, she stood up for her brother.

Lord Hamish ignored the comment and turned to Céline. "Will you read my future later?"

"It would be my pleasure," she answered smoothly.

He smiled and took a long swallow of his wine. He leaned close to Céline as if he was about to say something else.

No words came out.

He attempted to clear his throat and draw a breath. Alarm crossed his features.

"My lord?" Céline asked.

Panic filled Hamish's eyes as he stood and shoved back his chair, grabbing his throat and fighting to breathe.

In that instant, everyone began talking or crying out at once.

"Brother!" Lady Helena called, rushing toward him.

Rochelle was on her feet, but she looked wildly to the tall bodyguard standing nearby. "Maddox!" she cried. "It's happening again. Please make it stop!"

The Äntes guard bolted toward Hamish, catching him as he fell backward.

Céline was right there, pulling at Lord Hamish's collar to loosen it. "Don't fight it!" she told him. "Try to relax. Just let yourself breathe."

Hamish's eyes bulged in terror and agony. His face first turned red and then blue as he fought to breathe and failed. All Anton could do was stand there helplessly. Hamish's body began to convulse.

It took him several moments to die, but finally, he went still . . . with his eyes open.

The tall guard called Maddox lowered his body to the floor. He looked over to Rochelle as if he had just failed her.

She stared back at him.

Damek watched this exchange with a tight expression.

Céline knelt on the floor beside Hamish, and Anton couldn't help a rush of revulsion when she put her hands in the dead man's mouth and opened it, feeling his tongue and peering in at his throat.

"She did it!" Lady Helena shouted.

In confusion, Anton looked up to see her pointing at Johanna.

Johanna stepped back in fear.

"You told us yourself," Helena went on hysterically, this time speaking to Damek. "Nobody else touched the wine. It had to be her!"

Damek had not moved from the head of the table. "I assure you it was not Johanna."

Poor Lizbeth was struck speechless, and so was Heath as they both looked across the table and down at their dead uncle.

"It may not even have been the wine," Céline put in, and all eyes turned to her.

"What do you mean?" Anton asked.

Céline didn't answer. She stood. Hamish's half-full goblet was still on the table. Picking it up, she sniffed the contents.

"I don't see any signs that he was poisoned," she said. "His tongue is not swollen, his windpipe is open, and his throat appears normal. I don't know why he ceased to breathe." She paused. "But the only way I can think to test the liquid in this goblet for anything besides wine is to taste it myself, just a drop or two on my tongue. I may be able to taste a foreign ingredient."

"No," Anton ordered.

"I don't know how else to test it."

As of yet, Amelie had not spoken since Lord Hamish fell. Now she looked to the Lady Saorise and said, "She might."

Damek's face registered surprise at Amelie's comment, but then he, too, looked at Saorise. She raised one silver-blond eyebrow, and after a moment, he nodded.

With unhurried grace, Saorise walked over and reached out for the goblet. "May I?"

Wordlessly, Céline handed it to her.

Saorise held the goblet with both hands and closed her eyes. The great hall was silent when she opened them again. Before anyone could move, she dipped her finger in the liquid and then put it into her mouth.

"My lady," Céline cried.

"There is nothing in this goblet but wine," Saorise announced. As everyone stared at her, she took a long swallow as if to prove herself. "It is only wine."

Lizbeth found her voice. "Then what ... what killed Uncle Hamish and Carlotta?" Taking a step backward, she shook her head. "This is madness. We must sever this betrothal and go home."

"She's right," Heath said quietly. "We should have left before now."

Lady Helena straightened. "No. Your uncle would not have wanted that." She looked to Damek. "We must move the date of the wedding closer, as soon as it can be arranged."

CHAPTER SIX

Not long after, Céline found herself in Damek's chambers with only him, Amelie, and Anton present. Even Kochè and Rurik had been ordered to wait outside in the passage. Lord Hamish's body had been removed to the cellars, and the remaining members of his family had gone to their rooms.

Damek paced like a manic cat, all traces of the gracious host gone, as if he had been an actor playing a part downstairs.

Céline struggled to make sense of the chain of events she'd just witnessed. With the exception of the mystery of how Lord Hamish had died, she was most confused by Lady Helena's reaction ... of wanting to move up the wedding date as soon as possible. Hadn't she and the family threatened to leave Kimovesk after Carlotta died? That was what Damek had said in his letter to Anton. Had Damek lied, or had something changed?

Damek suddenly stopped pacing and whirled on Anton. "Your seers are useless! First they tell me there was no murder at all, and then they fail to stop the next one!"

Anton's entire body was rigid. "My task in coming here was to clear the way for your wedding to Rochelle, and yet it seems that two deaths in her family are no hindrance. I don't see any reason why I shouldn't take my people and leave in the morning. You'll be married inside the month."

"For once you're right," Damek hissed at him. "I don't need help from you. I can complete this marriage on my own, and then through my connection to the house of Äntes, I'll rise far beyond what you could ever hope for."

"We can't leave," Céline said quietly. "Two people dying for lack of air . . . for no apparent reason at the dinner table cannot be a coincidence. I don't know how these murders are being done, but there is a killer in this castle, and it seems to me that young Lizbeth is right. Someone is attempting to stop the marriage." She looked to Damek. "After Carlotta died, who took over negotiations for Rochelle's dowry?"

He paused a moment and calmed slightly before answering, "Lord Hamish. He was actually easier to deal with than Carlotta, and we had almost come to terms."

"And then Lord Hamish died," Céline finished.

She took a glance at Amelie and knew her sister well enough to see that Amelie was practically bursting to speak to her alone, but she didn't think Anton or Damek would pay much attention to Amelie's partially veiled expression of desperation. After all, they had just witnessed a death. Anyone might show some distress.

Anton ran his hands through his hair, and Céline could see that in spite of what she'd said, he was still considering packing up.

"If the goal is indeed to stop the marriage from taking place," she went on, "then Lady Helena's announcement tonight will only drive the killer to further action. Anton, what if he . . . or she decides to murder Rochelle next?

WITCHES WITH THE ENEMY   113

Or Damek? How will that look to your father if you've already abandoned the scene?"

Damek and Anton both tensed at her words, and Damek said, "Murder me?"

Had that not occurred to him?

Céline didn't answer and let her words sink in for a few moments.

Finally, Damek glared at her as if she was to blame. "And what is it you think you can do?"

"Amelie and I need to work up a list of people with possible motives, and then you need to back us absolutely should we ask to read someone."

"I have no authority over Rochelle's family or their guards," he answered.

"I know," she answered. "Let us worry about them, but if I ask, you'll give the order regarding anyone else?"

His eyes were still manic. "You think you can root out this killer?"

She shrugged, and it seemed that expectations for all forms of scraping and deference and calling Damek "my lord" had gone out the window. "We've done it before. Ask your father."

"Fine," he snapped. "Make your list and I'll give you a free hand, but I want this finished quickly, do you understand?"

"You'll need to string along the marriage negotiations," Anton put in. "As Céline said, if you rush it, you or Rochelle could become a target. Perhaps we should even say that the wedding is postponed?"

"No!" Damek closed his eyes and lowered his voice. "Perhaps. I need to think."

"The sisters will need some time to put a list together," Anton said as he started for the door, motioning

Amelie and Céline to follow. "I suggest we discuss further plans from there."

With his eyes still closed, Damek nodded. "Yes, now get out."

At long last, Amelie finally found herself at the door of their own room. Anton and Rurik had walked with them from Damek's chambers on the other side of the castle.

"We're in the room right next door if you need anything," Anton said.

"Yes, thank you," Céline answered. "Try to get some rest."

Without even waiting to say good night to the men, Amelie pushed the door of their own room open and went inside. Helga was there, amidst several glowing candle lanterns. She stood near the dressing table, arranging food on a tray: bread, ham, cheese, and steaming mugs.

Amelie was actually glad to see her. For some reason, Helga made the most bizarre situations feel normal.

"There you are," Helga said. "I was starting to worry after I heard another one of the hoity-toity had dropped dead at the table. But I figured dinner might be canceled."

"Oh, Helga," she said. "Will you get me out of this ridiculous gown? I can barely breathe."

As she turned to offer her back to Helga, Céline entered and closed the door.

"Amelie, I think you have a good deal to tell us," Céline said.

"Yes, I don't even know where to begin. Just let me get out of this gown."

As Helga deftly unlaced the back of the burgundy

silk, Amelie reveled in taking a long breath of air. Then she remembered the weapons strapped to her wrists and came to a decision.

"Céline . . . ," she began, sloughing the gown off her shoulders and letting it fall. She held out her arms. "Jaromir gave me these before we left Sèone. He told me to keep them a secret, but I'm tired of hiding them every time I change clothes. Don't ask me to take them off, because I won't."

"Why would you think I'd ask you to take them off?"

"I don't know . . . for the ruse, I suppose. We're supposed to be from a family of wealthy merchants."

Mildly affronted, Céline said, "Well, you needn't worry. I won't ask you to take them off. Not after tonight anyway. Now tell me what you know about Lady Saorise . . . and how you know it."

"You girls come and have something to eat first," Helga said, dropping Amelie's gown on the bed. "I know you've not had supper."

"In a moment," Amelie said, thinking where she might best start here. "Céline . . . first, you should know that Johanna is Damek's mistress, and I don't mean some servant girl he forces into his bed now and then. When I read her, I saw a scene of the night before Rochelle's arrival, and Johanna was threatening to leave him. Damek told her his marriage would change nothing between them, and then she said she loved him."

"Oh . . . my," Céline said, walking over and sitting down on the bed. "You're certain? There's no way you could have misinterpreted what you saw?"

"It was clear. But I couldn't expose her downstairs. You can only imagine what would have happened."

"No, of course you were quite right." Céline's brow

furrowed. "But that puts Johanna's name at the top of the list. She has a motive."

Amelie nodded. Now came the difficult part. "And the Lady Saorise . . . brace yourself . . ." She trailed off, struggling for the right words, and decided to just spit it out. "She created the elixir that turned all those soldiers into wolf-beasts up on Ryazan. She's some kind of sorceress."

"What?" Céline gasped, standing.

Helga stopped slicing cheese and turned from the dressing table. "A kettle witch? Here?"

That was Helga's term for anyone who practiced magic who'd not been born with a special gift as one of the Mist-Torn. But it was hardly helpful now.

On the sisters' last journey, up to the silver mines in Ryazan, they'd been engaged to discover why the soldiers there were turning into great, mad wolves. In the end, Amelie had done a reading of the man responsible, and when she looked into his past, she'd seen him with the Lady Saorise and Damek.

Saorise had used the blood of a dead Móndyalítko shape-shifter—who'd been killed for this purpose—and several body parts from a dead wolf to make an elixir. This was all part of an experiment Damek had wanted to try, but Saorise had helped willingly and shown not the slightest concern over causing suffering or death.

Amelie had explained some of this to Céline last summer, but she'd never described Lady Saorise or mentioned the name. There didn't seem to be a need.

Céline looked to Helga. "I don't know much about . . . Saorise would need to be quite skilled in order to make such a powerful elixir?"

Helga nodded. "I should say so. Move her to the top of your list."

"But what motive could she have?" Céline asked. "She's highly placed here, but her power is dependent on Damek's power. She'd want him to marry into royal connections."

That was true.

"She did seem awfully sure that wine hadn't been poisoned, and she didn't hesitate to drink it," Amelie put in. "If she'd used some kind of . . . spell to murder Hamish, she'd have known beforehand that the wine was safe."

"Yes, but she tasted a drop with her finger first. Perhaps she has knowledge of herb lore. Had Anton allowed me to do that, I could have told you if there was something more in the wine."

All three women went silent for a moment.

"Motive or not," Helga said, "I'd put her on your list."

"Yes," Céline said, turning back to business. "Of course." She reached out and touched Amelie's hand. "You've done well."

It embarrassed Amelie how much she liked hearing her sister's praise. For much of her life, Amelie had longed to be useful at something besides being good in a knife fight, and now she finally was.

"Two other people worth watching are that Captain Maddox and Captain Kochè," Céline continued. "Maddox never takes his eyes off Rochelle, and he looks lovesick to me. And Captain Kochè glares at her."

"Really?" Amelie asked. "I hadn't noticed. All right. We'll see what we can find out." She paused. "Helga, do you think you might learn anything from the other servants? Might they gossip?"

"Maybe," Helga grunted. "I can try."

"We can't discount the family, either," Céline said. "One thing that truly puzzles me is why the killer hasn't targeted Rochelle or Damek. If someone wished to stop the wedding cold, wouldn't they kill the bride or groom?"

"I know," Amelie agreed. "I wondered about that, too."

"Lizbeth is the most outspoken," Céline said, "and she was also the first one tonight to insist the family leave. Heath backed her up, but she spoke first. She seems fond of her two siblings, and Rochelle is too gentle-natured to argue with her mother or uncle. If someone tried to force you to marry Damek . . . I'm afraid I might be willing to kill in order to stop it."

Amelie glanced away. She'd certainly kill to protect Céline from such a fate—but she wouldn't do it by poison or arcane means.

"And what about the bride . . . this Rochelle?" Helga asked. "Is she truly so gentle? Could it be an act? What if she's trying to save herself?"

Amelie sighed. Perhaps they were trying to make *too* much progress in a single night?

As if reading her face, Céline drew her over to the dressing table. "That's enough speculation for now. Let's eat a little and get some sleep. We'll start fresh in the morning."

"What about Anton and Rurik's supper?" Amelie asked. "Is someone going to feed them?"

"Don't you worry," Helga answered. "Rurik knows what to do. He'll make sure the prince eats."

With some relief, Amelie reached for a cup of tea. It was probably cold by now, but she didn't care.

Late in the night, Céline lay awake in the bed she shared with Amelie.

Her sister was fast asleep, and Helga snored loudly as she lay on a palette on the floor. Though Céline longed for sleep, she couldn't stop trying to reason out how the deaths of Carlotta and Hamish had been arranged.

Amelie's news about the Lady Saorise was unsettling.

Could the victims have been murdered via some sort of spell? Even if so, there was no guarantee that it had been Saorise. Céline knew nothing of Rochelle or her family or their guards. Any one of them could have knowledge of the arcane arts.

If a spell had been cast, how much time would it need to take effect? Carlotta and Hamish had both died within moments of sitting down at the table—before the food had even been served. Where had everyone been standing just before dinner was announced?

Closing her eyes, Céline tried to re-create the scene in her mind . . . to place everyone, to try to remember who had been engaged in conversation and who had not. Amelie's reading of Johanna had brought most of the party nearer to the table.

Céline herself had been near Lizbeth, but she had not been watching the girl. Damek had been near Rochelle. Beyond that . . . lying there in the bed, Céline couldn't place everyone. She would probably need to be standing in the great hall for her memory to accurately re-create the scene.

As that thought passed through her head, she opened her eyes.

No . . . not at this hour, she told herself.

But then again, what time would possibly be better? Everyone would be asleep except perhaps a few Kimovesk guards on night duty. They were no danger to her. Damek had made sure of that. She would have all the time she needed to stand alone in the great hall and use it as a visual guide to re-create the events before everyone sat down. The more she considered this, the more it seemed her best course of action.

It was an odd thought that she would be safe walking around at night inside the home of Anton's enemy ... but she would. There was no one here who wished her any harm. Of course there was a killer somewhere in the castle, but as of yet, Céline was no threat to him or her, and Céline had no part in the marriage negotiations.

She would be risking nothing by going below and trying to set a few things straight in her mind. Anton was desperate to get this solved as quickly as possible, and she was willing to try almost anything to make that happen.

Quietly, she crawled out of bed and tiptoed to the wardrobe, which was cracked but not open. Thankfully, the hinges were oiled and after pulling open one door, she lifted out a wool gown that laced up the front.

In moments, she had it on. Then she pulled on the silk shoes she'd been wearing earlier.

Amelie had not stirred, and Helga hadn't ceased her snoring.

Céline slipped from the room and out into the passageway. Closing the door, she breathed in relief. The passage was empty, and she hurried for the stairs. Upon reaching the main floor of the castle, she peered out of the stairwell down the long passage to the great hall.

She saw no one.

If she ran into any of the Kimovesk guards, she would simply tell them she was unable to sleep and had decided to try a walk. They were under orders to treat her as a guest, and they feared Damek a good deal more than they might wish to interfere with her.

Though the passage along the backside of the castle seemed longer than it had earlier in the evening, she walked it swiftly and emerged into the great hall. The fire was dead, and the hall was now deserted—as expected. A few low-burning braziers on the walls provided light.

She stepped in slowly until she stood in the same spot she'd been in only moments before Master Lionel came to inform Damek that dinner was about to be served. Looking around, she tried to set the scene in her mind.

First, closing her eyes, she attempted to hear the voices of who had been speaking and who had been silent.

If someone had turned away from the group to do . . . *something* to set Hamish's death into motion, who might that person have been?

Johanna had been walking away from Amelie.

Rochelle had been standing near Damek.

Captain Maddox had been near the wall—and no one had been observing him.

Where had the Lady Saorise been standing? Had she been engaged in a conversation?

"Céline?"

She opened her eyes. Prince Damek and two guards in black tabards stood just inside the west entrance. Damek was still fully dressed, wearing the same clothes from dinner with the sheathed dagger at his hip.

"What are you doing here?" he asked, coming closer.

Suddenly, she was embarrassed. She'd thought him long asleep. She must look rather a fool standing there alone in the great hall at this hour.

"Forgive me, my lord," she said. "I couldn't sleep and thought to try and re-create where everyone had been standing just before . . . before . . ." She trailed off.

He didn't appear to even hear her words. Then he was directly in front of her.

"You are alone?" he asked in what sounded like disbelief. His eyes glinted.

Though his manner was unsettling, she wasn't afraid. At present, he needed her skills and abilities, and he wouldn't do anything to jeopardize his impending marriage.

Looking over one shoulder, he ordered his guards, "Get out."

Both men turned on their heel and strode out of the hall the way they'd come.

Though she still wasn't frightened, something about this alarmed Céline enough that she took a few steps backward. "I only sought to get a few things straight in my mind. Again, my apologies. I should be in my room."

In a flash, he cut off her exit, not touching her, but neither would he let her move past him.

"You're my brother's pet, aren't you?" he whispered. "I can see it when he looks at you . . . when he speaks of you."

The glinting in his eyes grew brighter, and Céline tried to step around him. "My lord, if you please—"

He cut her off again, and for the first time, fear began creeping into the pit of her stomach. He was staring at her as if he'd somehow come across an unexpected treasure.

"His pet, aren't you?" It was cold in the hall, but a few drops of sweat trickled down his temples. "Do you bring him comfort at night? Does he tell you his secrets?"

Now she could see madness behind the glint, and she bolted, dashing around him and running for the east archway. Before she'd gone three steps, something wrenched on her hair, and she was pulled at a rapid pace toward the wall.

The next thing she knew, he had her back against the wall, and he held her there.

Fighting for calm, she searched for anything she might say to make him stop. "I was brought here to ensure your marriage to a member of the royal family. Have you forgotten that?"

His body shook several times, and as his eyes bored into hers, she could see what looked to be a war taking place. A part of him had heard her, but another part couldn't seem to stop.

"So pretty," he whispered, touching her face. "Would he still care for you if you weren't so pretty?"

One of his fingernails raked down her cheek, and she couldn't help crying out and trying to push him away. He gasped in pleasure at her struggles, and when she got another look at his face, all semblance of reason was gone. He did not seem to see *her*. From the twisted words he'd been speaking, she realized he only saw something Anton cared for.

Was that Damek's sickness? A need to hurt or destroy whatever Anton cared for? Did he need to feed this hunger enough to ruin himself?

In terror, she realized that she was nothing to him in this moment. Nothing. He only wanted to cause Anton pain.

Leaning down, he brushed his face against the side of hers. "Push at me again," he whispered. "Or scream." One of his hands moved down her side, and he gripped her rib cage, pressing with his thumb. "We have all night."

Wild fear coursed through her. He cared nothing for anyone else's life, he enjoyed inflicting fear, and he seemed to have utterly lost himself. When she did not push at him or scream, he nuzzled her face again and took the lobe of her ear in his teeth.

He started to bite down.

At this, she pushed and struggled, knowing she was doing exactly what he wanted, but she couldn't stop herself.

"My lord, please!"

And then . . . he was wrenched off her.

Céline stumbled forward into empty air, and when she somehow stopped herself from falling and looked up, she saw Anton standing a few paces from Damek.

Damek appeared dazed, as if trying to understand what had just happened.

Anton was only partially dressed, in a loose shirt and pants. His feet were bare, but he gripped a dagger in his right hand. This confused Céline. Anton didn't carry a dagger.

Damek's eyes cleared slightly, and his right hand shot down for the sheath at his hip.

The sheath was empty.

The skin over Anton's cheekbones drew back, and he launched forward, slamming Damek against the wall. Anton's face was a mask of rage. He shoved his left forearm against Damek's throat, pinning his brother's head.

In equal rage, Damek tried to shove back . . . with no effect. Anton held him there and then pressed the point of the dagger low against Damek's abdomen. Céline stood frozen, watching.

She didn't even recognize Anton. The prince she knew was gone, replaced by a stranger.

He spoke directly into Damek's ear. "If you ever touch her again . . . I don't mean if you hurt her. I mean if you touch her. I will cut you from your groin to your rib cage, and then I'll drag you down to that little room we both know, and I'll lock you inside. If anyone asks me where you are, I'll tell them I don't know, and I'll leave you there in the dark to die over the next two days."

Horror passed through Damek's eyes, and he struggled to breathe with Anton's forearm straining against his throat.

"Do you believe me?" Anton asked.

No answer came, and it was possible Damek couldn't speak.

"Nod if you believe me," Anton said.

Damek tried to nod.

With one last shove against his brother's throat, Anton stepped back, still holding the dagger. "Céline, go into the passage," he ordered.

She ran for the east archway. Once inside the passage, she kept running for a few moments, and then she stopped and turned. Anton was striding after her, carrying the dagger.

She waited.

About ten paces away, he halted. His face was so tight and his eyes were so hard, she still barely recognized him.

"What were you doing down here?" he demanded.

Her body was shaking, and she couldn't stop it, and he was in no state to listen to rational explanations, so she just stood there.

"I told you not to walk alone," he said, his voice ragged. "There's something broken in Damek, and he can't stop himself once he . . . Do you understand what would have happened if I hadn't . . . if I hadn't . . . ?" He lifted the dagger and looked at it. Then he threw it across the passage.

When he turned back to Céline, the anger in his face was gone, replaced by pain, and he held one arm out to her. She ran to him.

He gripped her with both arms and pulled her tight against his chest. She was still shaking.

"Nothing like that will ever happen again. I swear. I'll make sure it doesn't," he said, holding her tighter. "Do you believe me?"

With her face pressed into his shoulder, she nodded. In that moment, she did believe him.

"How did you find me?" she whispered. "How did you know to look for me? I thought you were asleep."

"I was. Rochelle came and knocked on my door, asking permission to seek your help. It seems Lady Helena's brave face took a bad turn in the night when it finally hit her that her brother is dead. She's overwrought, and Rochelle hoped you could help. I went to get you . . . and found you gone. I ordered Rurik and Amelie to see if you'd gone to the kitchen, and I came here."

"Oh." With a rush of guilt that people had been looking for her, Céline pulled away from him. He let her go. "I'm sorry," she said.

He didn't answer.

"Does Lady Helena still need help?" she asked.

"I would think so."

With nothing else to say, they started back toward the east tower. Anton left the dagger where it lay. Céline assumed Damek had gone out the west archway of the hall and back to his own rooms, but she didn't care to think about him at all.

Upon reaching her room, Céline managed to put off an immediate scolding from Helga. Neither Rurik nor Amelie was there yet—as they were both still looking for Céline.

"Please just do what you can to let them know she has

been found," Anton interjected, leaving Helga sputtering.

Céline quickly found her box of medicinal supplies, and Anton took her back to the stairs.

"The family has rooms in this tower as well," he explained, "one floor above."

They hurried up one flight of stairs and as Céline stepped off the landing, she could see Captain Maddox and Heath both pacing in the passage, outside an open door.

Céline went right to them, with Anton on her heels.

"How is Lady Helena?" she asked.

Maddox remained silent and grim; perhaps he expected Heath to respond.

Heath shook his head. "I don't know what to do. Rochelle and Lizbeth are with her."

That wasn't exactly an answer, but Céline moved past him into the guest room. Inside, Lizbeth stood near the open door, with a blue cloak thrown over the top of her shift, looking lost and helpless. Rochelle was across the room, kneeling on the floor, wearing nothing but a white shift and a shawl.

"Please, Mother," she said, "come back to the bed."

Lady Helena was sitting on the floor with her back to the wall, her knees in her chest, and her face in her hands, whispering inaudible words. She also wore nothing but a shift. Rochelle must have heard Céline's entrance, because she looked over her shoulder, and her expression melted into relief.

"Miss Céline, can you do anything for her? She is distraught."

Céline walked over and dropped down, opening her box. "When did this start?"

"I don't . . . I don't exactly know. Lizbeth and I are sharing a room across the hall. Mother seemed fine when we went to bed. Of course she was troubled, but she was in control. I woke up to the sound of loud weeping, and I came in here, and I found her . . . like this, and she has not moved. I thought about asking Captain Maddox to lift her back into the bed, but I didn't know if that would be the right thing to do."

"You were wise," Céline assured her, reaching into her box and pulling out a bottle filled with a milky white substance.

"What is that?" Lizbeth asked from near the door.

"It's poppy syrup," Céline answered. "Your mother is in shock, and she needs to relax and sleep. When she wakes, she should be more herself again."

Céline opened the bottle and poured a wooden spoonful.

"My lady," she said gently. "Can you drink this for me?"

Helena took her hands away from her face and looked at Céline without recognition. With her hair down, the aging noblewoman seemed younger somehow.

"He was all I had left," Helena whispered. "I know he drank too much and sported with women too young for him, but he was all I had."

"No, Mother," Rochelle said, sounding hurt. "You have us. You have your children."

"All I had," Helena whispered again.

"My lady, please drink this," Céline said, and thankfully, Helena swallowed the spoonful.

She continued to mumble sorrow-filled words over the loss of her brother, but soon, the opium-laced liquid took effect, and she grew sleepy. Finally, Céline and Rochelle were able to help her back to bed, where she closed her eyes.

"Oh, thank you," Rochelle said to Céline. "I didn't know what to . . . Oh, you're hurt. Your face is bleeding."

Céline's cheek had been stinging where Damek had used his fingernail, but she'd been too occupied to notice much. After touching her cheek, her finger came away covered in blood. "It's nothing. I was careless and scratched myself."

Rochelle looked back to her sleeping mother. "I'll stay with her. Lizbeth, you should go back to bed."

Céline turned her head toward Lizbeth. "Do you think you could sleep?"

Wordlessly, the girl nodded, but she seemed so lost and distressed, nothing like the feisty creature from earlier this evening.

Céline stood and went to her. "Come with me."

Lizbeth allowed Céline to usher her outside into the passage where Anton, Heath, and Maddox waited.

"Lady Helena is sleeping now," Céline told the men.

Heath closed his eyes briefly. "Thank you."

"I'll see Lizbeth back to bed," Céline finished, heading across the passage with the silent girl.

Lizbeth opened a door and stepped inside.

Céline followed, went right to the bed, and pulled the covers back. "You should take that cloak off and come crawl under these blankets."

Like a child, the girl obeyed her and even let Céline pull up the coverlet to tuck her in.

"I didn't want to be right," Lizbeth said, her eyes bleak.

"About what?"

"About Carlotta having been murdered. I know I said that to you, but I didn't want to be right."

Céline sat on the edge of the bed. "Of course you didn't. You were a brave girl to speak up. Don't be afraid to say what you think when lives are at stake."

Some color returned to Lizbeth's face, and she rested on her pillow.

"Will you stay here until I fall asleep?" she asked.

"Yes." On impulse, Céline leaned down and kissed her on her forehead. The poor girl seemed to need some mothering. "Close your eyes."

A few moments later, Lizbeth was sleeping, and Céline stood and slipped out the door. Anton was waiting there to walk her back to her own room.

Near dawn, Anton lay in his bed, still unable to sleep. Rurik slept quietly on a pallet on the floor. Upon returning Céline to her own room earlier, he'd had some unwanted unpleasantness with Rurik and Amelie both demanding that Céline explain herself, but Anton was near the end of his self-control, and he'd squelched their questions and ordered everyone to bed—technically leaving Céline to deal with Amelie on her own.

Then he and Rurik had gone to their own room and fallen onto their respective beds in exhaustion. Anton had been lying awake since.

I attacked my brother.

The phrase continued to roll over and over in his mind, and he couldn't keep up with the emotions that accompanied this inescapable reality: triumph, a sense of freedom, guilt, betrayal, relief . . . and then back to guilt.

His history and connection to Damek were too long

and too complicated for anyone else to understand. Perhaps that was always the way with siblings?

When they were boys, their father had seemed like a god. As a warlord from a long line of warlords, Prince Lieven was a good father in the sense that he saw to his sons' education. Tutors were brought in to teach writing and mathematics. Prince Lieven made sure the boys spoke fluent Stravinan and Belaskian so they would never need to depend upon a translator in discussions with neighboring nations. Both boys could ride almost as soon as they could walk. They had a sword master, and Lieven himself drilled them on military history. He might have been a taskmaster, but their father wanted them prepared for their place in the world.

Their mother, the Lady Bethany, of the house of Yegor . . . she gave them love.

Anton's mother had been married to their father when she was only sixteen. Lieven had been a good deal older, but had finally gotten around to seeking a bride. The Lady Bethany was small and sweet-tempered, with a round face and a mass of chestnut-colored hair, and she never seemed to age. When Anton was quite young, he never fully understood that she was the wall between him and everything else.

By the time Anton was five, Damek had already begun small cruelties against him.

Once their father brought them each a tunic from Enêmûsk, and Anton had puffed with pride. The tunic made him feel manly, and he was so pleased to receive it. Before he had a chance to wear it even once, he found it shredded to pieces on his bed.

A moon later, one of their tutors had praised Anton's

handwriting, and Anton had beamed. Praise was rare in their world. Later that day, when he went to his room, he found that all his quills had been snapped into pieces, and someone had taken his entire supply of ink and poured it all over the floor.

Anton knew who had done these things.

But after every incident, his mother had come to him and cleaned up the mess. She'd comforted him and promised him a new tunic or new quills. Something about her dependable kindness made Damek's cruelties seem smaller.

Three years passed, and when Anton was eight years old, his father announced that he was taking Lady Bethany and the boys on a journey. Anton was so pleased by this news, he could barely contain himself.

The family home was Castle Pählen, and he'd barely set foot outside the courtyard except for riding practice. Prince Lieven owned other properties, and he'd decided on a trip to take stock of the new vassal he'd assigned to Castle Kimovesk.

Damek had taken note of Anton's excitement and frowned at him.

Although the journey took less than a day, it was tiring for Anton—though he never complained. He rode his pony proudly beside his mother's horse and remained determined to see and hear every new sight and sound.

On their arrival, the castle itself struck him as a disappointment, nothing so grand as their home, but he and Damek ate dinner in the great hall with the adults and this made him feel quite grown-up.

The next afternoon, Damek came and asked him if he wanted to go exploring. Since Damek never invited Anton to play at anything, Anton jumped at the invitation.

He wanted his brother to like him. He wanted them to be friends.

For the next hour, Damek behaved like a brother, and the two boys visited with some of the guards and were even allowed to walk the castle wall. Then Damek picked up a lantern and suggested they go down to look at the old prison located beneath the great hall.

Anton was enjoying himself so much, he followed his brother like a puppy. Damek led him through the castle to a stairwell leading down. Most of the villages had their own jails, and as the house of Pählen had been at peace with the other houses for some time now, the old prison at Kimovesk was no longer used.

As the boys emerged into what had once been the guardroom, Anton began to regret his agreement to come down here. The place smelled dank, and to him, it felt . . . sad. He walked through the guardroom and looked down a passage at the doors to the cells, and he thought about the past people who'd been locked away here.

"Let's go back upstairs," he said to Damek.

"In a moment. I came down earlier by myself and found something. I want you to see it."

Damek had come down earlier? Anton followed his brother down the passage between the cells, and at the end was a small door. Damek opened it.

"Come and look in here."

Anton wondered what there might possibly be to see, but he obeyed his brother and walked over to peer inside. He saw nothing but darkness.

Then he was shoved from behind, and he heard a loud click. After that, he heard nothing, and he saw nothing. He was alone inside the room. It was pitch-black, and the door had been closed.

"Damek?" he called in confusion.

No one answered.

In panic, Anton ran for where he guessed the door must be, and he found it, but it was locked from the outside. He pounded and shouted, still believing this to be some sort of mistake.

Again, no one answered, and no one opened the door. He had never been afraid like this in his life. He had no idea how large or small the room might be . . . or what might be in here with him.

"Damek!"

During the rest of the day and the night he spent in that room, he had no sense of the passage of time. He remembered becoming thirsty, and then his thirst became torture so that he could no longer call for help. After a while, his mind began to play tricks on him, and he imagined unseen things coming at him from the darkness.

At some point, he believed he would die in here . . . of thirst.

Then he heard a clicking sound, and the door opened, and Damek stood on the other side, holding a lantern.

"You can come out now," Damek said.

With his throat so dry he couldn't speak or weep with relief, Anton stumbled out the door.

"Father thinks you've gone missing," Damek said. "He's had a search going. I told him you were last seen walking on the wall, as we were playing up there, and that I ran to get us some apples and then could not find you when I got back. So no one has thought to look down here. When you and I go up, I'll say that you were a fool and came down here and managed to lock yourself in. I will say I saved you." He leaned closer. "If you say anything else, I'll call you out as a liar, and Father will believe me."

The tragedy was that Damek was right, and their father would not be able to accept the truth of what really happened down here. It was unthinkable.

Later, Anton learned that Damek had left him in that room from one afternoon to the next.

But that day, he was taken to his bed and fed water and broth so that he might recover.

When his mother came to him, her eyes were sad. She sent all the servants away and sat down on the bed.

"Did Damek do this to you?"

He began to weep. At least his mother knew.

"Why?" Anton asked. "Why would he do this?"

She gripped his hand. "Listen to me carefully. Your brother is jealous because you can feel things he cannot. He cannot take joy from a new tunic or from the praise of a tutor. He cannot . . . love in the way that you do, and so he seeks to hurt you for it. There is something broken inside him, and I fear he cannot help himself from trying to punish you. I never thought he would go so far."

"Can I tell Father?"

"No, that is the one thing you can never do. Your father respects only strength, and he would see your complaints as weakness. I would see you raised high, my Anton, and for this, you must have your father's respect."

She leaned over and pressed a cool rag to his forehead. "But *I* will watch your brother. He knows I love him well, and I will speak to him gently on this matter. I promise to put a stop to these cruelties."

In relief, Anton closed his eyes, finally able to rest in the knowledge that his mother would protect him.

And she did.

The family went home to Castle Pählen, and for the next three months, Anton did not suffer from a single incident instigated by his brother. His mother often touched Damek on the back or hugged him and called him her "sweet boy," and it seemed to Anton that Damek was striving to be the person she saw.

Then, one night at dinner, she looked queer and could not eat any food.

"Forgive me, my lord," she said to Prince Lieven. "I am not well. May I retire to my rooms?"

Their father stood, as such a request was unusual from their mother. "Of course," he said. "Do you need a physician?"

"No, just some rest, I think." She was holding her right side.

Before the middle of night, she was in agony, and by morning, she was dead. One of the serving women explained to Anton and Damek that their mother had been taken by something called the rupture, where an organ in her right side had burst and there had been nothing anyone could do to save her.

Anton was numb, in shock, but that proved a good thing, as their father made it clear he would brook no tears from two princes of Pählen.

The boys were allowed to see their mother's body laid out before burial, and Damek stood, stone-faced, staring down at her. Even then, Anton, who had depended so heavily on his mother, understood the depth of Damek's loss.

Damek reached down and touched her face. "Now she will never love me as she should have."

Stunned, Anton blurted out, "She did love you!"

Damek's eyes narrowed as he looked up. "She loved you more. Everyone loves you more."

A coldness settled in the pit of Anton's stomach.

The following month came the day that Prince Lieven bought the boys their first puppies . . . and Anton came to love his dog Arrow so much. On that night, later, when Damek had arrived at Anton's room, displaying brotherly affection, Anton had so wanted to believe in it.

But after that, Anton never let himself hope again, and over the following years, Damek seemed to take his only real pleasure in destroying or sending away anything or anyone that Anton cared for. Sometimes Anton wondered what would have happened if their mother had lived. Could she have saved Damek?

He never forgot her saying that there was something broken inside Damek and that he could not help himself.

Anton never told Prince Lieven of a single cruel act of Damek's.

He never would.

And yet tonight . . . on this night inside Castle Kimovesk, he had rammed his brother's head into a wall and threatened him with a dagger. For the first time, he was the one who had not been able to stop himself.

When he'd seen Damek gripping Céline and biting her ear, something inside him snapped.

A part of him regretted his loss of control, but at the same time, Anton knew without a doubt that he was capable of carrying out the threat he'd made to his brother . . . and of never looking back.

CHAPTER SEVEN

By midmorning the next day, Céline and Amelie were still in their room, but they'd formed a plan of action and decided that the first thing they needed to do was learn more about the dynamics of the family. After some discussion, they felt it might be unwise to go downstairs and ask permission to begin reading people like Captain Maddox or Johanna, as this might inadvertently—and incorrectly—shift blame.

Once the sisters knew a little more about the family, they would gain a better understanding of who indeed might have a reason to go to such lengths to stop the impending wedding.

"I think we must divide and conquer," Céline said. "I'll start with Lizbeth. She might be open with me. You try your luck with Heath. He seemed quite taken with you last night before . . . well, before his uncle died."

Amelie made a face. "He was not *taken* with me. I was simply one of the few people in the room who spoke to him."

Yes, poor Heath. He'd seemed so unable to assert himself. His uncle had been condescending, and his mother ignored him for the most part. Only his sisters seemed to welcome his company.

Helga pulled two wool dresses from the wardrobe, one brown and the other dark purple. "You two should wear somber colors today."

Céline agreed, and she took the brown dress. Although the Quillette women had been wearing bright colors last night, the family would be in double mourning now. Somber colors might be best.

"And no wandering off by yourself today!" Helga ordered. "I never thought you such a fool."

"Don't start," Céline warned.

Amelie glanced over but managed to keep quiet. There had been quite a scene last night upon her returning to this room, with Amelie demanding answers and Helga raising a fuss. Céline had decided to tell them the truth about what had happened . . . thinking they should both be better warned about Damek. But she had played down the danger to herself and the swiftness of Anton's arrival, and then she'd asked them both not to bring it up again.

Amelie took the dark purple dress and laced it up, pulling the sleeves down over her sheathed weapons.

Céline laced the front of her own gown and brushed her hair. The scratch on her cheek was still red, but it had stopped bleeding.

"I'm starving," Amelie announced.

Céline was hungry, too. "I'm sure something is being served in the great hall for breakfast. We can go down and see who else has arrived. Helga, would you like to come with us? If breakfast here is anything like in Sèone, it will be a casual affair with people dishing up for themselves."

"Nope," Helga responded. "I think I'll try my luck in the kitchen and see what gossip I might pick up."

"Oh . . ." Céline nodded. "Good idea. Should we let Prince Anton and Rurik know we're going down?"

Helga's already wrinkled face wrinkled slightly more in thought. "No, if they're sleeping, let 'em sleep. If they're not asleep, they're probably already downstairs."

Jaromir had been right to send Helga. She might be abrasive, but she was sensible—and determined to help.

With that, all three women set out for the day. At the bottom of the stairwell of the east tower, Helga headed off down a passage that ran down the shorter side of the center section of the castle, leading to the kitchen. Once again, Céline and Amelie started down the long passage running along the backside that led to the great hall.

Upon passing through the archway, Céline took stock of everyone present. For the most part, this looked like a typical breakfast in the hall of Castle Sèone. A number of guards—a mix of Väränj, Sèone, and Kimovesk—milled around, helping themselves to food that had been laid out. Servants were busy checking pots and bowls.

Céline continued scanning to see which nobles were present. To her relief, Prince Damek wasn't here, but she hadn't expected him to be. It seemed he seldom came out of his rooms during the day. Lady Helena was not in the hall. Anton and Rurik had not arrived, either.

However, Rochelle and Lady Saorise sat together near the end of the table. Saorise sipped at a cup of tea. Rochelle was working on a piece of embroidery. She wore a muslin gown dyed dove gray that complemented her red-gold hair. Lizbeth and Heath sat a short ways down the table, both looking somewhat at a loss and picking at their food.

Captain Maddox stood at attention against the back wall, watching Rochelle.

Just then, Captain Kochè walked in from the western archway. He looked around the hall, and then began to pass through, not stopping to eat. As he passed by Rochelle, she stiffened and her body moved in the chair as if to pull as far away from him as possible. He gave her a sidelong glance of hatred as he walked by, and Céline made a mental note to try as quickly as possible to find out what—if anything—had occurred between those two.

"Here we go," she murmured to Amelie.

The sisters went to Rochelle and Saorise first with a polite greeting.

"How is your mother?" Céline asked.

Rochelle's eyes dropped briefly to her embroidery and back up with a cast of guilt, as if she'd been caught out at something. "She's still asleep, and her maid is sitting with her. I . . . I had to get out for a few moments."

"You were right to let her sleep," Céline answered, "and you can't sit with her yourself all day."

Rochelle smiled. Saorise listened to the exchange with some interest, but offered no thoughts.

Breakfast consisted of oatmeal, boiled eggs, and stewed pears. The sisters dished up and sat down with Lizbeth and Heath. Lizbeth seemed glad to see Céline.

"The oatmeal's cold," the girl said.

"I don't mind."

Then Lizbeth noticed Amelie's shoulder-length hair—as it had not been pinned up that morning. "Your hair."

"Oh yes . . . I like to wear it like this," Amelie said.

"I wonder if Mother would let me do that. It would be so much easier to brush."

"I don't think so," Heath answered.

Amelie sat beside Heath and asked him if he'd gotten any sleep. Céline didn't hear the answer. She ate quickly, and then looked around for one of the guards from Sèone. Sergeant Bazin stood a few paces away.

"Sergeant," she said, "did you come in from the barracks this morning? How is the weather?"

"Not bad, miss. The sky is gray, but no rain yet."

She turned to Lizbeth. "I'm longing for some fresh air. Shall we take a walk in the courtyard? Maybe visit the horses."

Lizbeth's eyes lit up—as Céline knew they would. This was a girl who would be outside climbing trees if her mother would let her. She would jump at any chance to get out of this hall and do something . . . anything.

The girl was already on her feet. "Rochelle, may I go for a walk in the courtyard with Céline?"

This did surprise Céline a bit, first that Lizbeth would ask permission so politely, as she seemed rather headstrong, and second that she'd asked Rochelle and not Heath.

Rochelle hesitated and looked to Maddox. Céline wasn't certain why until Sergeant Bazin stepped forward and addressed Rochelle.

"I'll go with them, my lady. Make sure they are safe."

Then Céline realized Rochelle had been debating keeping Maddox here or sending him off with Lizbeth.

Céline shot Bazin a grateful look, and then she and Lizbeth headed out the west entrance, through the bottom of one tower, into the strange half tower, and out the front doors. Bazin followed at a respectful distance. Lizbeth practically skipped beside Céline as they stepped into the light morning air.

"Oh, thank you," the girl said. "Let's stay out as long as we can."

The courtyard was large, but activity was limited. Céline started down the front of the castle toward the stables, and Lizbeth fell into step beside her. Again, Bazin kept his distance, watching, but remaining out of earshot. Céline spent a few moments wondering how best to begin seeking a few answers. For one, no one could be discounted as the murderer, not even young Lizbeth. She appeared to be an awkward teenage girl, and Céline believed her to be innocent, but Céline had also met a few very good actors in her short time serving as Anton's seer.

Finally, she decided to fall back on honesty.

"Lizbeth," she began, "I hope you don't mind, but part of the reason I suggested our walk was so that you and I could speak in private."

The girl seemed undaunted by this confession. "Really? Why?"

"Because my sister and I have been engaged to find out who killed Carlotta and your uncle, and a few points are still hazy for me. I'd hoped you could help."

Here, Lizbeth hesitated for the span of a breath. "With what?"

"For one, after Carlotta's death, who was it in your family who threatened to pack up and leave?"

"Oh, that was Heath." The girl relaxed again. "And me. I think Heath even accused Damek of poisoning Carlotta."

"But your mother and uncle never made any such threat, to leave, I mean?"

Lizbeth snorted through her nose. "Of course not."

"At the time, did they protest or chastise you or Heath when you made this threat?"

"Did they ... No, they didn't. Maybe once we'd said something, they feared looking as if they didn't care that Carlotta was dead. Why do you ask?"

"We came because Prince Damek believed your family was on the verge of leaving."

"Oh, that would never happen." Lizbeth shook her head. "Mother and Uncle Hamish were set on seeing Rochelle married to Damek. Mother still is, believe me. Damek will be the next grand prince, and Mother is determined to have Rochelle seated as the grand princess."

Céline stopped walking. "That is pure speculation. There is no way to be certain who the next grand prince will be."

Lizbeth stopped as well. She tilted her head to one side. "In the past few years, better trade routes with Belaski have opened up, and the house of Pählen controls the western province of Droevinka. Belaski is a wealthy nation, and all the princes want a grand prince who can open trade even further. Prince Lieven will name Damek as heir, and the other princes will elect him when the time comes. Mother is never wrong about these things."

At first, Céline was so taken aback by the girl's grasp of politics that she wasn't certain how to respond. Then she said, "I think you've forgotten Prince Anton."

"I haven't. Everyone knows that Prince Lieven much prefers Anton—and who wouldn't? But the princes won't elect Anton. They think he's weak. Lieven may prefer Anton, but not enough to lose the chance of seeing his family in power. He'll name Damek."

"Anton is a better leader than Damek."

"Of course he is," Lizbeth sighed as if Céline were a simpleton. "You know that. I know that. Most of the people know that. But none of us get a say in the matter, and the princes won't elect Anton. Lieven knows it. He'll name Damek as his heir."

Céline's head was spinning. "So . . . your mother and uncle believe that by this marriage, Rochelle will indeed become wife of the grand prince? What does Rochelle think of all this?"

Lizbeth shrugged. "Who knows? Rochelle couldn't say boo to a goose. She'll do whatever she's told. Heath is the same way." She paused. "I love my brother and sister. They are good to me, but . . . neither one has an ounce of spirit."

"Did you love Carlotta?" Céline asked abruptly.

"No," Lizbeth answered just as readily. "No one did. Carlotta was not lovable. That's why she was so jealous of Rochelle."

Céline began walking again. "She was jealous?"

"It was awful to watch. For years, men would contact Father, making initial offers for Carlotta's hand, and then they would meet her. Even the most desperate of them decided tying their life to hers wasn't worth my father's money. Carlotta was bitter, coarse-faced, and bossy. No one liked her. But every man who walked through the door of our manor fell madly in love with Rochelle. She's the type they all want . . . beautiful, quiet, and she does what she's told."

Though Céline found that last part a rather unfair assessment of men, she pressed on. "But Carlotta was handling Rochelle's marriage negotiations to Damek. If she was so jealous, why would she work so hard to make her sister a grand princess?"

This time, Lizbeth stopped walking and raised one eyebrow. "Have you met Damek?" she asked sarcastically. "He's the type who probably keeps a pair of shackles and a riding crop beneath his bed."

"Lizbeth!"

"Well, he is. I think Carlotta wanted Rochelle to suffer for the rest of her life."

They began to walk again, and by this point, the stable loomed before them. Céline was still attempting to absorb everything she'd just heard.

"Céline . . . ," Lizbeth began slowly, and her tone had changed. Once again, she sounded like the uncertain teenage girl. "Can you truly read futures?"

"I can."

"Would you . . . would you read mine? With everything happening here, I want to know . . . I want to know that I even have a future."

"Oh, my dear," Céline breathed, and she meant it. In spite of her own necessary cautions, she couldn't help her growing affection for Lizbeth.

"Will you read me?" the girl asked again.

Céline looked around for someplace more private, and she spotted an alcove at the base of the east tower. "Over there."

After Amelie finished eating, she reached into the pocket of her dress and pulled out a deck of cards—which she'd stored there before leaving her room.

"You up for a game?" she asked Heath.

Startled by her offer, he looked at the deck for a moment, and then waved a serving girl over to clear their dishes. Amelie had a hard time getting a read on him. Though he was shy and unsure of himself, he was certainly used to being obeyed.

Sitting this close to him, she noticed he wore the same long-sleeved black wool shirt that he'd had on under his tunic last night. She could see every detail of his face and silky red-blond hair. His features were so delicate, just like Rochelle's, from his nose to his jaw. Amelie couldn't help feeling a sort of kinship with him. She herself lacked the feminine qualities that most men found attractive. While she didn't care about that, she did know what it was like to feel set apart.

However, she also couldn't help wondering how he felt about his uncle's death. She doubted he was in much of a state of mourning . . . and who could blame him? Hamish had done nothing but humiliate Heath the night before.

Looking at the deck of cards again, Heath said, "I was somewhat envious when your sister asked Lizbeth to go off for a walk. Perhaps you and I could do the same? It would be a relief to get out of this hall."

Amelie wavered. If they went out into the courtyard, Lizbeth and Céline might join them, and Amelie wanted to speak with Heath alone, hoping he might be more forthcoming. At the same time she didn't want to refuse his invitation.

"Where should we walk?" she asked.

"In my more desperate moments of boredom here, I've done some exploring in the lower levels. There are some interesting things to see down there."

She seriously doubted that, but at least she could get him off alone.

"Lead on," she said, trying to sound lighthearted.

He stood, lifted a small lantern from the end of the table, and then went to Rochelle. "I'm going to stretch my legs with Miss Amelie. Will you be all right here with Lady Saorise? Or perhaps you'd like to come with us?"

Rochelle smiled at Heath first and then turned the smile on Amelie. It was dazzling. "You two go on. I should stay here in case Mother wakes. I've left word for one of the maids to come and get me straightaway." She pointed to a pink rose on one side of her embroidery. "And Lady Saorise has been showing me a new way to finish the edge here."

Without thinking, Amelie looked to Saorise and asked, "You know embroidery?" Then she realized how insulting that might have sounded.

Saorise merely put one finger to her lips. "Don't tell anyone. It's a secret."

Amelie fought not to express a shiver. That woman made her skin crawl.

"Off with us, then," Heath said, motioning Amelie away from the table, and he called with mock gallantry back to his sister, "I promise to guard her with my life."

"I know you will," Rochelle answered.

While Amelie thought that in the unlikely event they should run into difficulties, she'd be the one defending him, she heard the open affection between him and Rochelle. After watching Damek and Anton together, she took some happiness from seeing two siblings who actually loved each other. Amelie loved Céline more than anyone and couldn't imagine a world without her. It seemed Heath and Rochelle were the same.

"Where to?" Amelie asked.

"Follow me."

He led her down the back passage. Toward the end was a side storage room with an open archway instead of a door. Heath walked through the room to a much narrower open archway near the back corner.

"Where are we going?" she asked, curious. What could

there possibly be below interesting enough to lure down a young baron?

He paused, holding the lantern. "This stairwell leads down to the old prison. I know it sounds ghoulish, but I like walking around down there. It's quiet. If you'd rather not go, though, I understand."

A prison?

Amelie shrugged. She'd seen old prisons before—in Castle Sèone. They didn't particularly interest her, but they didn't bother her, either, and this would give them a chance to speak freely. "No, it's all right. Go ahead. I'll come behind."

He led the way down a winding stairwell, and they emerged into what must once have been a guardroom. There was a hearth in one wall with an old decaying desk that faced it—about ten paces away. A set of keys hung near a heavy wooden door on the other side of the room. The door was open.

Heath walked straight through that doorway. Amelie went after him and found herself looking at a row of cells as he stood about halfway down. At the end of the row, she saw a small closed door.

Then he looked back. "You're sure you don't mind? This is the one place in the castle where I can be sure I'll be left alone."

"In the prison of Kimovesk?"

He grimaced. "Again . . . I know it sounds odd, but I don't mind the cells. There are days when I can think of nothing I'd like better than to be locked away someplace where no one can find me."

Amelie began to understand him a little better. Maybe it wasn't so strange that he liked it down here.

"Heath . . . ," she began. "I know this is none of my

concern, but does it worry you that your sister is being asked to marry Prince Damek?"

Thankfully, he didn't appear offended by the question. "Worry me? Of course it does. Damek is little better than an animal. But Rochelle has known her worth, and her place, since we were children. Her fate has always been to marry whatever prince or nobleman would raise my family the highest. My fate has been to inherit my father's title and play the part of baron. Neither of us can escape, and we both well know it."

He sounded so passive, so resigned.

As if reading her face, he added, "I do regret the life into which she is being forced, but I have no power to stop it. Neither does she."

"You could try to fight your mother."

He laughed without humor. "No one fights Mother. I sometimes think my father died on purpose." Turning, he looked again down the row of cells. "It's so peaceful here."

Amelie had no idea what to say. Somebody was fighting his mother. Somebody was willing to kill to stop this marriage. Who was it?

"Maybe we should go back up?" she suggested.

"You wish to?"

"I think so."

Somewhat reluctantly, Heath came away from the cells, held the lantern high, and led the way through the guardroom.

Before slipping into the alcove with Lizbeth, Céline turned and held one hand up to Sergeant Bazin, signaling him to keep his distance.

Inside the alcove, she saw a small stone bench. "Come and sit here."

"What happens now?" Lizbeth asked in a small voice. "You just touch me like Amelie touched Johanna?"

"Yes, that's all."

"And you promise you'll tell me what you see, no matter what it is?"

"I promise."

Reaching out, Céline took Lizbeth's hand in her own. Closing her eyes, she focused entirely upon Lizbeth, on the spark of her spirit within her. At first nothing happened, but a moment later, the first jolt hit.

Céline gritted her teeth in preparation. As the second jolt hit, she felt as if her body were being swept forward along a tunnel of mist, and she forgot everything but the sensation of speeding through the mists all around her as they swirled in grays and whites.

This journey was not a long one, and almost immediately, the mist vanished and an image flashed before her.

She was in the great hall . . . here at Kimovesk. The first person she saw was herself, wearing her favorite lavender wool dress, so she assumed this was a day set at some point in the near future and evening had not yet arrived. Lady Saorise sat in a chair nearby. Lady Helena, Amelie, Rochelle, and Heath stood by the hearth. Anton was close to the archway with Rurik.

Lizbeth was nowhere in sight.

How could that be? This was Lizbeth's future.

"No," Anton ordered. "I'll go back up and get her myself."

Before anyone else could speak, a scream echoed through the great hall, and everyone whirled toward the sound. Lizbeth came running in from the east archway with her hands and the hem of her dress covered in blood.

"He's dead!" she cried hysterically.

Inside the image, Céline watched herself run toward the girl. "Lizbeth!"

"He's dead!" Lizbeth cried again. "I leaned over to touch him, to make sure, but he's dead."

The scene vanished, and the mists closed in again, pulling her backward this time.

Céline gasped and opened her eyes and found herself sitting on the stone bench looking into Lizbeth's frightened eyes.

"What?" Lizbeth asked. "What did you see?"

Instantly, Céline calmed herself, as she had no intention of telling the girl what she'd just seen. The mists always showed her what was most important, what was a key to her questions, and she didn't understand the meaning of this image yet. There was no sense in terrifying Lizbeth with the news that she would stumble upon someone's death. The future could still be altered. That was one of the first things Céline learned after accepting the powers of her gift.

"Oh, forgive me," she said, smiling now. "Sometimes, when I come out abruptly, it can be disconcerting." She still grasped Lizbeth's hand. "I saw nothing to worry you. I saw you a little older than you are now, standing in a field of strawberries."

Anton had mentioned on the journey from Sèone that the Quillette family was also known for the fine strawberries they grew.

"Oh . . . then I was back home at the manor," Lizbeth said. "That is all you saw?"

"Yes, but at your request, I asked the mists to show me if you had a future. And they showed me that you do. You will leave this place safely, and you will go home."

Céline was determined that this *would* be Lizbeth's future. She was also now convinced of the girl's innocence in these murders. Should Lizbeth be involved, Céline would have been shown something else.

"Shall we go back inside and check on your sister?" Céline asked.

Lizbeth's open face flickered with guilt. "I suppose, but could we . . . could we go and visit the horses first? I like horses better than I like most people."

"Yes, we can certainly visit the horses first."

They stood and left the alcove, heading for the stables.

"I like dogs, too," Lizbeth added. "Have you noticed there are no dogs here? Prince Damek says he doesn't like them."

Indeed, Céline had noticed the lack of dogs, but she couldn't even pretend to understand Damek.

Anton and Rurik walked into the great hall.

Though Anton hadn't slept much, he was determined to assist Céline and Amelie in any way he could . . . so they could find the murderer and then leave this castle and everyone in it far behind.

As he looked around, a flash of alarm struck him when he did not see either sister. He and Rurik had checked their room before coming down, and it had been empty. If the sisters weren't here, where could they be?

Rochelle and Lady Saorise sat the table, speaking softly to each other.

Anton crossed the hall quickly, with Rurik on his heels.

"My ladies," he said, "have Miss Céline and Miss Amelie come for breakfast yet?"

"Indeed," Rochelle answered serenely, "and I am in their debt. Both Lizbeth and Heath have been quite miserable, and your seers were kind enough to try and engage them in some activity besides sitting in here."

Anton relaxed. "Oh, I see. Thank you. Where are they?"

"Miss Céline took Lizbeth for some fresh air in the courtyard. I'm not sure where Heath and Miss Amelie have gone off. He seems to enjoy exploring."

Some of Anton's alarm returned. The sisters split up? For a moment, he suffered indecision over which one to seek out first. This was solved for him as Amelie and Heath came in through the east archway.

"Please excuse me," Anton said, "I need a word with Miss Céline."

"Will you not have some breakfast?" Lady Saorise asked.

"Soon."

Without waiting to even greet Amelie, Anton headed toward the west archway—again with Rurik on his heels. They passed through the first west tower and into the strange half tower and out the main doors.

Squinting in the daylight, Anton scanned the courtyard and saw only soldiers. Then his gaze fell upon Sergeant Bazin standing near the doors of the stables. Anton and Rurik strode over.

"They're inside, my lord," Bazin said. "I've been watching out for them."

With a rush of gratitude, Anton said, "Thank you, Sergeant. Both of you wait out here."

Almost immediately upon entering the stables, Anton heard the sound of female voices, and he walked between the stalls to see Céline and Lizbeth up ahead, at the door to Sable's stall. The mare had her head stretched out of the top of the stall door and was eating grain from Lizbeth's hand.

"My lord," Céline said at the sight of him. "Is everything well?"

"Yes, quite well. I just . . . I wished to . . ." He stopped, uncertain how to continue. He'd wanted to discuss Céline's list of people with a possible motive.

Céline glanced from him to Lizbeth. "My lord, if you have questions pertaining to the investigation, you can speak freely. Lizbeth has been taken into my confidence and she has been most helpful to me this morning."

Still cautious, Anton wondered how much of that was true and how much was for the girl's benefit.

But Lizbeth said, "And last night, you were quite upfront about your reason for coming here, my lord. It's not a secret."

Anton sighed. "Céline, have you read anyone else? Prince Damek will sleep most of the day, but he's going to want answers when he awakens."

"She read me," Lizbeth said. "I asked her to."

Céline nodded once at him to confirm, but she added nothing else, and he knew better than to ask.

"Can you and Amelie do a few more readings today?" he asked. "I'll need something to tell Damek."

"There are several people in whom we have . . . an interest," Céline answered. "But I fear if we openly insist on a reading, we might cast blame in the wrong direction. I'd like to do this more quietly."

That gained Lizbeth's full attention, and she stopped petting Sable. "With who?"

Anton realized Céline was leading the girl, so he kept silent.

"Well . . . ," Céline provided, "Captain Maddox for one."

Instead of expressing shock, Lizbeth glanced away. "You want to read the captain?"

"I do, but only if he'll agree, and if I can do the reading in some privacy. Do you think you could assist us with our investigation?"

Anton found that tactic brilliant. The girl was both bored and ignored here. She might jump at a chance for something to do for someone who appreciated her.

However, Lizbeth hesitated. "I don't want to make any trouble for Captain Maddox. He lives with us, and he runs our household guard. He's been good to me. One day, after Mother was especially unkind about all my shortcomings, he took me outside and let me ride his horse."

"Then help me to do this in private," Céline said, "to at least clear him."

Lizbeth wavered a moment more and then nodded. "All right. I'll go and tell him that I need him to see something out here."

With that, she hurried out the stable door.

"You handled that well," Anton told Céline.

She glanced away. "I just hope Maddox is innocent."

Céline was prepared for some difficulty when not long after, Captain Maddox came through the stable door with Lizbeth.

"Lizbeth," the captain said, "what is it you wish to show me? I have left your sister alone in the hall."

He stopped cold at the sight of Céline and Anton.

"Forgive the ruse, Captain," Anton said. "My brother has authorized Miss Céline to do a reading of everyone connected to his impending bride's family, but we are striving to keep these as private as possible."

Maddox's expression tightened. "And you used Lizbeth to get me out here?"

"Only to clear you," Lizbeth cut in, sounding distressed. "Please, Captain."

"It has to be done," Anton said. "We can do it here or later, when my brother wakes up, out in the great hall with everyone watching."

That might be a hollow threat. Céline had no idea if Damek could order Maddox to submit.

With a hard shake of his head, Maddox exhaled through his teeth. "This is madness, but do what you must quickly. I need to get back inside. Rochelle is unprotected."

"Rochelle could not be safer," Céline countered. "She has a number of armed Väränj guards."

Maddox stared at her. "What is it you wish me to do?"

"Come and sit on this old chest," Céline answered. "We both need to be sitting. Then allow me to touch your hand."

Anton and Lizbeth both watched. Poor Lizbeth seemed distressed. Perhaps she regretted her part in this. Maddox himself appeared little more than angry. He showed no fear at the prospect of Céline reading him.

Either he didn't believe she was a seer or he had nothing to hide.

He sat down beside her, took off one glove, and offered his hand.

She took it and closed her eyes, feeling for the spark of his spirit. This time, though, she focused her attention on his connection to Lizbeth's family. If he had any part in these murders, his motive must be exposed.

The first jolt hit.

She braced herself. As the second jolt hit, she felt as if her body were being swept forward along the tunnel of mist.

Again, the journey was brief, even shorter than the one with Lizbeth. An image flashed before her. She found herself outside the entrance of the stairwell to the east tower, looking in, and she could not help feeling shocked by what she saw there.

Captain Maddox held Rochelle in his arms. She wore the same dove gray dress from breakfast, so Céline believed she was seeing something that would happen later this same day.

"You cannot stay here," Maddox said, holding her against his chest. His voice was agonized. "You cannot do this. You cannot tie your life to that prince."

"I have no choice," she answered, pulling back far enough to reach up and touch his face. "We both know that."

"I know nothing of the sort!" he whispered harshly. "I'll take you away from here. You need only agree to come with me. I can get us out the gate. We'll ride to Belaski and make a life there. You know I will care for you."

Céline's shock deepened. Maddox was asking Rochelle to run away with him. Céline had suspected he had feelings for Rochelle ... but she'd not anticipated this.

"And bring shame to my family?" Rochelle asked. "To my mother? I can't! Please, please don't ask me to do this! You only torture us both. If you loved me, you would let me do my duty."

She pushed him away, and he let her.

Then she ran up the stairwell. After watching her go, he turned and leaned his forehead against the wall.

The scene vanished, and the mists closed in again, pulling Céline backward this time.

She opened her eyes and stared at Maddox. At the sight of her expression, he shifted in discomfort.

This time, it was more difficult for Céline to fake a sense of calm, but somehow when she spoke she managed to sound apologetic.

"Forgive me, Captain. I saw nothing. This happens sometimes if there is nothing to be seen."

He wasn't a fool, and he studied her face. After a moment, he nodded.

"So he's been cleared?" Lizbeth asked anxiously.

"Yes, he's been cleared." Céline glanced at Anton. She had a good deal to tell him once they were alone.

Lizbeth rushed over and took the captain's arm. "I'm so sorry. Miss Céline thought this would be the best way."

"There's nothing for you to be sorry about," Maddox answered. "But you come to the hall with me now."

"Of course." Lizbeth looked back. "My lord . . . Céline, are you coming?"

Céline smiled reassuringly. "Right behind you."

CHAPTER EIGHT

The better part of the day passed quickly, although nothing else of note occurred. Upon leaving the stables, Céline, Lizbeth, Anton, and Maddox returned to the great hall. Damek did not make an appearance. Neither did Lady Helena. Around midday, Lady Saorise excused herself politely and departed for her rooms.

Had their host been anyone but Damek, Céline would have been surprised that he'd put no effort into planning amusements for his guests. It seemed he slept much of the day and paced the castle much of the night. Perhaps he was so self-involved that it never occurred to him to put himself out or alter his normal habits, even for his future bride's family.

So Céline, Amelie, and Anton remained in the hall with Rochelle, Heath, and Lizbeth.

No one mentioned Lord Hamish, and it didn't appear that his nieces or nephew would engage in a false display of mourning, so Céline decided to help pass the time as pleasantly as possible. No further progress could be made in the investigation until Damek was awake and she could have him order a few of his people to submit to a reading. She would have liked to read both Heath and Rochelle, but it was not the right time to ask, and she feared doing so might destroy any trust she and Amelie had established.

And . . . in truth, Céline had a difficult time seeing either of them as the killer. Although Rochelle *might* have a motive, to keep from marrying Damek, she did not seem averse to the prospect, and she did seem determined to do honor to her family.

Heath seemed almost incapable of taking any sort of action.

"Perhaps a game of cards?" Céline suggested to Amelie. "Something fun?"

Amelie organized a lively card game called Catch the Queen that provided a surprising amount of laughter. Three queens were removed from the deck, leaving only one, and then the entire deck was dealt. The players passed cards to the person on their left as everyone tried to match pairs and lay them down. When someone's hand was empty, he or she won the game, and was loudly pronounced "the winner," and whoever was holding the queen at the time was loudly pronounced "the loser." It was lighthearted and simple, and Anton was dubbed the loser most often. Lizbeth found this particularly amusing and proceeded to tease him—which he took with good grace.

Captain Maddox stood by the wall, watching, as did Rurik. But while Rurik smiled on occasion, Maddox did not.

Once the card game was exhausted, Céline told a few stories—comedies or adventures—and inspired by her performance, Heath ran to his room and came back with a lute. He played a number of songs for them, and Céline found him to be quite skilled. He must have had a good music master.

In the midafternoon, a servant came down to tell Rochelle that her mother was awake. Rochelle excused herself, and Maddox followed her out. Céline watched them go, and she wondered if the scene she'd read in the captain's future was about to take place.

Should she do something to stop it or let it happen? Should Rochelle be allowed to know that she had a way out should she decide to take it? Céline's ability differed from Amelie's. Whatever Amelie saw in the past was set in stone. But the future was still mutable. If Céline decided to take action, she could change it.

Indecision held her back, and she remained in the hall.

Rurik came over and spent some time teaching Lizbeth a dice game, and after that, Céline felt it was late enough in the afternoon that they might excuse themselves to rest for a while before dinner. If what she'd seen in Maddox's future had taken place in the stairwell, it was over by now.

"All right," she said, "I think we should all have a rest before dressing for dinner."

"Oh, just a little longer," Lizbeth begged. "This is the first fun we've had since arriving."

"No, Miss Céline is right," Heath said. "Come along, Lizbeth."

But he sounded regretful, too, and it seemed sad that two wealthy young nobles should find such pleasure in playing at cards and engaging in simple amusements for a few hours.

"We'll just clean up the card game," Céline said.

Heath and Lizbeth left the hall, heading for the stairwell in the east tower. Once they'd been given time to reach it, Céline, Anton, Amelie, and Rurik all left the hall together. This was the first opportunity that Céline had had to speak with them alone, and in the passageway along the back of the castle, she tried to fill them in as quickly as possible on what she'd learned that morning.

She left out the details of why Lady Helena was so certain Damek would be the next grand prince, but she related any news of the family dynamics she'd learned. She told them what she'd seen in the reading of Lizbeth, and then had to assure Anton twice that there was no clue to the identity of the man the girl had found dead. Finally, she told them of Captain Maddox asking Rochelle to run away with him.

Aghast, Anton stopped walking. "What?"

"It's true."

She described her vision, and although she couldn't be sure, it sounded as if Maddox believed Rochelle cared for him enough to consider fleeing this castle and making a life with him in Belaski.

"That does give him a solid motive," she finished.

Their quartet began walking again, and soon, they reached the stairwell.

"I don't know," Amelie said quietly. "Maddox doesn't strike me as the type to kill from afar."

"I agree," said Rurik.

He'd been rather quiet on this venture, but Céline thought them both to be correct. Maddox didn't strike her as the type to employ poison or the arcane arts, either.

All four of them climbed the east tower stairs to the

second level and walked down the passage to their rooms. Céline and Amelie's room came first.

"We'll see you both at dinner," Céline said to the men as she and Amelie slipped inside.

Helga was fast asleep on their bed. Her scarf half covered her face, and she snored loudly.

"Helga," Amelie said, sounding mildly annoyed.

The old woman sputtered a few times and opened her eyes, sitting up. "There you are. I wondered if you were ever coming back up."

Céline couldn't blame her for napping on their bed. There wasn't much else for her to do. It was not as if Amelie and Céline needed a ladies' maid.

"Did you learn anything in the kitchen?" Céline asked.

"Not anything that would help you," Helga answered, climbing off the bed. She gave a shiver. "Or anything you want to hear. But there are rumors aplenty about Prince Damek and a goodly number of missing girls and missing dogs."

Céline raised a hand. "Do spare us those. Since Prince Damek is not the one trying to sabotage his own wedding, we don't need to investigate him. The less we know about him, the better."

Helga nodded, but her face was bleak. Poor thing. Céline couldn't imagine having to listen to dark rumors about Prince Damek—which were all probably true.

Céline and Amelie rested for a while as Helga fussed about with gowns and silk shoes and stockings.

"All right, you two," Helga finally said, "time to get fancied up for dinner."

It seemed strange to Céline that after what had hap-

pened last night, they were all going to dress in their finest
and go downstairs for wine and dinner again . . . but apparently, that was the plan. Helga picked out a satin gown
of deep rose with a square neckline for Céline, and a midnight blue velvet gown with a scoop neck for Amelie.

Both young women were dressed and Helga was just
finishing Amelie's hair when a quick, purposeful knock
sounded on the door. Puzzled, Céline went to open it
and found the diminutive Master Lionel on the other
side. She hadn't seen him or Johanna all day.

"Yes?"

"Prince Damek has summoned you and your sister to
his private chambers. You will come with me."

Céline had no intention of allowing herself and Amelie to be trapped alone with Damek in his rooms, but
then she leaned farther out and saw Anton and Rurik
both waiting. Anton nodded to her once.

She turned and looked back inside the room. "Amelie,
you'd better come."

As Amelie once more passed through the door of Damek's
private chambers—following Céline, Anton, and Rurik—she wished she were not wearing this ridiculous
velvet gown. She didn't feel like herself when she was
forced to put on these costumes.

Had she been allowed to wear her pants and canvas
jacket and openly show her sheathed dagger on her hip,
she could have faced anything.

Inside, Damek was fully dressed, and he stood waiting
with his arms crossed by the hearth. Captain Kochè was
there as well. Amelie noted that Damek did not make
eye contact with either Céline or Anton, and he was
more agitated than usual.

"Well?" he demanded.

"Well what?" Anton returned.

"Don't play with me. What progress have your seers made today? Have they uncovered the killer? Or are we about to be treated to someone else dropping dead at dinner tonight?"

Amelie's mouth fell half-open. How could anyone have a rational conversation with him?

But Céline answered in a measured tone, "Amelie and I have begun putting together a list of people with a possible motive or who have been behaving strangely. I did find a way to read Captain Maddox."

"Maddox?" Damek repeated, but he didn't seem surprised. "And?"

"I saw nothing to suggest he has anything to do with these murders."

"Then what good are you?" Damek asked. "Start reading the others on your list. I insist you get to the bottom of this tonight!"

With both Carlotta and Lord Hamish gone, Amelie guessed that the Lady Helena would take over with the marriage negotiations, and she wanted to wrap things up as fast as possible. Damek probably wished to accommodate her.

"My lord," Céline answered. "This is not quite so simple a process as you—"

"You want us to start reading people?" Amelie interrupted, and then added, "My *lord*."

Damek stiffened, and Anton shot her a glance of warning, but she didn't care.

"Let us start with him," Amelie finished, pointing to Kochè.

Captain Kochè's expression shifted first to shock and

then to outrage. He took a step toward her, and she got ready to pull the dagger from her right sleeve.

But Anton stepped between them, and Kochè stopped, panting in rage

Prince Damek asked, "Why him?"

"Because he cannot walk past Rochelle without glaring at her," Céline answered.

At this, Damek met her eyes, and he appeared to be absorbing what she'd just said. Then he looked to Kochè and pointed to a chair. "Sit down."

"My lord!" Kochè protested.

"Now!"

Glowering, even shaking slightly, Kochè walked to the chair and sat down.

"His future or his past?" Anton asked quietly.

"Past," Amelie decided without even consulting Céline, and then she pulled a chair up in front of Kochè. The thought of touching him was so revolting that she wavered at first, but then she steeled herself and touched his hand, closing her eyes and focusing on the spark of his spirit.

Again, this time she wanted to go back only as an outside observer, and she tried to focus on the reason for his hatred of Rochelle.

The first jolt hit, and she gripped the arm of her chair with her free hand. The second jolt hit immediately, and she found herself swept backward in the swirling mists.

They cleared, and she found herself in an alcove with a stone bench. Damek and Rochelle were sitting on the bench and he gently gripped her hand. Amelie had not seen them like this before. She'd only seen them together last night, and while they'd each been exceedingly polite to the other, the only emotion Damek had displayed was pride. Now . . . now he looked more like a would-be groom wooing his lady.

"I know he is uncouth," Damek murmured, "but he is useful to me."

"Please, my lord," Rochelle whispered. "I've asked for nothing else. I cannot live in any place with so vile a creature. I feel ill, and I cannot eat if he enters the room. He must be sent away."

Though Damek's expression was troubled, he leaned over and kissed her forehead. "All right, my love. I did not think you quite so delicate, but I understand. Kochè will be gone before you come to live here. I do swear."

Her face melted into gratitude. "Thank you. I know it is a sacrifice, but it means so much to me."

"I'll find another captain."

Amelie had never seen Damek so accommodating to anyone, but she also wondered why she was witnessing this scene from Kochè's past. He was not here. Inside the vision, she moved from the alcove and found herself in the courtyard. It was twilight. She looked to her left.

There stood Kochè, his face awash in disbelief. He'd heard every word.

The scene vanished and the mists rushed back in. Amelie was pulled forward again, and she opened her eyes, staring at Kochè's stringy mustache. He watched her warily. Although she'd protected Johanna, she had no compunction about exposing Kochè.

Looking to Prince Damek, she said, "He overheard you promising Rochelle that you'd get rid of him before she came to live here permanently."

Damek stiffened again, and Kochè jumped to his feet. For a second or two, Amelie thought he would strike her, and she braced for a defense, but he contained himself.

"Spying at keyholes?" Damek hissed at Kochè. "Have you worked against my marriage plans?"

"No, my lord! I've done nothing. I think that girl you want to wed is more trouble than you know, but I've done nothing." Kochè stepped closer to Damek. "And if you want to seek out who is capable of casting spells to shut off someone else's breath, you ought to start with that witch!"

At first, Amelie thought Kochè was calling Rochelle a witch, but then she realized he meant someone else.

"Do you mean Lady Saorise?" she asked.

"Yes, you gypsy whore," Kochè breathed, running a hand over his face. "Why don't you go and read her?"

"Kochè . . . ," Damek said slowly. His tone dripped with warning.

Anton, Céline, and Rurik had been watching all this in silence, but now Céline looked to Damek. "My lord . . . perhaps you ought to summon the Lady Sao—"

A pounding on the door cut her off.

"Prince Damek!" Heath's voice called from the outer passage. "Come down to the courtyard at once. Summon your guards. Captain Maddox and my sister are gone. He's abducted her!"

Anton felt rushed along on a wave he couldn't stop as he found himself down in the courtyard with Céline, Amelie, and Rurik beside him.

Darkness had fallen, and large braziers on the courtyard walls provided enough light to see.

Everyone was out here.

Even Lady Helena was present, wearing a fine gown, but she must not have had time to put her hair up before the alarm was sounded, and it hung around her drawn face. Poor Lizbeth stood beside her, staring at Anton as if she thought he might be able to fix this crisis.

Väränj guards were already leading out saddled horses, but at least twenty Kimovesk guards stood around at a loss, as Kochè had not yet given the order to saddle up. Instead, he'd headed off to the stable.

Damek's expression was dark, angry, and thoughtful ... all of which made Anton nervous.

"I am telling you, Baron," Damek said to Heath with icy manners. "They are still here on castle grounds. None of my men would have allowed your captain to drag my betrothed out the front gate. You must see that."

"And I'm telling you they are gone," Heath shot back, grabbing the reins of a horse and swinging up. He wore a fine gray cloak clasped at his throat. "Maddox was a captain in the forces of the house of Äntes before he came to us. Do you really think he would abduct my sister and then hole up somewhere in this castle?"

"They could not have left the grounds!" Damek insisted.

Captain Kochè came jogging back from the stable and addressed his prince. "Both their horses are gone, my lord. A large roan stallion and a white mare."

Heath's back straightened, as if in triumph at this news, and Damek's features went still. Anton had no idea what his brother was thinking.

Two more Kimovesk guards in black tabards came up, dragging a third man—who was terrified—between them.

"It was him, my lord," the man on the right said to Damek. "He had the portcullis opened."

Damek's expression didn't change. He stared at the frightened man in the middle. "You opened the portcullis?"

"Your bride-to-be ordered me! It was still light out when

she came. She had her bodyguard with her, and she said she wished to go for a short ride. She will soon be mistress here. I could not refuse ... I saw no reason to refuse."

Damek was silent for a long moment and then said, "Take him away and lock him in the barracks."

Anton didn't wish to think about the man's fate.

Damek slowly turned to Heath—who was still mounted on his horse. "You keep saying that your sister was abducted ... and yet she was the one who ordered my man to let her out."

Heath's eyes hardened, and he did not seem so unassertive tonight. "Then Maddox did something to force her! He made her do it. Mount up, and we will recover them, and you'll hear it from her own lips!" His horse jumped to one side at the anger in his voice, and he pulled it in. "Either that or order the gate open and let me take my contingent to find her."

Though Heath sounded like a protective brother, Anton agreed with him about the course of action.

"He's right," Anton said, walking up beside Damek. "They can't have gone far. If we leave now, we might be able to catch them."

Damek took several quiet breaths and then turned to Kochè. "Have eight horses saddled, including mine, yours, and Anton's. Then choose five of your best trackers." He looked to Heath again. "Bring only five Väränj guards. We'll most likely need to split up to search, and larger contingents could give us away."

"Could my sister and I come?" Céline asked.

The courtyard went silent, and Anton couldn't believe what he'd just heard. But her eyes caught his, and he could see her pleading. Why would she want to come?

"I think it would be best, Baron," she said calmly to Heath. "Rochelle is undergoing a frightening ordeal. When she is found, she will need the comfort and company of other women, and I do not think your mother or young Lizbeth should go."

Céline never ceased to amaze Anton. In one fell swoop she had just given full support to Heath's insistence that his sister was abducted, and she'd given a valid reason for her and Amelie's inclusion in the pursuit.

With an expression of gratitude, Heath offered her a nod, and then addressed Damek. "Agreed?"

Damek was staring out at the gate now, as if thinking of something else. "Whatever you wish," he answered absently.

Lady Helena and Lizbeth watched all this in silence. While Helena had a shawl, Lizbeth stood shivering in a thin silk gown, and she was clearly distraught. Anton walked toward them.

"Rurik, come with me."

The girl watched them both with large eyes as they approached. "Oh, Anton, you'll find her? Promise you'll find her."

Somehow her use of his given name didn't bother him, especially when only hours before she had been laughing and calling him "the loser" every time he was caught with the queen in his hand.

"When did you first notice her gone?" he asked.

"Only a short while ago," Lady Helena answered. She sounded frightened, but he suspected her concern was different—and most of it pertained to Damek's suspicion that Rochelle had run off with Maddox.

"After leaving you in the hall," Lizbeth said, "Heath

and I went to our rooms to rest. Rochelle wasn't in the room I share with her, but I didn't think anything of it. I thought she must be with Mother." She turned and showed him the open back of her silk gown. "It wasn't until I went to find her or one of the maids to help me lace up my gown that I . . . I talked to Mother, and she'd not seen Rochelle. We started a search, and then Heath ran to Prince Damek's chambers."

Anton mulled that over. "Your sister and Maddox still couldn't have gone far. They didn't leave the hall until late afternoon."

Lizbeth shivered again, and Anton wished he had his cloak to offer her. He considered sending her inside but knew she wanted to be out here. Movement sounded behind, and he turned to see that Heath was off his horse, walking over. Heath stripped off the fine gray cloak and wrapped it around his youngest sister. Beneath it, he wore the long-sleeved black wool shirt. "Don't worry," he said. "We'll find them, and I'll deal with Maddox."

As opposed to reassuring, his tone was angry. Once again, Anton couldn't help noting how different he seemed tonight. He must love Rochelle to worry for her so—and to defend her honor so staunchly.

But if Anton had a sister, he would do no less.

Men began leading saddled horses from the stable.

Anton motioned to Rurik and spoke to Lady Helena. "Until Prince Damek and the young baron return, my man will stay with you and Lizbeth. You can depend upon him."

"My lord?" Rurik asked. "You cannot—"

Anton cut him off. "I know your place is beside me. But these ladies have lost their bodyguard, and the

Väränj are only here out of duty. You have my trust in this matter. I can look out for Céline and Amelie."

Though unhappy at the order, Rurik moved over beside Lizbeth. "Yes, my lord."

Céline's gray mare and Amelie's black gelding were led over to Anton.

"Wait!" a gruff voice shouted. "Wait a moment."

Helga came running out the main front doors of the castle carrying two cloaks. How could she have known Céline and Amelie would be taking part in the search? Anton sighed. He supposed it didn't matter. He was glad the sisters would have cloaks—as they were both still dressed for dinner and there was no time to change.

Helga got the cloaks over the sisters as men around them began to mount up.

Anton led Sable to Céline, and amidst the noise all around them, he leaned down and whispered, "What are you doing?"

Tilting her head toward his ear, she whispered back, "Damek and Heath are both on edge, near the breaking point. Can you not see? If either of them finds Maddox and Rochelle, I fear Maddox will be put to death instantly. With Amelie or myself there, we can offer to do a reading ... to prove the truth of what happened one way or another. If nothing else, this could provide a chance for cooler heads to interject and prevail."

He stayed there a moment longer, feeling her breath on his ear. He didn't answer ... but she was right.

"Keep me with yourself and Damek," she said, "and if we split up, send Amelie with Heath."

He gripped her waist and lifted her up into the sidesaddle. "Damek will set a fast pace. Just hold on and let Sable follow my horse."   ·

Amelie was already up on her black gelding, gripping the reins.

"Open the portcullis!" Damek called.

Anton grasped the reins of Whisper's bridle and swung up. Once again, he felt swept along on a tide he couldn't stop, and he had no idea how the rest of this night would play out.

CHAPTER NINE

Once outside the gate and on the dark road bordered by trees, Céline wondered why Anton hadn't pressed to be allowed to bring any of his own men. He hadn't even asked. Perhaps he felt that at heart, this search belonged to Heath and Damek, and that he was a mere appendage. He was most likely in no danger from his brother, who was focused on retrieving a lost bride. Still, Jaromir would have a fit if he ever found out Anton had ridden alone into the night with Damek, Kochè, and five Kimovesk guards.

As the pace of the horses increased from a canter to a gallop, she soon found herself gripping Sable's mane and trying to keep her seat. She hoped Amelie wasn't having too much trouble, and she wondered how some of these men would fare if they were forced to ride sidesaddle.

Beneath her cloak, she still wore the rose-colored satin evening gown.

Within a few moments, she was tempted to throw her leg over, grip with her knees, and let her skirts fly as they would.

She was just about to try this when Damek called, "Halt!"

He pulled his horse up abruptly and mild chaos ensued as everyone attempted to follow suit. They hadn't traveled far from the castle.

"What are you doing?" Heath asked, trying to hold in his mount.

Damek ignored him and waved a hand at the Kimovesk guards. "Start searching the sides of the road for signs where they might have entered the forest."

Heath rode up beside him angrily. "No. Searching the forest is a waste of time."

By the moonlight, Damek's eyes flashed as he wheeled his horse, but before he could speak, Anton spoke.

"Why is it a waste of time?"

"Because they won't be there," Heath answered. "Most people understand that my sister is delicate, but Maddox sees her as fragile porcelain. He would never even consider allowing her to sleep outdoors in the forest."

Damek went still, listening now. "Then where would he take her?"

"With Rochelle in tow, he knows he can't outrun a pursuit, so he'll opt for holing up and hiding her somewhere in at least adequate comfort. Most likely, he'll head for a large outlying village or town, someplace where he might find shelter and be able to disappear. He'll remain out of sight for a few days, possibly longer. He'll keep her there until he believes the search is waning, and then he'll try to slip away."

Céline absorbed this and glanced at Amelie. Everything he said made sense . . . but what if he was wrong?

"I do not know this area well," Heath continued, "and neither does Maddox. He would need information . . . directions to someplace both large enough for his needs and yet out of the way." He paused. "We should ride into

Kimovesk Village and ask the people there if Maddox and Rochelle rode through, and if they spoke to anyone."

Slowly, Damek nodded. "Yes . . . good."

Anton grimaced almost imperceptibly

With a lurch in her stomach Céline wondered what methods Damek might employ to *ask* the Kimovesk peasants if they'd seen or spoken to anyone.

As the horses around her broke into a trot, Céline looked back at her sister. "Amelie, throw your leg over the saddle."

Holding Sable's reins, Céline followed her own advice. There was no stirrup on the right side, but it didn't matter. She could grip much better with her knees.

The horses moved from a trot to a canter to a gallop in a matter of seconds, and again, Céline focused on nothing except holding on. The village soon loomed before them, and her worst fears were realized.

Damek thundered down the main path, shouting orders. Both Kimovesk and Väränj guards began leaping off horses, kicking doors open, and dragging people into the open.

Sable was breathing hard as Céline drew her up, and then Amelie's gelding was beside them.

"Oh, Céline," Amelie said in despair, watching the scene before them.

Dozens of bone-thin people in tattered clothes had been dragged or pushed out into the night at sword point. The whites of their eyes showed as they stumbled into the muddy main path between dwellings. Anton didn't try to interfere. There was nothing he could do.

A large number of people must still be huddling in their homes in the dwellings farther on, but Damek seemed satisfied with the few dozen kneeling before him.

Still on his horse, he called out. "Those of you in hiding! Listen to me! A man on a roan horse and a lady on a white mare rode through here in the late afternoon. The man would have spoken to someone and asked for information. I need only to know to whom he spoke."

Soft gasps sounded from the peasants on the ground, and Céline longed to be somewhere else, anywhere else. She had witnessed . . . she had lived through too many scenes like this one.

"Someone spoke to this man," Heath called out. "Who was it?"

An aged woman on her knees near Damek looked up at him. "My lord . . . the man and the woman did pass through, but they did not speak to anyone."

Damek jumped down off his horse and drew the dagger from its sheath on his hip. He pointed to a boy, perhaps twelve years old, kneeling in the mud beside the old woman.

"Bring that one," he ordered a guard.

Céline closed her eyes, but that proved a mistake, as she was instantly drawn into a memory she kept pushed down in the back of her mind. . . .

She was nine years old, living in Shetâna with her family. Her mother was the village apothecary and her father was a hunter—a good one. This was before Damek had been placed in charge of the province, but his predecessor, a vassal of Prince Lieven's, had been no better. Soldiers had free run of the villages, and the people feared them.

One day, three Kimovesk soldiers rode into Shetâna and began taking whatever they wanted. Céline knew they weren't collecting taxes, just taking things for themselves, probably to sell. One of them ordered a farmer to turn over all twenty of his goats. This would have left the man to starve, and he refused. Céline remembered when the shouting started, and she saw the farmer take a swing at the soldier. All three soldiers attacked the farmer, and Céline's father ran to help.

He shoved one soldier away, and as he was turning to push off another, the man drew a dagger and rammed it through Céline's father's stomach. She didn't scream. She stood there frozen and watched him die . . . over helping a farmer try to save twenty goats.

He'd failed.

The soldiers took the goats, and they stepped over her father's body as if it were rubbish lying on the ground. They'd probably forgotten him by the time they reached the edge of the village.

"Someone here spoke to this man." Damek's voice cut through her memory. "Who was it? Tell us, and we will leave."

She opened her eyes. Though he still held the dagger, he didn't seem intent on using it. Two Kimovesk guards held the boy between them. The boy panted in wild fear, and the old woman on the ground bowed her head, groveling.

"Please, my lord! They spoke to no one!"

Damek looked at one of the guards holding the boy. "Cut off his right hand."

Céline cast a desperate look at Anton. His whole body was taut, but he stayed on his horse and said nothing.

"Close your eyes again," Amelie warned.

The boy screamed as his arm was jerked forward and held out.

"Stop this!" someone called.

A young woman about Amelie's age walked down the

path toward them. Her clothes were as tattered as everyone else's, but her back was straight.

"I spoke to the man you seek," she said. "Let the boy go, and ask me your questions."

She walked right toward Damek and stopped about ten paces away. True courage was rare in a place like this, and Céline hope the young woman would not suffer for it.

Heath was still mounted, and he spoke first. "What did the man ask you?"

"He asked the name and direction of the largest town within half a day's riding distance." Her voice was clear.

Heath appeared so grateful that he lowered his voice. "And what town did you name?"

"Chekalin, to the north."

Turning quickly to Damek, Heath asked, "You know this place?"

Damek didn't answer him and studied the young woman. He'd not seen the boy's hand cut off, and he still wanted blood. Céline's stomach lurched again, but Heath seemed to see the danger as well and urged his horse between Damek and the young woman. "We have no time for this. Do you know the town?"

"Of course I know it," Damek bit off. "It's in my province."

"Then you lead."

Reluctantly, Damek turned, sheathed his dagger, and remounted his horse.

Céline looked down to see her hands shaking. After living most of her life in Shetâna, and then finding a safe haven in Sèone, she'd thought herself beyond sorrow or fear-induced flashbacks. She was wrong.

*　　*　　*

Halfway to the middle of night, Amelie heard one of the guards say they were approaching Chekalin. It had been a long, hard ride, and she was angry with herself over how much her current discomforts bothered her.

For one, she was hungry. After what she'd witnessed back in Kimovesk Village, she should not have the slightest interest in food, but she hadn't eaten much all day, and for the second night in a row dinner hadn't been served in the castle. Last night, Lord Hamish had died, and tonight, the meal had been forgone because of the news of Rochelle's abduction.

Both of these events were tragic . . . and yet Amelie could not ignore her hunger pangs.

Worse was the pain she felt from the skin on the inside of her legs. Céline had not been wrong to suggest riding straddle. At the fast pace they rode, gripping with their knees was the only option. At first, this had been a relief. A few hours later, Amelie's skin felt as if it had been rubbed raw.

Stupid dinner gown.

The dress offered no protection, and once again, she longed for her pants.

On the edge of town, the horses slowed. A wall of wooden logs surrounded Chekalin. There were two entrances within sight. As the wall would clearly not withstand any sort of serious assault and there were no watchmen on the entrances, Amelie assumed the wall's intent was merely to help channel incoming traffic to the main streets.

Heath rode up to the front of the contingent.

"Prince though you may be," he said to Damek, "this place is much too large for you to ride in and start torturing people. We might conceive a different strategy."

Amelie almost couldn't believe the change in Heath. He was panicked over his sister's disappearance, and it seemed to bring out the best and worst in him. While he was certainly more commanding than she ever could have imagined, his manner bordered on insulting.

Céline sat silently on her horse, and Amelie glanced at her in concern. Her expression had been queer, almost ill, since leaving Kimovesk. Amelie wanted to ask if she was all right, but then what could Céline possibly say? It didn't matter whether she was all right or not. They were in the middle of this now.

"And what do you suggest?" Damek asked Heath.

Amelie found his contempt unfounded. Without Heath, they'd probably still be searching the forests around Kimovesk.

Anton rode up to the front, keeping his voice low. "I think we should keep our arrival quiet, brother. If Maddox gets wind of us, he might take Rochelle and run."

At this, Damek's tight expression eased slightly, and he studied Anton. Then he nodded.

"How comfortable would Maddox wish to make her?" Anton asked Heath. "Would he risk taking her to an inn?"

"Possibly," Heath answered. "Though he is a most able soldier, he has a tendency to overestimate himself. If he and Rochelle are here, he probably views himself as safe . . . leagues away from our search."

"What do you mean *if* they're here?" Damek asked.

"I mean that we are following well-reasoned speculation and the word of a peasant girl. Nothing is certain."

The skin over Damek's cheeks tightened again.

"I suggest we split into two groups," Anton said, "and conduct a quiet search. Damek and I will take the west side of town. Heath, you take the east. We'll speak to every innkeeper and every tavern owner with a room to rent. I have some coin with me, and we can pay bribes if we must. Someone will have seen them or given them sanctuary."

Heath nodded at Anton's sensible counsel. "Yes, I have coin with me as well."

"I'll keep Céline with me," Anton continued. "You take Miss Amelie in case you find Rochelle first. Amelie can offer her comfort."

Mild surprise, followed by pleasure, passed across Heath's face. "It would be my honor."

Amelie found that a tad formal, all things considered, but she urged her black gelding toward his tall horse.

"We'll enter first," Heath said to Anton. "Give us a few moments before you follow."

With that, Amelie rode into Chekalin beside him, with five Väränj guards following. It bothered her to leave Céline, but Amelie understood why Céline had wanted to come, and at this point, the sisters had no choice but to split up.

They entered what appeared to be an open-air market that had been closed for the night with all the stalls covered. At this late hour, the town was quiet.

"We'll probably have to wake a few innkeepers from their sleep," she commented.

Heath turned east, and they rode down a well-maintained street past a row of neatly painted shops. As this town was in Damek's territory, Amelie hadn't expected it to look quite so prosperous—as most of his people were taxed near to death. Perhaps he'd overlooked it?

Amelie herself had no problem with taxes. She and

Céline paid taxes in Sèone, but Anton never overtaxed his people, and he always used the money for things like maintaining bridges, for helping the poor, for paying guards who actually guarded his people, and so on. He'd even funded a few small schools. She had no idea what Damek did with the taxes that Captain Kochè collected with such vigor.

"Up there," Heath said, pointing.

Following to where he pointed, she saw a white-washed two-story building with vines growing up a fenced porch.

Upon reaching the building, Heath dismounted. Without waiting to be asked, Amelie climbed down as well, but he offered no objection. The skin on the inside her legs felt on fire, and she tried not to wince.

"Stay out here," Heath ordered his men.

Amelie and Heath walked five steps up to the ivy-covered porch, and in the shadows of the front door, he stopped her with his hand.

"You do . . . ," he said quietly. "You do believe Rochelle was abducted, don't you? It matters to me what you think."

Why should he care what she thought? But she nodded to him. "Yes. I wouldn't blame any woman for trying to escape marriage to Damek, but I don't believe Rochelle would run off with Captain Maddox. She cares for your family far too much."

"Thank you." He didn't move. "And I know this is hardly the time, but I wanted to thank you for this afternoon, for staying in the hall and comforting my sisters with games and stories the way you did."

"Oh . . . you're welcome."

After this, she expected him to enter the inn, but still,

he hesitated. "It's been a long time since Rochelle, Lizbeth, and I all played together like that, and I have you to thank. I'm not comfortable speaking to most people, but I find myself at ease with you."

Amelie tensed. Was he about to express *interest* in her? She wasn't sure. Most men who met the sisters followed Céline with their eyes—but few men ever looked at Amelie. She had no idea how to properly respond and cut him off before he said something he might regret later.

Quickly, she took a step away from him. "Baron, we should go inside and wake the innkeeper."

He flinched, as if hurt, and then recovered. "Of course. I only wished to thank you for this afternoon."

Turning away, he opened the door, and they stepped inside. The foyer was dark, but some light from the outer streetlamps came in through the windows. There was no counter, but a long table stood in front of a closed door.

"Hello?" Heath called. "Is anyone here?"

A moment later, shuffling sounded behind the door, and a stocky man with a shiny head emerged, pulling a robe around his shoulders with one hand and carrying a lantern in the other.

He squinted at the pair of them and smiled sleepily. "Riding in so late? Do you need a room?"

Amelie wondered how this should be handled, and she let Heath take the lead.

"Yes and no," Heath answered. "My wife and I had arranged to meet my sister, along with our family's bodyguard, in this town, but I fear there was a miscommunication regarding the name of the inn. Do you have a lovely woman with my coloring, and a tall dour man with dark hair hereabout somewhere?" He smiled back.

Amelie was astonished at the ease with which he lied, but she much preferred his method of questioning to Damek's.

"Sorry, lad," the man answered. "I've only two guests here now, and both are older men, merchants, I think. But at this hour, you'd probably do better to stay here and find your sister in the morning."

"No doubt you're right," Heath answered. "But we'd like to try a few more places."

"Good luck to you," the man said, turning away to go back to bed.

Amelie led the way outside. "I believed him."

"So did I."

They headed back for their horses, to continue on and check the next inn.

"A lady about eighteen years of age, with red-blond hair, and she would be accompanied by a tall man in chain armor and a yellow tabard?" Anton explained to a sleepy woman in her nightdress and wrapped in a shawl. "The woman is my sister, and the man is her guard. We're traveling together, and I sent them on ahead tonight when my horse threw a shoe . . . but we neglected to name a meeting place here."

Anton, Céline, and Damek had entered the first inn they came across. As Damek had almost no capability for polite inquiry, he'd let Anton do the talking.

"No, sir," she mumbled back. "I've no one here like that tonight. The only folks I have staying here now are regulars who come through every autumn to sell goods."

He could see she spoke the truth, and he thanked her politely.

Turning, he saw Damek's expression darken, and he motioned his brother toward the door. "Out."

Thankfully, Damek obeyed, but the moment he was through the door and on the porch, he hissed, "This is madness. It will take all night."

Anton had not yet closed the door, and worry over his brother's mood gave him a spark of an idea. He looked back inside. "Madam?"

The woman was shuffling off, but she stopped, "Yes?"

"How many stables are there in town? If we find where they stabled their horses, it would help narrow our search."

Rubbing her eyes, she nodded in approval. "Oh, that's clever. We have three, all on the outskirts of town, one on the west side, one on the east, and one on the south. The east stable is the largest."

"Thank you."

When Anton stepped outside, Damek studied him curiously. Céline had not appeared to be listening, and he was becoming concerned about her. She'd been nearly silent and did not seem herself.

"What are you thinking?" Damek asked Anton.

"Exactly what I said. There are only three stables, so we should check those first. If we find a roan stallion and a white mare, we'll know for certain that Maddox and Rochelle are here, and we'll have narrowed the search zone."

Damek tilted his head. "Sometimes I underestimate you."

"Sometimes?"

Anton walked toward his horse, Captain Kochè, and the Kimovesk guards, but he glanced back at Céline, who followed him without really looking where she was going. Something was wrong. He suspected it had to do with the scene back in the village.

"We need to head west for the outer edge of town," Damek ordered the guards. "We'll start with the closest stable."

Anton helped Céline onto her horse and then he mounted up. She didn't speak or look at him. His concern grew.

They headed west and began doing a search for the stable on the outskirts of town. It didn't take long to find. However, at this hour, the large double doors—wide enough to drive a wagon through—were barred from the inside, and the stable master had long since retired for the night.

Captain Kochè walked to a small door near the left front corner of the stable. "My lord?"

Damek walked over and Anton followed.

"I could break this one quietly," Kochè said.

Damek nodded.

Kochè gripped the latched, put his shoulder to the door, and shoved a few times. The door cracked and broke inward.

"I'll take a look," Anton said. "You stand watch out here."

He knew Damek would have no interest in mucking about inside a stable, so he expected no argument—and neither did he get one. But then he reached out with one hand and motioned Céline toward him. "Come with me."

At that, Damek did raise an eyebrow. Hopefully, he would assume that Anton simply didn't wish to leave her alone with the men from Kimovesk.

She came to him and followed him inside, but her expression was still lost.

He pushed the door back in place as well as he could and then started toward the back of the stable. "This way."

They walked down a long row of stalls, and he peered over the tops of the doors. There were no roan horses. He did stop at the stall of a white mare, but she was older and her coat was rough, and Anton knew the animal would not belong to Rochelle.

The final few stalls were empty. The door of one was open, and there were crates stored inside.

"Come in here and sit for a moment," he said.

"What?" She spoke for the first time, since leaving Kimovesk Village, and her eyes cleared a bit.

He sat on a crate and pulled her down beside him. "We don't have much time, and I need you to tell me what's wrong."

Her dark blond hair hung forward over her face, and her cloak was askew, revealing the shoulder of her gown. "There's nothing wrong."

He wasn't good at this . . . at drawing things out of people. He was highly skilled at concealing emotions, but he had no idea how to draw them out of someone else.

"If we find Maddox and Rochelle tonight, you will be needed. You'll need to be my seer, and right now . . . you are not. Tell me what is wrong."

She stared at the straw on the floor. "I'd just forgotten how very little life or suffering counts for here. I've been in Sèone too long. Damek could have cut that boy's hand off and then ridden away, and by the time he reached the edge of the village, he'd have forgotten the boy existed. But the boy would have spent the rest of his life maimed."

"I would have spared you seeing that if I could."

"I've seen worse, much worse. I've lived through worse."

Here, he was on dangerous ground. He knew that she and Amelie had suffered much at the hands of Damek's soldiers, but the truth was . . . he wasn't certain he wished to know *how* much they had suffered. He knew this was cowardly and self-centered, but he couldn't help it. He had his own demons from the past, and he wasn't sure he could effectively wrestle with the demons of someone else.

"They killed my father," Céline whispered. "Soldiers from Kimovesk."

He turned on the crate to look straight at her.

"I saw it," she added.

"Oh, Céline." Instead of awkward discomfort, a pity he could not describe washed through him. "How old were you?"

"Nine."

Without thinking, he reached out and pulled her against his shoulder. "I'm so sorry." And he was.

"He was trying to help someone else," she whispered with one side of her face pressed against him, "and one of the soldiers stabbed him and then just left him there like he was nothing. There was no one to whom we could complain or report. There was no one like Jaromir to deal out justice. Those men rode away and forgot him, leaving two daughters without a father and a wife without a husband."

With nothing he could possibly say, he laid his face on the top of her head.

Pulling back slightly, she looked up at him. "If you were grand prince, could you change things? Could you protect the people in a province like this one?"

"I don't know," he answered honestly. "But I would try."

Her mouth was inches from his, and the pain in her

eyes cut through him. Unable to stop himself, he touched his mouth to hers, and to his absolute wonder, she kissed him back and moved her hand up to the side of his neck, brushing it with her fingertips.

It had been so long since anyone had touched him like this. He opened his mouth and kissed her more deeply. She responded, but the pressure of her mouth was soft and gentle, eager and unsure at the same time. His whole body felt alive, and he moved his right hand inside her cloak, feeling her small rib cage. She pressed in closer to him, and he'd never wanted anything in his life more than this.

Then bells of warning rang in his head.

She had been in a sorrow-filled and vulnerable moment. . . .

He was taking advantage. . . .

He could not marry her. . . .

Damek and Captain Kochè were right outside.

With a strangled cry, he jerked himself away and stood up.

"Anton?" she asked in confusion.

"We can't . . . Céline, we can't. Not like this."

She stared at him, beyond hurt. He knew he could never erase what he'd just done, but there was more here at stake, and he dropped to his knees. "I need you to be my seer tonight," he begged. "I need you to come back to yourself. Please, Céline."

She blinked. "Is that why you . . . ?" She stood up.

He'd said everything wrong. He had not kissed her or been kind to her so that she would recover herself and be useful to him.

"Of course, my lord," she said stiffly.

"I didn't mean—"

"Anton!" Damek called from the front of the stable. "What are you doing? Have you found anything?"

"No. We're coming," he called back.

Céline wouldn't look at him. "Which stable next?" She sounded so cold, but maybe that was best. At least he couldn't hurt her if she wouldn't let him get close.

"The one on the east side. The innkeeper said it was the largest."

She walked away, heading for the front of the stable.

After trying several inns with no success, Amelie and Heath spotted a two-story tavern with what looked to be separate rooms on the upper floor—or at least from what they could guess by peering up through the windows.

The bottom floor was well lit, and voices came from inside.

Amelie shrugged. "It's worth a try."

She had opted to walk and lead her horse, as she couldn't bear the thought of climbing into the saddle again. So Heath walked beside her, leading his mount as well. They both passed their reins up to a Väränj guard.

"Wait out here," Heath told the men.

He and Amelie headed for the front door of the tavern.

Inside, it was less populated than she'd expected. There were only four patrons inside, all at the same table, but they were laughing loudly and appeared nearly drunk. A spindly man with an equally spindly beard stood behind the bar.

Heath walked up to the bartender. "Good evening. Do you rent the rooms above-stairs?"

The man glanced at Amelie, back to Heath, and smiled. "I do, sir. Clean rooms, and I'll give you a fair price."

"Do you have any guests already tonight?"

The man's smile faded. "Why do you ask?"

Something about this caught Amelie's attention, and she watched the bartender as Heath repeated his story about the miscommunication with his sister. When he described Rochelle and Maddox, the man's expression flickered.

He shook his head. "Sorry, I can't help. I don't have any guests and haven't seen ladies with red-gold hair. I'd remember if I did."

This time, Heath smiled. "One moment, please."

He motioned Amelie to remain where she was, and he walked over to the door, cracking it and peering out. "Lieutenant?" he called, and held up two fingers.

As he came back to the bar, two Väränj guards in red tabards walked in and the table of drunkards fell silent. The bartender began backing away, and like lightning, Heath grabbed his wrist and slammed his hand down on the bar.

The action caught Amelie by surprise. Heath didn't look strong enough to pin another man like that.

With his free hand, Heath pointed to a dagger on the belt of a Väränj guard. The guard drew it, and Heath turned back to the now terrified bartender.

"I am here in the company of Prince Damek," Heath explained calmly.

"Prince Damek . . . ?"

"So you will understand that I have leave to do anything I wish," Heath went on as if he'd not been interrupted. "If you have the two people I am seeking upstairs in your establishment, or if you know where they are, you'd better tell me now. If you don't"—he pointed to the guard with the dagger—"I'll have him begin cutting off your fingers, one by one, starting with the thumb on this hand."

The man's eyes went wide, and Amelie fought back a gasp. At the moment, Heath sounded just like Damek.

"Not here," the bartender babbled. "They're in the stable . . . a few blocks east. I own part of it, and I put 'em in a room in the back. But that soldier paid me well to keep quiet, and I'm no welcher. You understand . . . I didn't know Prince Damek was lookin' for him and the lady."

Heath smiled again and let the man go. "Of course I understand, and I thank you for your trouble." He turned on his heel and walked to the door.

With little choice, Amelie followed him and the Väränj guards back outside. Before reaching the horses, she caught his arm. "Heath, you wouldn't really have cut that man's fingers off?"

He stopped. "Cut his . . . good gods, no. I thought you knew I was bluffing. I've no idea what I'd have done if he hadn't begun talking."

Taking this in, Amelie couldn't help laughing once. He was certainly unpredictable.

But then she grew serious. They had found Rochelle and Maddox, and she feared he'd not be so inhibited when it came to dealing with Maddox.

She was ready for anything.

"Let's find that stable," she said.

Riding in front of Damek and the Kimovesk guards, Céline and Anton located the stable on the east side of town with fair ease. Anton put a hand up and halted the small contingent about a block away.

The stable was huge, built of solid oak with glass in the high-set windows.

Céline was both on edge and miserable at the same

time. She knew she had to be at her best here, gauging a rapidly changing situation and being at the ready to protect Rochelle, or possibly Maddox, depending on how all this played out. And yet, for once, her mind was not on the crisis. She'd been wallowing in self-pity on the ride here, mourning afresh for her lost father, and feeling angry at the lack of justice that had prevailed for so long in this province. Then ... Anton had shown amazing kindness, followed it up by kissing her, and she'd let herself become lost in him, in the warmth and pleasure of his touch. She'd been startled and hurt when he pulled away.

Moments later, no matter how shattered she'd felt inside about so many things, she understood why he'd pulled away. Now she wished she could talk to him. She knew him well enough to know he'd be racked with guilt. In truth, it still hurt when she thought about him drawing away from her, but here, in enemy territory, they both needed to keep their wits about them. Getting lost in each other was a pitfall that could not be risked.

Even from a block away, Anton's eyes moved up and down the large, well-maintained stable. The wide front doors were open.

"This town," he said slowly, "appears rather prosperous."

"You mean for a town under my control?" Damek returned. Anton said nothing, and then Damek confessed, "The mayor is a good friend of Father's, a friend of old, and I've thought it wise to take a light hand here for now."

Anton dismounted. "The front doors are open, so there is most likely someone on watch inside. I'll check for the horses."

Without waiting to be asked, Céline climbed down off

Sable. Damek and Captain Kochè watched her join Anton.

"Try to be a little quicker this time," Damek said dryly.

Anton started toward the stable and Céline followed. They didn't speak as they walked, and Céline resigned herself that any further words—about themselves or each other—would have to wait.

A single hanging lantern just inside the wide stable doors provided some light. Various tack and harnesses hung on the walls, and two wagons were parked here up front. Céline followed Anton past two empty stalls, and then he paused in front of a third stall. Its door was open, and Céline peered in to see a youth of about sixteen years sleeping on a matt on the stall floor. He didn't even stir. If his job was to guard the horses from thieves, he wasn't much use.

Anton put his finger to his lips and then motioned Céline forward.

They walked quietly on, looking over stall doors, but they found no roan stallion or white mare in the front section of the stable. They reached a stout support wall with a doorway and passed through into the back half of the building. Here the only illumination was moonlight coming through the upper windows—along with any residual light from the lantern glowing through the door behind them.

Four stalls down, Céline peered over the top of the door to see a fine white mare with slender legs and a silky mane. "Anton."

He looked in and then went to the next stall. "A big roan."

For the next moment, they both stood there. They'd found the horses. That meant Heath's speculations had been correct all along. Maddox and Rochelle were nearby ... somewhere.

Movement sounded from the front of the stable and a young male voice called out, "Hallo? Is anyone there?"

Anton frowned. Down at the end of the row of stalls was a closed door. "Out the back," he mouthed silently.

She followed him down the remaining stalls, but when he reached the door and tried to turn the latch, the door didn't budge.

"It's locked," he whispered. "And I'd rather not alert anyone to our presence here yet." Turning back, he put his shoulder to the door and was about to try to force it when it jerked open in his hand from the other side.

Captain Maddox stood there, his face awash in shock, holding a sword with the blade pointed toward the ceiling. He struck out, catching Anton in the face with the fist gripping the hilt. Céline couldn't help gasping and rushing back out of the way. Somehow Anton hit the floor, rolled up almost directly beside her, and drew his own sword in the same motion. His mouth was bleeding.

Céline looked beyond Maddox into a small room behind him with a table that sported a glowing candle lantern. Rochelle stood by the table with her hand at her throat.

Maddox roared and rushed Anton. He was the larger man by far, but Anton stepped aside at the last second, and Maddox stumbled past where he'd been standing.

However, as Maddox brought his sword down at the same time, he almost hit Céline. She felt the air moving past her when the blade swung.

"Maddox, stop!" Anton shouted.

Rochelle ran out from the small room where they had been hiding, looking from Céline to Anton.

"The women are in close quarters here!" Anton rushed on. "Do you want us both swinging swords?"

Despite the desperation in his eyes, Maddox froze, glancing at Céline, and she knew Anton had made the correct appeal.

"Rochelle!"

Céline half whirled to see Heath standing about twenty paces down the row of stalls. Amelie and the Väränj guards were just behind him . . . and Damek and the Kimovesk guards were behind them.

"Heath!" Rochelle cried. "I knew you would find me."

Amelie had been taken aback when she and Heath approached the stable . . . only to find Damek and his men waiting. Without asking why they were here, Heath explained they had reason to believe that Maddox had hidden Rochelle in a room at the back.

Heath led the way, and upon entering the front section of the stable, they had all heard Anton shouting for Maddox to "stop."

Breaking into a jog, Heath hurried toward the back with Amelie right behind him . . . and there, they found Anton and Maddox squared off with their swords drawn. Céline stood near a stall close to Anton.

Rochelle was just outside a small doorway in the back wall. "Heath!" she cried. "I knew you would find me."

A few breaths of silence followed. Maddox's expression was tortured and confused at the same time.

"Put down that blade!" Heath spat at him.

Rochelle was looking beyond Heath . . . behind Amelie to someone farther behind. Slowly, Damek came forward, moving down the right side of the stalls, slipping past the Väränj guards. His face expressed nothing. His eyes shifted from Maddox to Rochelle, but he offered no emotion at all.

"My lord!" Rochelle said, with a hint of fear. "He stole me from the castle. He forced me!"

"And how did he force you to charm one of my guards into opening the portcullis?" Damek asked.

Her breaths came fast. "He threatened me."

"With what?"

As those words left Damek's mouth, Heath whirled toward him in a rage. "How dare you treat her like this . . . after what she's endured?" He pointed to Maddox. "I'll execute him myself! He's the one who has been trying to stop this wedding."

"That's not true," Maddox said raggedly, lowering the point of his sword in defeat. "But I did force Rochelle to come with me. I tried to save her."

Damek ignored Heath and continued to study Rochelle. Amelie had a bad feeling that Damek was most dangerous when he was calm like this.

"My lord," Céline said, slipping past Anton and moving to Damek. "My sister can tell you without a doubt exactly what happened."

Thankfully, Céline sounded like herself again. Something had woken her up.

"Please allow Amelie to read one of them, and then you'll know the truth," Céline went on.

Finally, Damek turned his eyes to her, letting them rest briefly on her face. He looked back first to Rochelle and then Maddox. "Have her read . . . *him*."

He still sounded dangerous, but Céline had accomplished what the sisters had come here for. As of yet, no one had killed Maddox on the spot, and now Amelie had the chance to find out what had really happened. The tricky part here was that she and Céline had been charged with the task of making certain Damek's marriage was completed. If Maddox turned out to be innocent . . . and Rochelle had run off with him, how in the world would Amelie be able to save him and the marriage?

Still, she had to learn the truth. She didn't know Maddox well, but anyone deserved that much.

Walking forward through the small group of people ahead, she went straight to him. His eyes were filled with despair, and a trickle of sweat ran down his face.

"How did you find us?" he whispered in disbelief.

"Heath seemed to know what you would do," she answered. "We followed him for the most part."

"Heath?"

The shocked manner in which he repeated Heath's name bothered Amelie. Was it so unthinkable that Heath should have a brain in his head? She looked past Maddox into the room. "Are there chairs in there? We should sit, but drop your sword out here."

A flash of rebellion passed across his features. It was gone just as quickly as he looked over at Rochelle. In defeat, he dropped his sword and walked through the doorway. Amelie followed, finding herself in a narrow but fairly comfortable looking room with a bed, a table, chairs, and even a porcelain washbasin. Not bad for the back of a stable.

"Sit down," she instructed. "I only need to touch your hand."

"I know."

Damek now stood in the doorway, watching them, and Amelie tried to shut him out. She grasped two of Maddox's fingers and closed her eyes.

She felt for the spark of his spirit.

Although it was a terrible invasion, she knew she couldn't go back as only an observer this time. She needed to see and feel the past as Maddox had felt it. Merely watching events as they had played out would not be enough.

The first jolt hit. Amelie fought to latch on to Maddox's spirit, and when she had it, she forced it to mesh with her own. She could feel anxiety flooding his mind, but she didn't let go. She struggled to see through Maddox's eyes and feel what he had felt . . .

Until she was Maddox.

The second jolt hit.

The room around them vanished, and they were swept backward together through the gray and white mists.

CHAPTER TEN

Maddox had never known such joy.

Rochelle lay beneath him. Her slender, perfect body was naked, and her arms were around his neck. They were in the same small guest room they sometimes availed themselves of when they both could arrange an excuse to sneak away. Today, they'd made good use of the past hour, and he was nearly spent.

These stolen moments had become the center of his life. He'd had women over the years, and he'd cared deeply for some of them, but he'd never been in love.

He hadn't even known what the word meant until now.

She ran her nose along his cheek, and he breathed in pleasure while moving his hand from her hip up her side to cup one of her small, rounded breasts.

"Rochelle," he murmured.

Even after three weeks of this, he sometimes still couldn't believe it. Every unmarried nobleman who walked into the manor made an offer for Rochelle, and yet she'd given herself to him, to a soldier with no title and no fortune ... and twelve years older than her.

How could he be so lucky?

"We have to tell your parents soon," he said. "This is beginning to feel dishonorable."

"Does this feel dishonorable?" she asked playfully, brushing her fingers from his neck all the way down his back.

His whole body tingled, but he pulled away and rolled onto his side. "I mean it. We need to tell them and arrange for our marriage."

Daylight came in through the window, glinting off her beautiful red-gold hair.

She sat up in bed, letting the covers fall so he could look at her. The sight never ceased to astonish him. His eyes moved from her narrow, rounded hips up to her fragile shoulders. Her white skin was flawless.

"Not yet, Maddox. I haven't thought of a way to tell them yet ... to explain. I fear if we choose the wrong time, I could be locked in my room, and you could be dismissed from service."

"Your mother wouldn't dismiss me."

His place among the family was somewhat ambiguous. He'd basically been a "gift" from Prince Rodêk three years ago: a captain of the Äntes guard to oversee their manor. Although Maddox was in service to Lady Helena, and her brother, Lord Hamish, they treated him as a near equal in their daily lives, and he often ate in the dining room with them. He only played the part of bodyguard, standing at attention by the wall, when they had guests.

"She would dismiss you if we don't choose our moment and our words correctly," Rochelle said, "and I couldn't bear that. Please, wait a little longer, and we'll think of something. I cannot be the cause of anything that injures you."

"But soon?" he pressed, picturing their wedding day in his mind.

"Soon." She smiled and lay down, stretching her slender body. "Put your hands on me again."

A week passed and they were able to meet two more times. Rochelle was only eighteen, and she knew nothing of the world. Maddox marveled that so young and innocent a girl could be so insatiable in bed. She could not seem to get enough of him.

He loved it.

He'd found the perfect woman.

Still, though, he had pressed her again to let him speak to her mother and uncle, but she so feared the prospect of his dismissal that she'd begged him to wait.

He knew he couldn't wait much longer. He was trusted in this house, and the thought of some of the things he and Rochelle had done in back corners of the manor filled him with heat and guilt at the same time.

Evening had fallen, and he was dressed for dinner, but when he walked into the dining room, he wondered if he'd forgotten a special occasion. There were elaborately arranged roses on the table, along with the good silver candelabras that Lady Helena used for company.

Yet only the family was present, already seated. Of course his gaze first went to Rochelle, who was resplendent, wearing a muslin dress of pale yellow. Her hair was loose and fell around her shoulders.

Sitting next to her was the eldest daughter in the family ... Carlotta. She was as different from Rochelle as snow from fire. Physically, she took after her father's side of the family, large-boned with sinewy hands. Though she was only in her mid-twenties, her coarse dark hair had begun going gray, and she wore it in a severe knot. Her nose was sharp, and her mouth was perpetually turned down at the corners. She wore dark gowns with high necks and long sleeves. Maddox had never heard a kind word come from her mouth.

Across the table from her sat Lizbeth, and his heart went out to the girl in a different way from how it beat for Rochelle. Poor Lizbeth. In the three years he'd lived here, he'd watched her grow from an awkward twelve-year-old to an awkward fifteen-year-old. She lacked any sort of grace. There were often red spots on her cheeks and forehead, and her hair forever seemed to be falling out of whatever attempt she'd made to pin it up or pull it back. Her dresses never quite fit her properly, and she was always fidgeting and pulling at her sleeves. But it was impossible for him not to feel a fondness for her. She was open and honest and had a good heart. She was kind to horses, and she loved to run and climb trees. Unfortunately, Lady Helena never failed to point out the girl's faults, and Lizbeth had become self-conscious.

Maddox pitied her now, but he had a feeling that with time, she might grow into her own brand of beauty and perhaps take the world by storm.

Heath sat to the left of Lizbeth, and at the sight of him, Maddox's pity increased. At eighteen, Heath was more like a child than a man, and he rarely spoke. He looked like a male copy of Rochelle, but on him, the effect was . . . unsettling.

Maddox had tried to do what he could for the young man, including arranging private lessons so he might

learn to use a dagger, but Maddox had never been comfortable around Heath. The situation had been better
when Baron Alexis was still alive—for both Heath and
Lizbeth. Their father had exuded a warmth their mother
lacked, and he'd balanced out the family. But when
Heath and Rochelle were sixteen, their father had died
after a short illness. Heath had been named baron, but
this had only caused him to vanish further inside himself.
Lord Hamish openly despised his nephew and dispar-
aged him at every opportunity.

"Am I late?" Maddox asked as he walked in, still wondering about the roses and the silver candelabras.

"Not at all, Captain," Lady Helena answered smoothly.
She wore red silk tonight with jewels in her ears.

"Come and have some wine," Lord Hamish said, ges-
turing to Maddox's usual spot at the table.

Maddox sat. He'd never cared much for Lord Hamish.
This manor had belonged to his brother-in-law, and now
Hamish treated it as his own, even though it technically
belonged to Heath—along with the wine business.

Heath was allowed no say in the running of either the
house or the business, but he didn't seem to mind. He expressed no other interest than being left to spend time
with Rochelle or Lizbeth. Maddox supposed it was because the girls accepted him as he was.

"Pour some wine for Captain Maddox," Lord Hamish
called to a servant.

Lady Helena leaned forward. "Lizbeth, do not slurp
your wine like that. Set it down and sit up straight. Your
uncle has an announcement."

Lizbeth set down her goblet.

Lord Hamish stood, and to Maddox's puzzlement, the
man beamed at Rochelle. "My dear niece," he said, rais-

ing his own goblet. "Your mother and I have such news for you . . . news for the entire family. We've been in quiet talks with the house of Pählen. Your sister Carlotta received a letter this morning from Castle Kimovesk, and we have now entered formal marriage negotiations between you and Prince Damek . . . who we all know will be the next grand prince of Droevinka." He held his goblet toward Rochelle. "My dearest girl . . . you will be the grand princess of our nation."

Maddox sat frozen, thinking he hadn't heard correctly.

Rochelle stared at her uncle and then looked down at her plate.

"Are you not happy, my sweet?" Lady Helena asked. "Is this not the best news?"

"Yes, Mother," Rochelle answered. "I am overwhelmed."

Then it hit Maddox that this was really happening. Surely, Rochelle would speak up now. She'd have to. She couldn't allow such negotiations to continue. Then he saw her glance at Lizbeth and Heath.

Of course she would not wish to speak of her love for Maddox . . . of her relationship to Maddox in this mixed company. She would request a private counsel with her mother and uncle . . . and Maddox himself.

He understood this, and he relaxed in his chair.

"You cannot be serious?" Heath's voice carried down the table. The young man had risen to his feet and looked to his mother. "Damek? Prince Damek? You know his reputation."

Maddox had never seen Heath show anything close to this kind of spirit.

"*Sit* down," Lady Helena ordered, "and conduct yourself as is proper at this table. We have great cause for celebration, and you will drink to your sister's impending marriage."

With his eyes downcast, Heath sat. He took a sip from his goblet. Still, Maddox wished he could ease the young man's mind. This talk of Prince Damek would soon be over.

The rest of dinner was a quiet affair, broken only by Lord Hamish's occasional question to Carlotta about Damek's initial dowry request. Maddox didn't listen to the answers, but he realized that Carlotta had been put entirely in charge of negotiations.

As the meal ended, Maddox grew more anxious to speak with Rochelle alone so they could make a plan for speaking with Lord Hamish and Lady Helena. He was well aware of the disruption and disappointment they were about to cause, but it had to be done tonight.

"Rochelle, did you still wish me to look at your mare's hoof?" he asked. "You mentioned earlier that she was limping."

For the first time since dinner began, she looked at him. "Yes . . . yes, that would be kind."

"I apologize for not seeing to her sooner. Will you walk out with me?"

He could not read her face.

"Must you go now?" Lady Helena asked her daughter. "I wanted to discuss the wedding feast."

"I should have the captain see to Mira's foot, Mother, and I'd like to hear his thoughts on treatment. We won't be long."

Everyone knew she was fond of her horse.

"Can I come?" Lizbeth asked.

"No, you'd best stay here," Maddox answered. "It's a cool night."

Rochelle fell into step beside him as they walked through the manor, but the instant they were out the front doors and alone in the courtyard, he drew her to one side.

"We must speak to your mother and uncle tonight," he said. "We should have spoken up weeks ago, and now Carlotta will be caught in an unpleasant situation with Prince Damek as she breaks things off."

"We can't speak to anyone," she whispered, keeping her eyes downcast so he couldn't see them.

"What?"

"Don't you see?" she went on quietly, regretfully. "My family is on the verge of royalty. A great deal of work has already gone into this. I cannot destroy it for my mother. I will not."

He stepped back. "But surely you don't mean to marry Prince Damek? You and I . . . we belong to each other. We must marry." Anger began rising inside him. "And what if I go to your mother and your uncle myself and I tell them everything?"

"If you do that, one of two things will happen. Either my uncle will do anything necessary to hush it up and he'll have you quietly killed as soon as possible, or . . . he will explode in a rage, call me out as a whore, and send you back to Prince Rodêk while calling you out as a seducer of young daughters. I will be ruined, and you will never hold a position in a great house again." She sobbed once, and tears streamed down her face. "Which of those outcomes would you prefer?"

He took another step back, reeling. "Then you . . . you intend to marry Damek?"

"Forgive me. I have no choice."

Nearly two weeks passed, and the manor was abuzz with nothing but talk of the marriage negotiations. It pained Maddox when he realized that Rochelle was going out of her way to avoid any chance of being alone with him.

He began making excuses not to attend the family dinners.

A part of him believed that Rochelle might still somehow find a way to end the negotiations, and once that happened, he and she might have a chance to speak to her mother and uncle without fear of destroying the family's interests.

He couldn't stop thinking about the hungry way Rochelle used to seek him out, and they would hide in guest rooms or storage rooms or once in the tack room of the stable, and she would struggle halfway out of her dress before he got the door closed. She'd wanted him so badly. Now . . . she barely spoke to him.

It was torture.

The manor had a small contingent of private guards—with few duties, as Quillette Manor was located in one of the safest areas of Droevinka—and one of Maddox's duties was to oversee the watch rotation.

He lived in a small room on the upper floor of the manor, and he was in his room, sitting at his writing desk, attempting to concentrate on the watch rotation—and failing—when a knock sounded on his door.

He swiveled his head. Had Rochelle come to him? She'd never come to his room before, but no one ever knocked on his door. Getting to his feet, he strode over and pulled it open.

Lady Helena stood on the other side, looking frazzled and distracted.

"I do apologize for disturbing you in your room, Captain," she said, "but it couldn't be helped. It seems that via written communication, the negotiations for the betrothal have come to a standstill. We are willing to dower Rochelle quite generously, but Prince Damek is asking too much. He wants a portion of the wine income for life. Lord Hamish thought a meeting in person might help with matters, but of course he would never be coarse enough to say that."

Maddox didn't understand where this was going. Why would suggesting a personal meeting with Damek be considered coarse?

"So Lord Hamish arranged for a family visit at Kimovesk. Prince Damek welcomed the idea as charming." She paused. "I told my sister, and Prince Rodêk instantly assigned a contingent of Väränj soldiers to accompany us. They arrive tomorrow afternoon. You'll be in command of them. I regret giving you such short notice, but we leave in two days."

The Väränj guarded the family of whoever was serving as grand prince during any given nine-year period. For Lady Helena, arriving with a contingent of Väränj soldiers in red tabards would only give more credence to her claim of royal connections.

Yet Maddox still didn't quite understand the situation.

"My lady . . . the family? You don't mean Lizbeth and Rochelle?"

"Of course Rochelle. Once Prince Damek sees her, he will . . ." She trailed off and gave him a hard look, as if he was being impertinent. "You will act as bodyguard to the children. We leave tomorrow."

She swept away down the upper passage.

Maddox fully grasped the scheme now.

Prince Damek was asking for more than they were willing to pay, and Helena and Hamish were banking on what would happen as soon as Damek saw Rochelle . . . spoke to Rochelle. He'd probably drop half his demands. Helena was using her own daughter's beauty and sweet nature as a bargaining chip . . . but she was doing so on the pretense of a seemingly innocent family visit to meet an impending new member.

Gripping the door latch, Maddox felt so ill he considered packing up and riding away. He couldn't bring himself to take part in this. A moment later, he changed his mind. This wasn't going to be some garden party in the company of a handsome prince. The most common term he'd ever heard applied to Damek was "twisted," and his soldiers had the worst reputation for violence in Droevinka.

Maddox couldn't let Rochelle be forced to walk into this without proper protection, not to mention Lizbeth.

No, he had to go.

Then he thought . . . perhaps this was for the best after all. Once Rochelle saw the reality of the future her mother and uncle were creating for her, she might be shocked enough to forgo her duty to the family and refuse.

That thought gave him comfort as he began to pack.

After a two-day journey, the entire family arrived at the gate of Kimovesk in the late afternoon with Maddox and ten Väränj guards riding at the front and another ten guards bringing up the rear. The family and their personal servants rode in the middle.

The party was expected and accorded with an instant entrance through the gatehouse tunnel.

Prince Damek was not in the courtyard to meet them.

Instead, they were greeted by a strange, small man with a birthmark—who introduced himself as Master Lionel—and a paunchy captain with an unkempt mustache named Kochè.

The castle was ugly and forbidding, and there was no one in the courtyard but guards in black tabards. Maddox knew his instincts had been right. Even before meeting Damek, who should be out here, Rochelle could see the trappings of the dim future before her.

Master Lionel informed them that Prince Damek was not yet ready to receive guests, but that they would all be shown to their rooms. They were taken through the castle to the third floor of the east tower. The family was assigned rooms nearest to the stairwell, and Maddox was assigned a small room a good distance down the passage, all the way at the end. He didn't mind; he wouldn't be using it much.

He noticed the air throughout the entire castle smelled dank.

While the family rested from their journey, he went down to make sure the horses and Väränj guards were properly housed and fed, and by the time he got back, he knocked on Heath's door to check in and learned that the family was dressing for dinner.

Not long after that, a gong sounded, and then everyone began emerging from their rooms. Lady Helena and Lord Hamish were both dressed in their finest, complete with jeweled rings on their hands. Heath wore a simple blue tunic over the top of a black wool shirt, and he looked as if he'd rather be anywhere but here. Lizbeth had put some effort into her appearance, dressed in a light green satin gown with her hair in a neat braid.

Carlotta wore black with her hair in its usual severe bun. She also wore a tight, determined expression as if she were about to head into battle.

And then . . . Rochelle stepped out from her room.

She, too, wore black, but it was a velvet gown with a scooped neckline that exposed the white skin of her throat and collarbones to the tops of her breasts. The dress fit snuggly around her small rib cage and waist, and then draped to the floor at her hips. He'd never seen it before, so he assumed it must be new.

Her hair had been brushed until it shone and then left to hang loose, but her long bangs had been pinned back at her forehead with a small, jeweled clip.

"Perfect," Lady Helena said approvingly. "You are a vision, my dear."

She was.

Master Lionel appeared from nowhere and escorted them down the stairs, and then down a long passage along the back of the castle that emptied into the great hall. A single table had been prepared at the far end. A fire burned in the hearth.

With the exception of a few downcast-looking servants and Captain Kochè, the hall contained only one occupant. He stood by the fire with his back to the archway, but he turned as the family entered.

Prince Damek.

Revulsion flooded Maddox at the sight of him. Damek was slender and sleek with long, dark hair. His skin was nearly white, and his narrow features could certainly be called handsome. But his face had a feral merciless quality, as if he was incapable of understanding the suffering of others.

He smiled, revealing straight white teeth. "Lord Hamish," he said, sounding like an actor in a play. "What a pleasure to see you again."

Maddox assumed they had met somewhere before.

"My prince," Hamish answered, returning the smile.

Lady Helena was to his right, and Carlotta was to his left. Damek greeted Lady Helena, who introduced Carlotta as her daughter, and as Damek's eyes shifted to Carlotta, a look of undisguised horror passed through them.

He must think she was the intended bride.

Damek's expression was so obvious that Helena rushed to correct the misinterpretation. "Oh, my prince, this is my eldest daughter, Carlotta, to whom you have been writing." She stepped aside. "May I present Rochelle?"

As Rochelle moved into Damek's view, an entirely different expression altered his face. He looked stunned.

"My lord," Rochelle said gently, keeping her eyes on the floor.

Prince Damek had the manners of a peasant. First he had openly insulted Carlotta by not bothering to hide his revulsion, and now he stared at Rochelle like a hungry wolf.

Maddox hated him already, but again, prince of Pählen or not, at least Rochelle could see how hopelessly unsuitable he was.

Heath and Lizbeth were quickly introduced, but Damek barely glanced at them. He went to Rochelle, took her hand, and kissed it. "My lady."

Maddox wanted to run him through.

Carlotta watched Rochelle with a stony expression, but to Maddox's surprise, he also caught a glint of hate. This took him aback. It had never occurred to him that anyone could hate Rochelle.

"Am I late?" a silky voice said from behind.

Maddox turned to see a slim woman with long silver-blond hair, wearing a long purple robe, glide in through the east archway.

"You're always late," Damek responded, but his tone was light, and he gestured to the woman. "My counselor, the Lady Saorise."

As she approached, Damek introduced her to everyone, and her gaze lingered on Rochelle. "Oh yes . . . yes."

Something about her gave Maddox the shivers.

"Please," Damek said, motioning toward the table, "come and sit and we'll have wine before dinner." He called to a servant, "Johanna, bring the pitcher."

Looking over, Maddox saw a striking young woman with black hair and slanted eyes. In her own way, she was almost as lovely as Rochelle—which was rare. Johanna carried a large pitcher toward the table, but she stole a few glances at Rochelle, and in her eyes . . . Maddox saw alarm.

He noticed Lizbeth watching Johanna, too. Lizbeth didn't miss much.

The family sat where Damek directed them, with Carlotta as far down the table as possible.

Maddox stood against the wall, invisible. On this occasion, he was only a bodyguard.

Somehow he managed to keep himself expressionless and standing at attention through dinner and into the late evening. At some point, Carlotta and Prince Damek went up to his private chambers for further bargaining.

Maddox believed their efforts would be a waste of time, and he believed that by morning, Rochelle would have privately informed her mother she could not possibly wed Damek and become mistress of this dank castle.

But the following day, the family gathered in the great hall in the late morning, and they ate breakfast, and they waited out the day. Damek never appeared. No one even mentioned leaving. Heath wandered the castle for lack of anything better to do, but for the most part, everyone else seemed in limbo.

And Maddox realized they were not leaving.

Rochelle was going to be sacrificed to Damek.

In the late afternoon, the family went upstairs to change for dinner, and a repeat performance took place once they all went down to the great hall in the early evening.

Before any food appeared, Damek asked his guests to be seated.

Goblets and plates had been laid out on the table, and Johanna went from guest to guest, pouring dark red wine. Maddox paid no attention to the Lady Helena's attempt at polite conversation, but he knew this was going to be another long night.

Carlotta had not said much and appeared to be at odds. Once again, she was seated as far down the table as possible. She'd been the one handling negotiations with Damek, and perhaps she had expected a bit more respect and attention than she was receiving. With her mouth more downturned than usual, she took a sip from her goblet.

"Is the wine to your taste?" Prince Damek asked Rochelle.

She murmured a polite reply, but then Maddox noticed Carlotta was in some distress, attempting to swallow and apparently failing. She attempted to swallow again, and her eyes began to widen as she struggled to breathe.

"Are you well, my dear?" Lady Helena asked, with a tone of mild embarrassment.

Carlotta turned red and struggled halfway to her feet with one hand gripping her throat and the other gripping the table. Her eyes bulged, and Maddox took a few steps forward, but he was uncertain what to do.

Other people jumped up and moved to help. Lord Hamish reached her first. A barrage of questions and cries filled the air, and Maddox heard Rochelle cry her sister's name. He felt helpless, but he was a soldier, not a healer.

Carlotta grunted and choked a few more times. Her features contorted and she fell backward into Lord Hamish's arms.

Prince Damek strode toward them, his face exposing both his confusion and his alarm.

Carlotta made one final struggle to breathe, and then her body went stiff.

"She's dead," Lord Hamish said, raising his gaze to Damek and then lowering it to Carlotta's wine goblet.

"Did you have her poisoned?" Heath demanded. "Over the dowry negotiations?"

Damek's mouth fell open, and Lady Helena gasped. "Heath!"

"I want to go home," Lizbeth said. "We can't stay here."

"Yes, this is over," Heath said. "We are leaving."

Again, the passive young man showed surprising spirit, and hope rose inside Maddox that Heath might prevail.

Neither Hamish, Helena, nor Rochelle spoke. They

were all still looking down at Carlotta's body and bulging eyes.

"Please," Damek said, holding both hands up. "Let me find out what has happened here."

By the following morning, Maddox's hopes were again dashed. No one had packed a thing, and it was clear the family was still not leaving. Damek had Carlotta's body moved down to a cold cellar, and he promised Lady Helena he would find out who was responsible for Carlotta's death and see the culprit punished.

This appeared to soothe both Lord Hamish and Lady Helena.

Several days passed slowly. Damek either slept or remained in his private chambers most of the day, coming out only at twilight. To Maddox's disgust, dowry negotiations resumed, with Damek and Lord Hamish meeting after dinner.

No amusements or entertainments were planned. Rochelle took this serenely, as was her way, but Maddox could see that both Heath and Lizbeth were miserable. Once, Maddox attempted to speak to Rochelle, to see if she was considering breaking with family honor now that she could see what her mother and Hamish intended for her. But his words only caused a tear to run down her face, and she turned away. After that, she began making certain they were never alone.

He was helpless.

On the fifth night after Carlotta's death, Maddox escorted the three siblings into the great hall to see a few new soldiers wearing tan tabards ... and then he saw three new guests, a man and two young women.

The man bore an uncanny resemblance to Damek,

except that his hair was shorter and not quite as dark. His eyes were different, too. As opposed to cruel, they struck Maddox as ... cautious. Both women were pleasing to look at, especially the one with dark blond hair. She certainly didn't have Rochelle's ethereal beauty, but she was indeed unusually pretty.

Lady Helena introduced the man as Damek's brother, Prince Anton. Then Anton introduced Miss Céline and Miss Amelie as his personal seers. Maddox had no idea what that meant, but it seemed they had come to help Damek investigate the matter of Carlotta's death.

Almost immediately following this, Miss Céline admitted that she had examined the body and was uncertain if this was a case of poisoning or not.

Maddox seethed inside as Lady Helena jumped at this news.

After that, he tried to stand by the wall and ignore anything being said. He kept his eyes on Rochelle.

While everyone remained standing, Johanna served wine, and at some point, Lady Saorise arrived.

Some silliness followed as Miss Amelie pretended to "read" Johanna's past—but this was done at Lizbeth's insistence. And shortly after that, Master Lionel entered the hall, and Damek asked everyone to take their seats.

Maddox followed them as they all drifted across to the table, and he took another position against the wall.

Miss Céline attempted polite conversation, and Lord Hamish aimed a few insulting comments at Heath—at which Lizbeth defended her brother. Rochelle sat near Damek, and the prince leaned over to whisper in her ear. She smiled.

Maddox's whole body stiffened.

Lord Hamish appeared to have set his sights on the

pretty Céline. "Will you read my future later?" he asked her.

"It would be my pleasure," she answered.

With a lecherous smile, he took a long swallow of his wine and seemed on the verge of saying something else, but no words came out. He attempted to clear his throat and draw a breath. His expression grew alarmed.

"My lord?" Céline asked.

In panic, Hamish shoved back his chair and stood, grabbing his throat and fighting to breathe.

"Brother!" Lady Helena called, rushing toward him.

Rochelle was on her feet as well.

Again, Maddox had no idea what to do, but then a miracle happened. Distraught, Rochelle turned to him and cried, "Maddox! It's happening again. Please make it stop!"

She was afraid and needed help, and her first instinct was to call for him. He bolted, running to Lord Hamish and catching him as he fell backward.

Céline was suddenly kneeling beside them and pulling at Lord Hamish's collar to loosen it and begging him to try to relax.

Hamish's eyes bulged in agony. He fought to breathe and failed. Maddox desperately wanted to help—to show Rochelle that he could help—but there was nothing to be done. Hamish's body began to convulse.

A few moments later, he died with his eyes still open.

In despair that he had failed Rochelle somehow, Maddox looked up at Rochelle, and she stared back at him.

He was well aware that this exchange was not lost on Damek.

By the following afternoon, Maddox's opinion of Céline had somewhat altered. She had angered him in the late morning by using Lizbeth to lure him out to the stable so she could "read him." But no harm had come from that, and he'd not seen young Lizbeth so happy since their arrival in Kimovesk.

Charlatan or not, tool of the Pähden princes or not, Céline had a kindness about her that couldn't be denied—and Maddox couldn't help liking anyone who was kind to Lizbeth.

At first it struck him as unsettling that no one except Lady Helena made an attempt to mourn Lord Hamish. But after a while, even that began to make sense. Hamish had never done anything but disparage Heath and Lizbeth, and he'd only valued Rochelle for what she could gain him via her marriage. Why should his nieces and nephew mourn him?

Then, in the early afternoon, in the great hall, Lady Saorise excused herself, and once she'd left something . . . happened.

It started simply enough.

Miss Céline asked her sister to organize a card game. Maddox expected Prince Anton to make his excuses and leave, but he didn't.

He stayed.

Miss Amelie explained the rules of a silly-sounding game, and Lizbeth's face lit up. Soon, Lizbeth, Rochelle, Heath, Amelie, Céline, and Prince Anton had gathered at one end of the table, and they were passing cards to each other at a rapid pace, apparently attempting to make pairs and lay them down as quickly as possible. Rochelle emptied her hand and called, "I'm out!"

Amelie looked up. "Winner! Who has the queen?"

Anton showed his hand, and there was the queen of spades.

"Loser!" Amelie called.

Maddox could not help his shock when Anton smiled slightly. "Deal the cards again."

After several more hands, it appeared Anton had a penchant for ending up with the queen, and by that point, most of the players were laughing as they passed cards as fast as they could. Anton didn't laugh, but Maddox thought it possible that he didn't know how to laugh.

Yet after that first hand, every time he was caught with the queen, Lizbeth would clap with glee and shout, "Loser!" at him.

He'd smile, just slightly, and he let her tease him mercilessly . . . as a proper future brother would.

On the sixth hand, Rochelle laughed as she went out again, and her eyes came up to meet Maddox's. She held his gaze. Unbidden and unwanted, his mind flashed to an image of her writhing beneath him with her arms stretched up over her head as she made small, animal sounds in his ear.

Biting the inside of his mouth, he pushed the image away.

When the card game finally lost its appeal, Céline put on a show, telling stories. She was quite good at this, and Maddox found himself so caught up that he had an hour's reprieve from the pain inside him.

After that, Heath ran to get his lute, and once again, Anton astonished Maddox. The prince clapped after each song and politely praised Heath for his skills.

Until that point, Maddox had been taking at least some enjoyment in seeing Rochelle and Heath and Lizbeth so happy as they reveled in these common amusements. But then . . . it hit him that what he watched was an illusion, a fleeting moment in time that would vanish as soon as Anton took his people and left.

Then once Rochelle was married, Lizbeth and Heath would leave, and Rochelle would be alone, sitting in this hall with no laughter and no stories and no music.

He couldn't stand it.

He had to stop it.

A maid came into the great hall and announced that Lady Helena was awake.

"I should go to Mother," Rochelle said. "Everyone else, please stay."

Maddox saw his chance. As she went to leave, he strode after her and no one even looked up. Rochelle glanced back, but there was nothing she could say, and they walked in silence down the back passage.

Inside the stairwell, he caught her gently and pulled her up against himself. She let him, and he almost couldn't believe the physical relief of having her in his arms.

"You cannot stay here," he whispered. "You cannot do this. You cannot tie your life to that prince."

Again, she told him that she had no choice.

In part this angered him, but he also knew that he'd provided her with no real choice before, and so now he did. Shedding every last ounce of pride, he begged her to run away with him to Belaski. He had skills and he could make a life for them there.

If she would only agree, he could still save her.

"And bring shame to my family?" Rochelle asked him. "To my mother? I can't! Please, please don't ask me to do this! You only torture us both. If you loved me, you would let me do my duty."

She pushed him away and ran up the stairs.

He leaned against the wall in despair. Then he straightened. Rochelle was still young, almost like a child at times. She might cite family honor and duty, but she had no idea what a future in this place would hold ... what her life would hold.

It was up to him to stop this.

Turning, he took the stairs three at a time, and when he got to the top, Rochelle was just down the passage. He caught up to her before she'd reached her mother's room, and he grasped her arm.

"Maddox?" she said in alarm.

He'd never used his strength against her before.

But he propelled her into the room she shared with Lizbeth and he closed the door, blocking it with his body.

"Pack what you need," he ordered. "We're leaving."

"I am not."

"Yes, you are," he said slowly. "And if you don't leave with me now, I will go straight to the inner west tower, wake up that unnatural prince, and tell him everything you and I have been to each other. I'll tell him everything we've done together and in which rooms of your family's manor we did them. I'll describe every inch of your body, and I'll tell him all the things you beg me to say when I'm inside you."

"You wouldn't."

"I would. I don't care what happens to me anymore."

He meant it. He was taking her out of here.

She stared at him, and for the first time, there was a cast of anger in her eyes.

"Get a cloak and pack up or I'll take you as you are," he said.

The anger on her face turned quickly to anxiety, but she did what he said, and he took her back downstairs, up the passage to the kitchen, and then outside. Once they were in the courtyard, it was a short walk to the stables. The few Kimovesk guards they passed barely glanced at them. They were a familiar sight here now.

He saddled both their horses.

"Mount up."

"We'll never get out the gate," she said. "Have you thought of that?" All the normal sweetness in her voice was gone, and she sounded like a stranger.

"You'll get us out," he answered, "or I'll make good on my threat."

Her eyes narrowed, and she swung up onto her white mare. Maddox mounted his roan, and they rode to the front gate. It was late afternoon, but there was plenty of daylight left.

Rochelle took the lead and rode through the gate-house. She smiled down at the Kimovesk guard on duty there.

"Please have the portcullis opened," she said, sounding like her charming self again. "I'd like to go for a short ride."

The guard on the ground shifted weight between his feet. "I'm . . . I'm sorry, my lady, but Prince Damek said nothing to me about anyone going out for a ride."

She laughed, and the sound was like music. "I hardly think the prince needs to inform you if his future bride wishes to go for a short ride. I have my bodyguard with me." Her tone altered slightly, becoming more serious. "And I will be mistress of this castle soon."

Maddox was both surprised and unsettled by how well she handled this.

The guard still appeared torn, but he called up, "Open the portcullis!"

The sound of grinding followed and the gate rose.

Rochelle and Maddox cantered out and down the road, and he began considering what to do next. He hadn't had much time to plan inside.

Rochelle rode around in front of him and pulled up her mare. They were alone on the open road. "It doesn't matter where you take me," she said. "*He'll* find you, and he'll get me back."

"I think you overestimate the effort Prince Damek might put into anything."

"Damek?" she returned scornfully. "He couldn't find his own horse if it got lost. I'm talking about Heath."

"Heath?"

Again, as Maddox looked at Rochelle, she was like a stranger . . . someone he didn't even know.

"Well?" she asked. "What now?"

Grabbing her reins, he decided to ride into Kimovesk Village. He needed information and directions.

CHAPTER ELEVEN

The image vanished and the mists closed in, pulling Amelie only a short distance forward. She opened her eyes to see Maddox staring at her. He gagged once and fell forward out of his chair, catching himself with his hands and then gagging again.

Amelie couldn't help feeling pity. One of the drawbacks to seeing the past through someone else's view was that the person had to relive all of it.

"Well?" Damek demanded, standing in the doorway of the small room. Heath and Rochelle were right behind him. Heath was still angry. Rochelle appeared nervous.

Amelie had to think fast. The emotions and physical sensations of all that she'd just seen and felt still filled her mind. But she couldn't reveal Rochelle and Maddox's past. Prince Anton's task here was to ensure that the marriage took place, and she could do nothing to endanger that without speaking to him first.

And yet she couldn't just leave Maddox to Damek's mercy, either. What could she say?

Moving from her chair, she pretended to support Maddox where he'd fallen. "Whatever I say," she whispered so softly she hoped he could hear her, "just go along."

Looking up to Damek, she said clearly, "He abducted her. He forced her to talk her way past the guards, and she did so out of fear."

Rochelle closed her eyes in relief.

"But he meant no harm," Amelie rushed on. "I saw the events through his eyes, and he truly believed he was rescuing her from unhappiness." She got up and stood in front of Maddox. "He did not take her for himself. He is their family's guardian, and he thought he was doing the right thing. Heath, surely, you can understand that?"

Heath did understand. She could see he did.

"That is not his place to decide!" Damek spat, and Amelie felt the danger building again.

From somewhere behind them, Céline spoke. "My lord Damek. I believe Captain Maddox is in service to Lady Helena, and this is a family matter. I suggest we bring the captain back to Kimovesk, lock him up, and then let Lady Helena decide his fate."

Amelie couldn't see Céline, but Damek's expression wavered. There was much in what Céline had said. First, that Maddox indeed belonged to Lady Helena. Second, Rochelle was Helena's daughter, but she was not yet Damek's wife. An execution right here could have repercussions.

Turning his head, Damek looked to Heath, who hesitated and then nodded.

"All right," Damek said, "we take him back. The lady has been recovered, and that is what matters to me."

Amelie didn't believe that for a moment. Damek wanted blood, but at least he'd sounded like a prince.

Thankfully, Maddox had the good sense to keep silent, and he spilled no tales. No matter what he'd said to Rochelle back at the castle, perhaps he did still care what happened to him and thought his chances were better with Lady Helena.

"Do we find shelter for the night or ride out now?" Anton asked.

"We ride out now," Damek answered.

Amelie wanted to groan at the thought of hours more in the saddle, but she turned to see if Maddox needed help up.

As she leaned down, he grasped her wrist briefly.

"Watch Rochelle," he said quietly. "She is not what she seems."

The horses were nearly spent, so Damek set a slower pace on the ride home, and Céline opted for riding sidesaddle.

Maddox had his hands tied and was surrounded by the Väränj guards.

It was nearly dawn before they arrived in Kimovesk. Rochelle rode beside Damek all the way, and the two spoke softly for part of the journey. By the time it was over, he was treating her like a tragic maiden who had suffered a terrible ordeal, which she had.

By that point, Céline was so weary she barely noticed Anton lifting her off her horse. She remembered him taking her and Amelie up to their room. She'd been starving on the way back, but now she was too tired to eat. She let Helga unlace her gown, and then she fell onto the bed. She remembered Amelie falling beside her.

Then the world went dark.

She had no idea how much time passed, but a delicious scent woke her sometime later in the day, and she opened her eyes.

"There you are," Helga said.

"What time is it?" Céline asked, still groggy.

"Late afternoon, but you need to wake up and eat. You've had nothing since yesterday."

Amelie opened her eyes. "What smells so good?"

Helga set a tray on the dressing table, and she brought over two plates piled with scrambled eggs, bacon, and steaming rolls. Just the sight made Céline's mouth water, but when she tried to sit up . . . she groaned.

"Oh, I'm so sore I can barely move."

Amelie was in a similar state as she tried to sit up as well. "My legs hurt the worst."

Somehow they managed to get some pillows arranged against the headboard and for the first time in Céline's memory, they ate breakfast in bed like two spoiled ladies. Céline didn't care how it looked. She wolfed down the scrambled eggs first, and then Helga brought the sisters steaming mugs of spiced tea with generous amounts of milk.

Amelie ate just as fast, but toward the end of finishing her plate, she began to talk. They'd had no chance to speak last night, and after hearing only a few sentences, Céline stopped eating to listen. Helga stood by the bed and listened as well as Amelie spilled out the story of Maddox and Rochelle, from stolen moments in back rooms, all the way to the attempted abduction last night.

"She was playing with him," Helga said. "That girl never had a mind to marry him."

Céline concurred, but something else—concerning herself—had her on the edge of real anxiety.

"Amelie, I read Captain Maddox yesterday morning. I saw his almost immediate future . . . which was his past by last night. The only image I saw was the brief scene at the base of the stairwell where he asked her to run away with him. That's all I was shown. Why didn't I see him forcing her to leave with him? Had I seen, we could have stopped it."

Amelie stopped eating as well.

"Maybe you weren't meant to stop it," Helga put in. "Maybe something had to happen last night for you to find the real killer."

Céline tried to think of anything that might have happened last night to reveal the identity of the murderer, but her mind went straight to Anton's mouth pressing gently on her own.

"Well . . . ," Amelie began. "Right before Maddox was dragged out of the stable, I leaned down to help him up and he told me to watch Rochelle. He said she's not what she seems."

"From what you told us about her tryst with Maddox," Céline responded, "that would certainly appear to be the case, but she doesn't seem averse to marrying Damek, so what would be her motive?"

Amelie's face was still thoughtful. "You know who else was different last night? Heath. When I read Maddox, Rochelle seemed sure he would be the one who'd come after her."

"Yes, I noticed the difference in him, too. But I think he was driven by getting his sister back. His family only benefits from a connection to Damek, so I don't see his motive, either. I need to find a tactful way to suggest us reading the both of them."

"While you're thinking about that, maybe you ought to speak to that fool of a captain?" Helga suggested. "Find out what he meant about Rochelle."

The thought of getting out of this bed and walking

downstairs was hardly appealing, but the sisters couldn't stay here all day.

"Have you heard where they took him?" Amelie asked Helga.

That was a good question. Helga must have gone down to the kitchen for the food.

"Nope," Helga grunted. "Either none of the servants know or they aren't talking."

Céline swung her legs over the side of the bed and then winced. "Well, we must find out. Someone in the family will know."

Helga walked to the wardrobe. "I had your lavender dress laundered, and Amelie's light blue one. I've also got wash water, and you'll both need clean shifts."

"Oh, thank you," Céline said, and she was grateful. The lavender wool was her favorite dress. It was comfortable and warm, and it fit her perfectly.

Sore as she was, Céline did feel better after eating. She hoped Rurik had managed to get Anton some food by now.

Amelie crawled out after her to wash up. As soon as the sisters were both dressed, they headed out the door and down the stairs into the back passage. As they walked, Céline couldn't help being bothered by the fact that they were no closer to even a hint of learning whoever had killed Carlotta and Lord Hamish. They should have learned *something* by now.

Although she still had no motive for Rochelle or Heath ... or Lady Helena for that matter ... she was going to have to find some way to let all three of them submit to a reading. How could that be done without insulting them? And even if she cared about insulting them, what power could she use to make them agree? Prince Damek couldn't order them.

When Céline passed through the archway into the great hall, with the exception of a few Väränj guards, the only people present were Helena, Saorise, and Rochelle. All three women sat at the table, speaking softly.

Céline's gazed paused on Saorise. There was someone else she needed to read—and as of yet had had no opportunity.

"Amelie," she whispered. "Do what you can to draw off Helena and Rochelle."

The sisters crossed the hall. Lady Helena looked drawn and weary, but she smiled at their approach. "I hope you got some sleep. Rochelle tells me you were a great comfort to her last night."

I'll bet she did, Céline thought, especially considering that Amelie had convinced Damek of Rochelle's abduction.

"Are you well this morning?" Céline asked Rochelle.

"As can be expected," Rochelle answered with her eyes downcast. "I only woke up a short while ago myself. Lizbeth is still sleeping, and I didn't knock on Heath's door."

Amelie crossed her arms and shivered. "And where . . . where is Captain Maddox being held?"

Lady Helena glanced away uncomfortably. "I understand he was locked in a cell in the old prison below the castle. He is being guarded."

That didn't bode well. Céline had hoped he might be locked in his room. A prison cell branded him as the worst of criminals. But at least he was alive.

Amelie looked over to the burning hearth. "I fear I'm

still feeling the cold. Lady Helena, would you and Rochelle care to accompany me to the fire?"

"Of course."

Both women stood up, and all three of them made
their way across the hall to the hearth.

Lady Saorise tilted her head up at Céline. "That was
deftly done."

Céline sat down in the chair Lady Helena had occupied. "Prince Damek has authorized me or my sister to
do a reading of everyone in his service. I'd like to handle
it as quietly as possible."

Saorise smiled, and the sight brought an uncomfortable feeling to the back of Céline's neck.

"I assure you that I am not exactly in Damek's service," Saorise answered, "but I've no objection to you
reading me."

She must have once been quite beautiful, and Céline
couldn't help wondering how this woman and Damek
had met, how Saorise had become his counselor when
he allowed so few people to normally live here in the
castle.

Still smiling, Saorise asked, "And how do we begin,
my dear? I admit I've been wondering about you and
your sister since the day you arrived. I assume you're
both Mist-Torn, and Anton picked you up from a gypsy
caravan somewhere."

Céline stiffened, but she refused to take the bait.
"You'll have to ask Prince Anton about that yourself.
May I touch your hand?"

"By all means."

Céline glanced over at Amelie, who had the other two
women engaged by the hearth, and for an instant, she
felt a wave of trepidation. From what Amelie had told

her, Saorise was a cold-blooded killer who had created an elixir that would turn men into beasts. Céline had expected anyone in Damek's inner circle to be dangerous, but she was on uncertain ground here and had no idea what she was about to see.

Still, she touched Saorise's hand. Then she closed her eyes and reached out for the spark of a spirit. She focused all her energy on receiving answers as to who was carrying out the murders in this castle.

The first jolt hit her immediately, followed by the second, and she was swept forward on the mists. The journey was longer than she had expected, and when the mists cleared, she found herself in a large windowless room with walls of stone. Small braziers lined three of the walls, providing a good deal of light. Spears and crossbows lined the fourth wall.

There was a long table to her right with various objects scattered across its surface: faded books, brass urns, unlit candles, quills, ink, bottles, small daggers, and a mortar and pestle. Light more intense than the braziers drew her eye and she turned to see a burning hearth—large enough to stand in—at the other end of the vast room. An iron hook had been set over the flames, and a small metal cauldron with symbols etched around the outside hung from the hook.

Saorise stood before the cauldron with her eyes closed. Her mouth was moving, but Céline could not hear the words.

Inside the image, she moved across the room to study Saorise, who appeared almost in a kind of trance. Her hair was uncombed, as if she'd not been attending to herself recently, and her face was pinched with exhaustion.

"Munimentum," she whispered. *"Tutamen* . . . Damek."

Without opening her eyes, she reached out and dropped several strands of long dark hair into the cauldron.

The image vanished, and the mists closed in, rushing Céline forward again.

When they cleared, she found herself in an even larger room, an enormous hall, only this one was crowded with well-dressed people and guards. Looking to the guards, she saw tabards of red ... and light blue ... and dark blue ... and green ... and orange. She lost count of the various colors of the great houses of Droevinka.

"Prince Damek of the house of Pählen," someone boomed.

Inside the image, Céline turned to see Damek, wearing a sleeveless black tunic, dark pants, and polished boots. He looked both handsome and confident. Standing beside him, Rochelle was a vision in pale pink silk with small pearls in her ears. Her red-gold hair floated around her like a cloud. From all around the hall, men turned to stare. She was like a sweet confection.

Lady Saorise stood on Damek's other side, and she, too, was lovely, in her shining robe, with her silver-blond hair arranged on top of her head.

A striking man in his late forties with a close-trimmed beard strode over to greet them. "Prince Damek, welcome to Kéonsk." He bowed to Rochelle. "And to your lovely wife."

"Thank you, Lord Malbek," Damek answered smoothly. "I see we already have quite a gathering."

"Yes, but the vote won't take place until tomorrow. Tonight we should enjoy ourselves."

"Has my brother arrived?"

"Not yet."

Inside the vision, Céline gasped. She was in Kéonsk ...

two years in the future at the gathering of the great houses for the vote of the next grand prince. Although of course she'd never met him, everyone knew that Lord Malbek was chancellor to Prince Rodêk.

With another low bow, Malbek turned to Saorise and took her hand. "My lady," he said, "what would Prince Damek be without your counsel?"

"Oh, I'm certain he would do fine on his own." But her tone suggested that she believed nothing of the sort.

Lord Malbek kissed her hand.

The image vanished, and the mists closed in, pulling Céline backward in time. When they cleared, she opened her eyes to find Saorise watching her intently.

"What did you see?"

Céline struggled to make sense of what she'd just seen. First, she looked over to the hearth. Amelie still had Rochelle and Helena engaged in conversation, and at some point Heath had entered the hall, and he now stood with them. Lizbeth had not come down yet.

Céline was so puzzled by what she'd seen in Saorise's future that she decided to share some of the truth and hope for light to be shed. After all, the future had not yet happened and it could be changed. "I saw you, Rochelle, and Prince Damek two years in the future . . . in Kéonsk, at the vote for the next grand prince."

Saorise went still in her chair. Then she asked, "Had the vote taken place?"

"No, it was scheduled for the next day, but . . . Lord Malbek kissed your hand."

She thought on the first part of her vision, and she decided that speaking up and hoping for clarity was a wiser course than silence. "But before that, you were casting a spell. You used the words *Munimentum* and *Tutamen*, and then you spoke Damek's name and put several strands of long, dark hair in a cauldron."

"Ahhhh." Saorise nodded. "I was casting a protection spell on Damek, to ensure his safety." But she seemed uninterested in this and pressed for more information about the second part of the vision. "But you saw me, Rochelle, and Damek all in Kéonsk, the day before the vote, and Lord Malbek kissed my hand?"

"Yes."

"Then you have your answer as to my involvement in the deaths of Carlotta and Lord Hamish." She lowered her voice. "You see, my dear, like you, I come from less ... auspicious beginnings myself and yet now I am counselor to Prince Damek of the house of Pählen, who controls a portion of the western provinces. He will marry a beautiful first cousin of Prince Rodêk, and in two years' time, Lord Malbek will be kissing my hand in recognition of my influence over Damek, who I believe will be the next grand prince."

Without meaning to, Céline drew back in her chair.

Saorise smiled again, and the sight was as eerie as before. "I would do nothing to stop this marriage from taking place. Were it in my power, I'd conduct the ceremony myself."

Feeling as if she'd just been trumped, Céline couldn't argue with that logic. It appeared highly unlikely that Saorise would do anything to sabotage Damek's marriage to Rochelle.

And yet something about the smug look on Saorise's face drove Céline to say, "The future is not set, and on several occasions I have managed to alter it. You should not be so certain of yourself ... or Prince Damek just yet."

Saorise's smile vanished.

Céline stood up.

She had a feeling Saorise was about to say something further when the sounds of shouting echoed from the east passage, and she heard the sound of pounding boots.

"Inform Prince Damek!" The voice belonged to Anton. "Now!"

Two Kimovesk guards ran into the hall and kept running without pause out through the west archway. Two breaths later, Anton and Rurik ran into the great hall.

"What has happened?" Lady Helena asked, her hand to her breastbone.

"We stepped out from the bottom of the tower to find those men coming up from the prisons. They told us Captain Maddox has killed his guard and escaped his cell," Anton answered.

Rochelle drew in a loud breath. The Väränj and Sèone guards in the hall walked over to hear better.

"It's all right," Anton went on, speaking to Rochelle. "You are well protected here, and I've ordered a search. Prince Damek should be down in a moment, and he knows the castle better than I do. He'll be able to hone where we look."

"But what of Lizbeth?" Heath asked in alarm. "Is she still asleep in her room?"

"Oh," Helena answered, "she is! Heath, you must go and get her."

"No," Anton ordered. "I'll go back up and get her myself."

Before he'd taken a step, a scream carried from down the hall and everyone whirled toward the sound.

Lizbeth came running in from the east archway with her hands and the hem of her dress covered in blood.

"He's dead!" she cried, shaking her hands and sobbing.

Céline ran to the girl. "Lizbeth!"

"He's dead!" Lizbeth cried again. "I leaned over to touch him, to make sure, but he's dead." Céline caught her and pulled her close as several other people reached them

"Who is dead?" Anton demanded, sounding like a Pählen prince.

Lizbeth sobbed again. "Captain Maddox!"

Anton stood over a dead body on the third floor of the east tower.

Amelie was there with him, as was Damek, Heath, Rurik, and Captain Kochè. Céline and the other women had remained downstairs to comfort Lizbeth.

Maddox lay exactly where he'd been found, on the floor positioned between Heath's guest room and the one shared by Rochelle and Lizbeth. Maddox had been stabbed only once, through the hollow at the base of his throat. A pool of blood surrounded his shoulders and head.

"This doesn't make sense," Rurik said, kneeling on the floor beside the body. "Why would Maddox kill his own guard, escape from the prison . . . and then come up here to the family's rooms?"

"To assault my sister again, of course," Heath answered.

Anton glanced at Damek and shook his head. "I don't think so. Maddox was desperate last night, but he's not mad. He wouldn't attempt to abduct Rochelle again."

Damek said nothing.

Amelie crouched beside Rurik, looking at the wound

first. "This was made by a thin blade." She looked down at Maddox's side. "His sword isn't drawn, so there wasn't a fight." She turned to see Heath. "You didn't come down to the great hall very long before Anton. Did you see anything when you left your room?"

"No, this passage was clear. I didn't know Lizbeth was still sleeping in her room. I woke up, dressed, came out of my room, and went downstairs."

"Then whatever happened must have been quick," Rurik said. "Or Lizbeth would have heard a scuffle." He frowned. "So Maddox arrived after Heath went down, and someone killed him?"

"What about one of the Väränj guards?" Damek suggested, speaking for the first time.

"The men on duty are in the hall, and the others are in the barracks," Anton answered. "And if a Väränj guard had killed Maddox, he'd have reported it right away. Besides . . . even in that case, there would have been a fight. I can't imagine anyone getting the jump on Maddox like this. Before going into Lady Helena's service, he was a captain in the Äntes forces."

"So, what are you saying?" Amelie asked.

"I'm saying either he knew the person who killed him, so he wasn't on guard . . . or he didn't feel he needed a reason to protect himself."

Everyone fell silent, and Anton almost wished he hadn't spoken. A third murder had been committed, and he had no more answers for this one than the first two. In addition, almost everyone's whereabouts were accounted for except Lizbeth . . . and he hardly suspected her.

Amelie looked around the passage. "Again, why would he come here? Why didn't he try to run? Climb the wall and go on foot if he had to? But he came up here, to the family's rooms. Why?"

Anton had no answer. Poor Maddox. "I think the body has told us all it can for now. Perhaps we should have it—"

"My lord Damek!" someone called from the stairwell. A Kimovesk guard in a black tabard came off the landing and hurried toward them.

"Oh, what now?" Damek breathed.

"My lord!" the guard called again. "Your father has just ridden into the courtyard with a large party. He has Lord Malbek with him!"

Anton went cold, not certain he'd heard correctly. Their father never personally interfered in any of their affairs unless he believed they were about to fail at something he considered important—and thereby disappoint him.

Looking to his brother, Anton said, "Father is here? What can that mean?"

Damek's face was tinged with gray.

CHAPTER TWELVE

Early that evening, Céline and Amelie were in their room, feeling almost as if they were hiding. The mood in the castle had altered greatly in the past few hours, taking on a kind of frenzied energy.

The door to their room opened. Helga came in quickly and closed it again. "The kitchen is a madhouse," she said. "You should see what's going on down there."

Upon the news that Prince Lieven had arrived, all talk of Maddox's death stopped. Céline had not yet seen Anton's father, as apparently upon his arrival he and Lord Malbek went straight up to Damek's private chambers. Shortly after, Damek and Lady Helena were summoned to join them.

After that, Saorise excused herself, and then Rochelle, Lizbeth, and Heath slipped away to their own rooms. No one knew what was happening, and it seemed no one was ready to speculate. Céline and Amelie opted for mutual solitude in their own room as well.

Céline had no idea what Anton might be doing, but at present, she felt it best for her and Amelie to keep out of sight until he came to them.

What was Prince Lieven doing here?

Worse, Céline was once again troubled by the limited scope of the future vision she had seen yesterday from Lizbeth. From the emotions expressed in the image she saw, she'd been fairly convinced that Lizbeth was no murderer. But if the vision had continued only a few moments more, Céline would have learned that it was Captain Maddox whom Lizbeth found dead. Why had the vision cut off?

Could it have to do with what Helga had said about Captain Maddox's desperate attempt to steal Rochelle away? If Céline had indeed known that Maddox would die, would she have tried to alter his future, and in doing so, would she have kept him from abducting Rochelle? Helga seemed to think that the night's journey was important, that something had happened that would help lead the sisters to the truth. But . . . did Maddox have to be allowed to die for this? The possibility troubled Céline.

The remnants of the afternoon passed.

Finally, in the early evening, they'd sent Helga out to see what she could learn, and she'd not been away long.

"Did you hear anything about why Anton's father is here?" Céline asked her.

"No one knows, but he brought a pack of Pählen guards and some of Prince Anton's relatives. Master Lionel's in quite a state, ordering guest rooms prepared. The cooks were told to make a big . . . and I mean big dinner. Since two formal dinners have been canceled in a row, there's a good deal of leftover roasted chicken and beef. The cooks are using some of that to make meat gravies to pour over bread and potatoes. They got more brook trout to bake than I could count."

"A dinner?"

"Yup, for Prince Lieven and all his fancy guests.

You're both expected. Master Lionel was on his way up to let you know, and he told me instead. He also told me to get you two dressed up before the gong sounds."

Céline swallowed hard. She and Amelie were expected to dine with Prince Lieven and Lord Malbek? Well . . . they certainly couldn't refuse.

"I'm going to put you back in that amber velvet," Helga said to Céline, "and Amelie in the burgundy silk. I know those gowns have been seen before, but they're the finest I brought."

For once, Amelie didn't argue or raise any kind of fuss, and she let herself be dressed. Helga pinned up her hair.

"We're leaving yours down, Céline," Helga said. "You both need to look as fetching as possible tonight. You'll need to fit in with the folks of Lieven's court."

"Don't make it worse, Helga," Amelie warned.

The gong sounded, followed a moment later by a knock on the door.

Helga walked over and jerked it open. Anton and Rurik stood on the other side. Anton had clearly taken time with his appearance; he wore a dark brown tunic with an embroidered diamond pattern done in silver thread. His boots had been freshly polished. Although his beard did not grow quickly, Céline could see that he'd just shaved.

Behind him, Rurik wore his usual tan tabard, but his boots had been polished as well.

"Are you ready?" Anton asked. He both looked and sounded tense.

"Yes," Céline answered. "Have you spoken to your father?"

"No, he's been in a private conference in Damek's chambers since he arrived."

Amelie followed Céline out into the passage, but at

the last moment Céline looked back into the room. "Thank you, Helga, for everything. I wish you could come down with us."

"Oh, those fancy folks aren't for me. Make my skin crawl. But you girls bring me back the gossip."

Someday, Céline was going to learn of Helga's past, and how she had come to serve in Castle Sèone. Tonight was not that night.

Anton led the way down the stairs and the back passage. Even before they'd reached the great hall, they could hear a chorus of voices in conversation ahead. Anton stopped walking. "Céline and Amelie, I want one of you on each side of me. Rurik, walk directly behind."

No one argued or asked what he was doing. Céline assumed he knew how to make an entrance. She stood at his right, with Amelie at his left, and they entered the great hall.

It was crowded . . . teeming with people. In addition to all the guests, there were now even more guards—the new ones wearing the dark brown tabards of Prince Lieven's men. Three more tables had been set up and countless chairs had been carried in from somewhere.

Céline scanned the room. Prince Damek, Lady Saorise, Rochelle, Lady Helena, Lizbeth, and Heath were already there. As Damek turned to greet one of the guests, Heath reached out and grasped Rochelle's arm. He pulled her closer and whispered in her ear. She shook her head once and drew away.

Continuing her scan, Céline stopped her gaze on a figure in the center of the hall. He was muscular with graying hair and a proud bearing. He wore a loose red jerkin accented by a gold thread. Three jeweled rings on each hand adorned his fingers.

Prince Lieven.

She had never seen him in person before, but she had seen him once while doing a reading of the future.

Lieven looked over as soon as they entered, and his eyes rested on Anton. Without hesitating, Anton went to him. Through the crush of people, Céline and Amelie each managed to remain at his side.

"Father," Anton said, and Céline could hear his affection.

"My son," Lieven returned, and his eyes softened.

Céline was not certain what she'd expected, as Anton never talked about his father, but it was clear the two men cared for each other.

"May I present my seers, Miss Céline and Miss Amelie?" Anton said. "These are the sisters who provided help in your recent . . . difficulties up in Ryazan."

When Lieven's gaze shifted first to Amelie and then to Céline, his surprise could not be misread. "These are your seers?" He didn't sound entirely pleased, and his eyes moved down Céline's velvet gown. Then he studied her face and hair.

"Is something wrong?" Anton asked.

"No, they are simply . . . not as I pictured."

While Céline had no idea what that meant, Anton didn't press. Instead, he stepped closer to his father. "I'm glad to see you, but I apologize that you had to come here yourself. I hope you did not doubt I could bring matters to a close."

Lieven touched Anton's shoulder briefly. "Not at all. You know my faith in you. But this matter is of such importance that after some thought, I decided my own presence was necessary."

They spoke so easily to each other. Céline hadn't ex-

pected that. Anton was normally so closed off, and
Lieven had a reputation for being cold and arrogant.

"Now that you're here, I'm going to get this started,"
Lieven said, turning to walk away. Three guards in dark
brown tabards followed him.

He went to the first table at the head of the hall. When
he faced the crowd, everyone fell silent. "Take your
seats," he ordered.

Watching him now, Céline saw the calculated, steely-
eyed man she had expected.

"Where do Amelie and I sit?" she whispered to Anton.

"With me."

Her stomached tightened as he led them both toward
the head table. She had not anticipated this. She wondered what she would have said a year ago, had someone
told her she would soon be wearing a fine gown and dining at the head table of Kimovesk with three princes of
Pählen.

Another man came walking toward them. He was
well dressed, in his mid-forties with a close-trimmed
beard. She recognized him from her reading of Saorise:
Lord Malbek, chancellor to Prince Rodêk.

Lieven took the head of the table, with Damek and
Rochelle sitting on his right. Lady Helena and Lord Malbek sat on his left. This was some relief to Céline. At
least she, Amelie, and Anton would be far enough down
the table they wouldn't be expected to converse with
Anton's father. Lady Saorise, Heath, and Lizbeth also
took places at this head table.

Other guests began taking their seats around the hall,
and when the last guest had found a chair, Prince Lieven
remained standing.

"Wine," he called.

Servants hurried forward, pouring wine into goblets. Céline could not help noticing the lovely Johanna was serving at the head table.

Once everyone's goblet had been filled, Prince Lieven picked up his own and raised it.

Again, the hall fell silent, and he addressed his audience.

"With great joy, I announce that marriage negotiations have been completed and signed for the betrothal of my son Prince Damek of the house of Pählen to Rochelle Quillette, first cousin to Prince Rodêk of the house of Äntes." Despite his words, there was no joy in his voice. He sounded more like someone who'd just finished a deal for a large tract of land or a new silver mine. "As the young couple has expressed a wish to join their lives as soon as possible, the wedding will take place here at Castle Kimovesk tomorrow afternoon. The house of Pählen is honored that Lord Malbek himself will officiate the ceremony."

Tomorrow? Céline couldn't believe her ears. The ceremony would take place tomorrow?

Lieven raised his goblet higher. "Let us drink to their happiness."

A chorus of cheers rang out and everyone drank, but Céline could hardly swallow.

If the murderer was in this hall, how would he or she react?

As large trays of food were carried into the hall, Amelie sat in silence.

Anton sat stiff as a board beside her, and Céline was on the other side of him. Amelie badly wished to speak

to her sister, but she could hardly look around Anton to
do so.

What had just happened?

It was as if almost everyone involved here had forgotten the deaths that had taken place over the last week.
There was no mention of Carlotta or Lord Hamish ... or
Captain Maddox. Prince Lieven behaved as if this were
all a normal marriage agreement and that rushing the
wedding was merely due to the happy couple's wish not
to wait ... as opposed to a political marriage being
moved forward over the bodies of three people.

Though the guests at the other tables were all chattering away to one another, this head table fell awkwardly
quiet, and Amelie was thankful for the servants setting
food down, as it gave them all something to focus on.

Only young Lizbeth shook her head in open and honest puzzlement. "Tomorrow?" she said. "Here? I thought
Rochelle had decided to have the ceremony at home at
the manor ... outside in the autumn garden if weather
was clear. She won't want to be married here. This place
is awful."

"Be quiet," Heath said tightly.

She winced, hurt. Amelie had never heard him speak
to her like that.

Anton sat directly across from Lizbeth, and he leaned
forward. To his credit, his tone was light but his voice low
enough that it would not be overheard. "My father has a
few things in common with your mother, and I suspect
they both pressed Damek and Rochelle to rush things.
Trust me. He is difficult to refuse."

Lizbeth nodded in understanding, and Amelie's esti-
mation of Anton rose. He'd said the exact thing to make

the girl feel as if she were an adult who had made a perfectly rational comment, for which he had an answer.

Yet on the inside, Anton must be just as panicked as Amelie was . . . as Céline must be. What was Prince Lieven thinking? Did he want to drive the murderer to an even more desperate act?

Glancing across the table at Heath, she could see he was just as troubled. He sat straight in his chair and began to eat a small helping of baked trout, but his light brown eyes were glassy, and she knew he must understand the risks of Prince Lieven's decision as well.

Somehow . . . and later, she was never quite sure how . . . they all made it through three entire courses without speaking much.

A peculiar observation suddenly struck her. This was the third night upon which she'd dressed up for a formal dinner, and the first time they'd made it as far as having the food served. Normally, she at least enjoyed the richly prepared foods at these events, but tonight she hardly tasted them.

Finally, as the last of the plates were being cleared away, Amelie thought she might be able to get Céline alone for a few moments so they could discuss what to do next.

To her astonishment, Prince Lieven stood up again.

"I brought musicians from Castle Pählen," he announced. "Tomorrow will be the true celebration, but we can all enjoy some dancing tonight."

Dancing?

Looking across the hall, Amelie could see a group of six musicians taking chairs. They began to play, and Prince Lieven looked down at Damek. His eyes were cold and expectant at the same time. Damek stood up and held his hand out to Rochelle. "Will you join me?"

She flashed him a beautiful smile and stood to take his arm.

Other couples were moving to the open area of the floor near the musicians, and Prince Lieven's gaze shifted to Anton. It seemed he was expected to join in. Anton stood, and for an instant he looked at Céline with a hint of longing, as if picturing himself dancing with her, but he didn't ask her.

Instead, he offered a bow to Lizbeth. "My lady?"

Until that moment, Lizbeth had still appeared somewhat lost and puzzled by everything happening around her, and Amelie suspected the girl was quite shaken by Maddox's death. But at Anton's invitation, Lizbeth jumped to her feet and nearly ran around the end of the table to join him.

She liked Anton. And who could blame her in this place?

As soon as they were off for the dance floor, Céline turned in her chair and caught Amelie's eye. How could they possibly search out the murderer before tomorrow afternoon . . . if the killer waited that long?

Amelie glanced around for someplace where she and Céline might be able to speak, and to her frustration, an aging man with a white beard approached the table and offered a bow to Céline.

"My prince," he said to Lieven. "Would you introduce me to this lady?"

"Baron Menchan, this is Miss Céline Fawe, personal seer to my younger son."

"A seer." The baron smiled at Céline with real humor. "Delightful. Would you dance with an old man, my dear?"

Amelie wanted to scream in frustration, but they were still playing their part here, and so Céline smiled. "It would be my pleasure. But I warn you, our mother neglected our dance training, and I'm not very skilled."

Instead of being put off by this, Baron Menchan seemed pleased. "Oh, not to worry. My mother was over-zealous. I'll teach you."

With little choice, Céline was whisked away to the dance floor. Prince Lieven fell into a low conversation with Lord Malbek. Lady Helena was speaking to Sao-rise, and Amelie found herself looking across the table at Heath.

She fervently hoped he would not ask her to dance — as she knew even less about dancing than Céline.

But he stood abruptly and said, "Excuse me." Then he walked away.

His manner was so odd that Amelie watched him cross the hall. He stopped near the edge of the dancing, and he watched Rochelle with Damek.

The first song ended, and people applauded. Damek and Rochelle came away from the dance floor. Several guests flocked to them, offering congratulations — or that was what it seemed to Amelie. As Damek became en-gaged in speaking with a middle-aged couple, Heath slid up beside Rochelle and whispered something in her ear. She frowned and shook her head, and he leaned in and spoke again, more insistently.

This time, Rochelle allowed her brother to draw her away. They walked the short distance to the east arch-way, and then they left the hall, stepping out of sight. Was Rochelle leaving her own engagement celebration?

Amelie found that hard to believe.

No one was watching her, so she stood and casually

made her way to the east arch. She'd intended to pass right through, but as she approached, she heard the sounds of an argument. Moving closer, she leaned against the outer right side of the archway, near the edge so she could hear the words clearly.

"You can't," Heath was saying. "You must put a stop to it."

"I cannot stop it now," Rochelle answered. "It's done."

"Marry Damek? Tomorrow? Do you understand what that means?"

"I know what I'm doing. I can handle Damek. I put him to the test, Heath. I asked him to dismiss the captain of his guards, the head of his castle security, and he agreed. He'll do anything for me."

"That was before the wedding. Things might be quite different after tomorrow." Apparently, he was not so resigned to this marriage as he'd claimed.

"Everything is going as planned, better than planned," Rochelle said, and her tone was soft and soothing now. "I know it sounds awful, but with Carlotta and our uncle gone, there's only Mother to try and force my hand once I'm in power . . . and I can handle Mother. I'm going to be the grand princess of Droevinka, and Damek will do anything I ask. I can make you lord chancellor, Heath. We won't be separated, and I'll give you any position at court you want."

"I don't want a position at court!" His voice rose, and then it lowered. "Listen to me, Rochelle. If you go through with this, you'll be in Damek's bed tomorrow night. His *bed*. I know you know nothing of . . . men and women, and you can't possibly understand what that means, but by the time you do, it will be too late."

"Don't be crude," she said. "Now stop this before

someone comes looking for us. I'm going back to the hall."

Her footsteps sounded, and Amelie hurried away from the side of the arch, walking back toward the crowd to try to disappear. Once she had a few people behind her, she looked back. Rochelle had rejoined Damek, but Heath didn't return to the hall.

Amelie tried to make sense of what she'd heard pass between them. Her thoughts kept rolling over the same sentence.

With Carlotta and our uncle gone, there's only Mother to try and force my hand once I'm in power . . . and I can handle Mother.

What if the motive had not been to sabotage the marriage? What if Rochelle had known her mother wouldn't sever negotiations no matter what happened, and Rochelle was trying to strengthen her own position before the wedding took place? And who besides Rochelle had a stronger motive for killing Maddox? He'd threatened to make their history known and to ruin her.

The question was . . . how? Even Céline still didn't know exactly what had killed Carlotta and Hamish, and Rochelle could not have killed Maddox. She'd been in the great hall when he died.

Still, another sentence echoed through Amelie's mind: the last words she'd heard from Maddox.

Watch Rochelle. She is not what she seems.

After two dances with Baron Menchan, Céline was relieved when Anton suddenly appeared at her side.

"May I borrow my seer, Baron?" he asked politely.

"Oh, by all means," Menchan answered, panting. "I'm not as young as I once was."

He was a good-natured soul, and on any other occasion, Céline would have enjoyed his company. But now she was glad to let Anton steer her back in the direction of the table. They didn't get far.

Prince Lieven had left his place and was walking toward them. Céline glanced around for Amelie but didn't see her sister in the crowd.

Lady Saorise, Damek, and Rochelle all moved to join them as Lieven reached the small party, and he somehow seemed to assess them all at once. Céline began to suspect that rumors of his failing health had been greatly exaggerated.

Rochelle offered her future father-in-law a sweet smile. "My lord, I'm told I have you to thank for completing the contract today. Prince Damek told me you stood well against my mother."

Any other man might have melted at both her smile and her compliment, but Lieven only glanced at her and then addressed Damek. "I suppose you have enough in your wine stores to satisfy this lot tomorrow? A few of them can drink half a cask by themselves."

There was no warmth in his eyes and no affection in his voice.

With equally coolness, Damek responded, "I'm certain we have enough, Father. But I'll check with Master Lionel if it pleases you."

Lieven grunted. "You do that, and make sure everything's ready by tomorrow afternoon. The sooner we get this over with, the better."

Rochelle stared at him, and even Lady Saorise appeared taken aback by Lieven's manner toward Damek. Had she never seen them together before? It was possible she had not. She probably didn't travel to Castle Pählen when he was summoned there for a rare family visit, and from what Céline understood, Prince Lieven hadn't visited Kimovesk in years.

Lieven looked to Anton. "You'll stand witness for your brother, won't you?" Both his tone and expression softened.

"Of course, Father. If you wish."

"I do."

Although Céline cared deeply for Anton, and she feared Damek, she found Prince Lieven's treatment of his elder son to border on inappropriate in this company. This was the night before Damek's wedding, and Damek was marrying exactly as his father had wished.

Damek cast Anton a look of pure hatred. "I would be honored to have you act as witness, little brother."

"My love . . . ," Rochelle said to Damek. "Would you dance with me again?"

Damek allowed himself to be led away.

Lady Saorise's normally serene face was not so serene.

"My lord," she said to Lieven, "I do congratulate you on Damek's marriage. And I hope that someday you will be able to marry Prince Anton to someone so advantageous as Rochelle Quillette."

Lieven turned his icy gaze on her. "I wouldn't saddle Anton with that sugarcoated she-wolf, but she'll do for Damek. Pählen now has a close connection to Prince Rodêk, and that's what matters."

"Father . . . ," Anton murmured. "Don't be so mercenary. You'll have a new daughter tomorrow, and you should welcome her."

"Should I?" Lieven challenged. Then he relented. "I suppose you're right. You usually are."

Saorise turned to Anton. With a honeyed tone, she said, "Yes, in these past few days, Prince Damek and I have welcomed Anton's good counsel here." As she said this, she reached up to touch the side of his face, and when she drew her hand back, he flinched.

Céline didn't know what to make of her false praise or of her touching Anton.

"Will you excuse me?" Saorise said. "There are a few other guests I've not yet had a chance to greet."

As she turned away, her pleasant expression wavered, and Céline could see that she was shaken, possibly more than shaken.

Amelie stood at a loss among the crowd of nobles and the varied collection of guards. Looking over near the musicians, she saw Céline trapped in a conversation with Prince Lieven and Anton. There was little hope Céline would be able to extract herself from that any time soon.

Watch Rochelle. She is not what she seems.

Amelie couldn't get those words to leave her thoughts, nor could she stop wondering about the possibility that she and Céline had been wrong about the killer's motive.

Her mind kept turning to Captain Maddox.

From what she'd seen in his memories, he was an honorable man, and yet he'd killed a Kimovesk guard to escape his cell, and instead of fleeing, he'd gone up to the guest rooms of the family he served. Why?

If he'd been captured after killing one of Damek's men, his own execution would have followed swiftly. What could be so important that he'd risk his life to go back to those rooms?

Did he think to find something there? Was it possible that during his final night with Rochelle, his opinion of her became so altered that he'd begun to suspect her of something darker than casting his love aside?

Had he intended to search her room? If so, he never made it that far. Lizbeth had been asleep in there at the time, and if he'd opened the door, he would have disturbed her. Amelie shook her head. This was all speculation. Maybe he'd been attempting to go all the way to his own room for something and been caught by someone who wanted him dead? But that made no sense, either. They'd already established there'd been no fight in the passage. He hadn't even drawn his sword. So either he knew the person who killed him or he'd been caught unawares.

Still . . . Amelie scanned the great hall. Rochelle and Lizbeth were both here. Heath was not, but he'd most likely gone to his own room. He'd seemed quite upset about the announcement of Rochelle's overly rushed marriage to Damek, and he probably wanted to be alone.

If Amelie was quiet, she could go upstairs, sneak into Rochelle's room, and search it herself, just to be sure.

Looking over, she saw that Céline's back was turned, so there was no way to signal her sister. Still, this had to be done.

Causally, Amelie strolled to the east archway and slipped away from the great hall, down the back passage.

CHAPTER THIRTEEN

Céline stood politely as Anton and his father turned to discussing estimated tax income from Sèone once the last of the autumn harvest was in. Though she tried to appear interested, she never stopped watching Lady Saorise from the corner of her eye. Céline had thought the woman impossible to rattle, and yet Saorise had been badly shaken by Prince Lieven's strikingly different interactions with Damek and Anton.

Before Céline's true powers had manifested, she'd made part of her living by reading people's faces and emotions, and she'd seen fear in Saorise's face. Perhaps the woman had solidly believed that Lieven's determination to procure Rochelle Quillette as a wife for Damek was proof that Damek would be named heir.

Now ... it seemed possible that Lieven wanted to claim a strong Pählen connection to the house of Äntes, and that was all.

Céline watched as Saorise made her way around the hall, greeting some people briefly, and talking at greater length with others, but when she finally neared the east side of the hall, she walked through the archway and vanished down the passage. No one else paid attention as she left.

"Forgive me," Céline said to Anton, "but I fear the dancing has made me a touch dizzy. Do you mind if I go and sit for a short while?"

He turned and looked down at her. "Dizzy? Are you all right? Should I take you to a chair?"

She realized she'd chosen the wrong excuse. "Oh no, please. Stay and talk with your father. I just need a moment."

With a smile, she left them, and then she made her way past the musicians to the east archway. Unfortunately, it had taken too long to extract herself from Anton and Lieven. Saorise was nowhere in sight, and Céline had no idea where she might have gone. Perhaps to her private chambers? But where was that?

Amelie thought Saorise to be highly dangerous, and Céline knew her to be a power seeker. Why had she left the hall on such an important occasion? And why had she touched Anton first?

Light footsteps sounded from ahead, and Céline looked up to see Johanna coming down the passage toward her, carrying a tray of sugared confections. With a jolt of guilt, Céline had an idea. She didn't like it, but it was all she could come up with.

"Johanna?" she said, stepping into the passage and walking to meet the young woman. "Could I have a word?"

Johanna would know the location of Saorise's private chambers, and Céline knew Johanna was Damek's mistress. If she had to, she could threaten to tell Rochelle the truth . . . and then Johanna's position here would not be long-lived once Rochelle was Damek's wife.

"Yes, miss," Johanna said. "How can I help?"

Though her words were polite, as she spoke she sounded so unhappy, so miserable, that Céline's resolved weakened. Instead of making a threat, Céline couldn't help asking, "What's wrong?"

"Nothing, miss."

Céline moved closer and lowered her voice. "I know you are Prince Damek's mistress . . . No, please don't be alarmed. I assure you I'm not one of those nobles in there, and I can see you are troubled. Tell me what is wrong."

Johanna looked into the great hall, where Rochelle could be seen dancing with Damek. *"Her,"* she whispered. "My lord said that her coming here would change nothing between us, and I think . . . at the time he meant it. But he had never seen her. Of course he'd been told by her family of her beauty, but all families say that when offering a daughter in marriage." Johanna dropped her gaze. "Then he saw her . . . met her, and he's not called me to his chambers since. Worse, I think she knows about me. Once she has power here, I'll be thrown out the gate and sent to starve in the village . . . and my lord will not care."

A better idea, a much better idea occurred to Céline. "Johanna, I need to find the Lady Saorise right now, and I don't know where her private chambers are located, but I must know. If you show me, I promise, when we leave here I'll make certain Prince Anton takes you with us, and I'll find you a good position in Castle Sèone."

Johanna's eyes flew up, but she was cautious. "Why can you not ask Master Lionel?"

"Because I don't think he'll tell me, and I fear Saorise may be up to something . . . harmful, and if so, I want to stop her."

This was all rather too honest, but it seemed best in the moment.

Johanna didn't react to—or seem to doubt—the suggestion that Saorise might be up to something harmful. "You swear? You swear you'll take me to Sèone and find me a position in the castle?"

"I swear."

Another few breaths passed, and Céline grew worried.

Then Johanna nodded. "Lady Saorise is not in her chambers. I passed her on my way here, and I know where she was going. She spends most of her time in the lesser hall, down below the kitchen."

"The lesser hall?"

"Yes, in the days of war, the castle housed more soldiers. They ate in the lesser hall, but now Lady Saorise uses it as her sanctuary. None of us wish to know what she truly does down there."

"Take me there."

Again, Johanna paused. "Wait here a moment. We'll need a key."

With that, she hurried into the great hall and set her tray of confections on a table. Master Lionel was near the west wall, giving a servant instructions. Johanna went to him and spoke in his ear. He frowned but took a set of keys from his belt and handed them to her.

She hurried back to Céline. "I told him the cooks need to get into the locked stores in preparation for tomorrow's wedding feast. I'm often trusted with the keys."

They set off down the passage.

"Where to?" Céline asked, still uncertain about exactly what she was doing, but knowing she had to do something.

"Through the kitchen," Johanna said.

*   *   *

When Amelie reached the third floor of the east tower, she walked past Heath's room as quietly as possible.

Grasping the latch of Rochelle and Lizbeth's room, she opened the door slowly, slipped inside, and closed it again. For the most part, the room was similar to the one Amelie shared with Céline: a wide bed, a wardrobe, and a dressing table with a chair. The wardrobe was much larger here, and the dressing table was covered in a variety of objects. There were silver brushes and combs, crystal bottles of perfume, boxes of bracelets and earrings. Walking closer, Amelie picked up a jar of pale pink rouge powder. She assumed most of these things were Rochelle's, but they were all typical paraphernalia of a noblewoman.

Once she'd finished examining the top of the dressing table, Amelie began going through the drawers, finding nothing but stockings and undergarments. She searched the bed thoroughly, above and beneath, even under the mattress.

Nothing.

Finally, she turned to the wardrobe. It was packed with hanging gowns. She searched each one carefully, looking for . . . something. She didn't know what. She only knew that Maddox had come up here for a reason and he'd ended up dead.

Three wool cloaks hung to one side of the wardrobe, rather smashed in among the dresses. The smallest one was blue. Amelie took it down and went through the pockets, finding nothing. The next one was longer, and dyed dark green. The pockets and lining were empty as well.

The last one was a rich shade of gray, and while it was

too long for Lizbeth, it looked too heavy for Rochelle. Amelie pulled it out and felt nothing sewn into the lining. Then she put her hand in the right pocket.

She touched something soft and coarse at the same time. Closing her fingers around whatever she'd found, she withdrew her hand and found herself looking down at a handful of hair. The hair seemed familiar. It was dark and very dry with strands of gray.

"What you are doing in here?"

Amelie whirled to see Lizbeth standing in the door.

"Why are you holding Heath's cloak?" the girl asked.

"This is Heath's?"

Then she remembered. Last night, before the search party had ridden out, Lizbeth had been shivering, and Heath had covered her with his cloak.

"Yes . . . ," Lizbeth answered. "Why are you in here, and where is Heath? I noticed him gone from the hall, and I came up to check on him. I think he's sad. But he's not in his room."

Amelie dropped the cloak, strode over, and held out her hand. "Lizbeth, do you recognize this hair?"

The girl tensed. "That's Carlotta's. Where did you—?"

"Did you say Heath wasn't in his room?" Amelie interrupted.

Lizbeth seemed to understand that something was terribly wrong, and she nodded wordlessly.

Where would he have gone?

And then . . . Amelie knew.

"Lizbeth, stay here and lock the door behind me when I leave. Don't open it for anyone but Céline, Prince Anton, or me. Do you understand?"

"No, I don't! Tell me what is—"

"Just do it!" Amelie ran out the door and pulled it closed. "Lock the door," she called.

Then she bolted for the stairs.

Johanna took Céline down the back passage of the castle. At the base of the east tower, she turned and led the way up the shorter passage into the kitchen. The place was alive with activity.

"Get those pots scrubbed!" shouted an exhausted-looking woman in an apron. "I need them for tomorrow."

Several young girls ran for the pots, and only a few people glanced over as Johanna led Céline down the backside. Once they exited the kitchen, they descended three steps and turned into another short passage. Johanna stopped in front of a heavy door, and she held up the ring of keys.

"I'll open it, but I'm not going down there," she said.

"You needn't. I owe you a good deal for getting me this far."

"And you'll keep your promise?"

"I will. You'll like Sèone. It's a good place."

"Be careful," Johanna warned. "Lady Saorise frightens me." With that, she unlocked the door and opened it.

"Leave it unlocked," Céline instructed, and then she passed through the door into a dim stairwell. She descended the distance of a single floor and emerged from a narrow archway into a large windowless room with walls of stone. Small braziers lined three of the walls, providing a good deal of light. Spears and crossbows lined the fourth wall.

She had seen this place before . . . in the vision of Saorise casting the protection spell over Damek.

As Céline entered the long chamber, she noticed differences from her earlier vision. The table was nearly empty now, with only a few stacked books on one end.

There were similarities, too.

She turned to see the hearth at the other end of the vast room. The fire was lit. The iron hook had been set over the flames, and the same small metal cauldron with symbols etched around the outside hung from the hook.

Saorise stood before the cauldron with her eyes closed and her mouth moving. She appeared in a trance again and seemed to have no awareness of Céline's presence in the chamber. She held a small dagger in her right hand.

Unlike the vision from Saorise's more distant future, her appearance was pristine, as if what she did tonight took little planning and little effort.

This thought brought Céline no comfort.

Could Saorise be the killer after all? If so, why had Céline not seen this when she'd done her reading? And what possible motive could there be?

"Breath . . . ," Saorise whispered. "The breath of life cut off . . . *prosterno* . . . *eroado*." Without opening her eyes, she pricked the point of the dagger into her wrist and several drops of blood trickled into the cauldron.

This was all Céline needed to see and hear. Whatever Saorise was casting in this moment, it was no protection spell.

The spears on the walls were taller than Céline's head, and she doubted she could lift one. The crossbows weren't loaded. But there was a short, stout javelin on the wall. Walking over, she took it down and gripped it.

Then she strode toward Saorise.

*   *   *

Amelie ran down to the storage room that Heath had shown her near the base of the east tower. Crossing the room swiftly, she passed through the doorway at the back and descended the stairs. She could hear the crackling of logs and see a glowing light before she even emerged into the guardroom of the old prisons.

Although she had no idea what she would find, at the bottom of the stairs, it took her a moment to absorb the sight before her.

A fire crackled in the small hearth. Heath sat crosslegged on the floor in the center of a triangle that had been drawn in black chalk. His tunic and wool shirt lay a few paces behind him, and his chest and arms were bare.

He was perspiring, and his skin glistened.

There was a dagger strapped to his left forearm. Directly above the sheath, she saw several deep cuts that had just begun to heal. There wasn't a single hair on his smooth torso, but the muscles in his arms were more defined than she would have expected. A short hook had been placed over the fire, and a small iron cauldron hung from the hook.

About six strands of red-gold hair, the same color as his own, lay on the floor beside him, but these were longer, much longer.

He was in the middle of pouring something from a white bottle into the cauldron.

"Heath?" Amelie said.

His head whipped toward her. His expression was still, but his light brown eyes held a glint of madness.

"Amelie?" he said in turn.

"Whatever you're doing, stop doing it," she said.

He dropped the bottle and jumped to his feet.

She'd wanted to find him as quickly as possible, but

for the first time, she wondered about her wisdom in coming down here alone.

"I have to finish," he said. "I have to save her. I tried everything else ... everything, and if I don't save her now, she'll be in his bed tomorrow. She doesn't understand what he'll do ... and I have to save her."

Though she'd never suspected Heath, looking down at the long red-blond strands on the floor, Amelie realized that somehow he had killed his older sister and his uncle, and he was about to kill Rochelle.

She held up her hand, still gripping the dark, gray-streaked hair. "Like you saved Carlotta."

Heath's eyes widened at the sight. "No! I was trying to save Rochelle. Carlotta was behind all this. We wouldn't be here if not for her poisoned heart. I don't want to do this, Amelie. I never wanted it. But there's no other choice now, and you must let me finish. You must see I'm right."

"No."

His expression went still. Drawing the dagger from its sheath on his wrist, he took a step closer. "Move away from the stairwell."

She had two choices: fight or flee.

If she fought and lost, he'd finish whatever he was doing here and kill Rochelle. If she fled, she might make it up the stairs before he caught her ... at least she'd get far enough to call for help.

Whirling, she jumped back up the stairs. But she was laced into a floor-length evening gown, and she made it only four steps when a hand grabbed her arm from behind, jerking her backward.

He pinned her against the wall near the bottom of the

stairwell and held the dagger a few inches from her throat. He was stronger than she'd imagined.

"I'm sorry," he said. "I would never have hurt you."

The madness in his eyes and the resignation in his voice filled her with fear. He had one of her arms pinned, but her other hand was free. Falling back on the only defense she had in the moment, she grabbed his jaw.

In a flash, she reached for the spark of his spirit, trying to rip his awareness from this moment, to trap and disorient him in the mists of time. She found his spirit instantly, and she latched on.

The first jolt hit, and she focused as hard as she could on why he had done these terrible things. The second jolt hit, and they were both swept into the gray and white mists, moving backward. She fought to mesh her spirit with his, as she'd done with Maddox. She needed to see through Heath's eyes, to feel what he felt, to understand his tortured mind.

He fought back, trying to break his spirit free, but she held on. In here, she was the stronger one.

The mists cleared.

CHAPTER FOURTEEN

Heath's fifteenth year was the happiest of his life.

His father, Baron Alexis Quillette, was not only titled, but also one of the most prosperous wine merchants in Droevinka, and he worked hard. But Alexis had been forced into "learning the business" at the age of twelve by his own father, and as a result, he'd missed a good part of his childhood.

He wanted more for his son.

"Enjoy these years," he told Heath. "Learn what you must from your tutors, but otherwise let yourself be young. Do as you wish."

And so Heath did.

However, the only thing he wished to do was spend time with two of his sisters. He learned writing and mathematics and music from his tutors, but every other spare moment was spent with Rochelle and Lizbeth. When the weather was foul, they would hide in the attic and put on plays for one another, acting out the characters with great flair and drama.

When the weather was fine, they rode their horses all over their family's lands, sometimes—when they had no lessons—disappearing from breakfast to dinner. Out in the forest around the manor, they played make-believe games in which Rochelle was a princess and Lizbeth was a cruel villain who abducted her. Heath was the hero who rescued Rochelle.

They took delight in stealing clothes or other items from the manor to use in their games. Rochelle seldom required any sort of costume. She looked the part of the princess all on her own.

Heath loved his younger sister, Lizbeth, who had just turned twelve that year, but he adored Rochelle.

She was the most perfect thing he'd ever seen. Sometimes he thought this sentiment might seem vain, as she was his twin, younger than him by ten minutes, and they looked so much alike, but he made most other people uncomfortable. He put them off. Rochelle dazzled them. No one could see her, listen to her voice, and not fall in love.

So Heath's life was filled with imaginary games and putting on plays in the attic and riding his horse . . . all in the company of his two favorite sisters.

His father paid little attention to how he chose to spend his days so long as he was happy.

His mother said little but made it clear she did not approve of the arrangement. Nor did his elder sister, Carlotta.

Heath had a difficult time speaking to anyone besides his father or his younger sisters. With everyone else, he could rarely think of a proper response or anything to say, and attempting to speak to his mother was most difficult. For one, she rarely spoke to him unless it was to criticize or offer a correction, and for the first fifteen years of his life, he didn't remember saying anything to her other than "Yes, Mother."

Carlotta almost never spoke to him at all.

It didn't matter. He had Rochelle and Lizbeth, and the three of them would hide and talk and play for hours.

But as midsummer approached that year, one day, their mother was out, and they took advantage of playing on the main floor of the manor. Lizbeth was the villain, as always, and Rochelle was the princess.

"You won't escape me!" Lizbeth shouted. She wore an old pair of their father's pants, rolled up, and she'd drawn a mustache on her upper lip with charcoal.

Rochelle pretended to struggle, and then Heath ran into the dining room with a wooden sword.

He was about to call to Rochelle to take heart when he saw one of the hired house guards standing on the far side of the dining room. The man stared at Heath with a look of measured disgust.

Heath stopped. "Let's go up to the attic."

Rochelle and Lizbeth followed him out.

Later, he was still troubled, with a knot in his stomach, and he asked Rochelle, "Did you see that guard's face when he looked at me?"

She shrugged. "What does it matter?"

"Was I doing something wrong?"

"Of course not. He's a grown-up. He probably thinks it's strange for a young man your age to spend all his time playing with his sisters. Ignore him."

Young man? Was he a young man now? He didn't want to be. His father had spoken to him of the adult world, and it sounded awful, filled with accounts and ledgers and worry and toil and duty.

Heath wanted nothing in his current life to change.

Yet, that year, he did learn that not all change was a bad thing, and two new men entered his life. The first was Captain Maddox.

Heath's mother, Lady Helena, had suddenly seemed to think the family would be doing more traveling in the near future—Heath had no idea why—and she wanted a bodyguard who was a tad more impressive than their hired men at the manor. Captain Maddox was apparently some sort of "gift" arranged by Aunt Clarisse, who was mother to Prince Rodêk. Maddox arrived in shining boots, wearing a long sword and the pale yellow tabard of the Äntes.

Lady Helena was pleased, as she loved all things Äntes, and she informed the family that Maddox was not to be considered a servant, and that he would live in the manor and dine with them. At first, Heath had great trepidation over this news. Captain Maddox was tall, muscular, and ruggedly handsome. He was the type of man other men wanted to be. Heath had never been at ease with men like that—or rather, they'd never been at ease with him.

But the captain was unfailingly polite to Heath and quickly proved himself interested in little else than protecting the family. He oversaw the hired guards and kept most of them out of the house. Soon, Heath was glad for his solid presence.

There was only one drawback to his arrival.

Heath wasn't aware of it until he noticed his parents arguing more than usual. Lady Helena and Baron Alexis had never liked each other, or at least not in Heath's memory, and they learned to arrange their days so that they only need be in the same company at dinner. Even then, they barely spoke.

But of late, Heath had heard them shouting behind closed doors, and one day, he came into the house to see if he could sneak some bread and cheese to bring back outside to Lizbeth and Rochelle for lunch, and he heard raised voices on the main floor, coming from the drawing room.

"You do him no service and no favors!" his mother shouted. "Do you see how our own guards look at him? Do you see how our friends look at him when they dine with us?"

"I'll not force him into manhood too fast!" Heath's father returned. "I've told you that."

"How long will you wait? Until he's shaving every morning, and all the young men of the other families have years of training behind them?"

Heath froze. They were arguing about him.

Slowly, he crept back outside, worried. It sounded as though Mother was pressing Father into forcing Heath to take his place in the adult world.

A few days later, Captain Maddox approached him. Heath watched him cautiously, sensing something was up.

"Your father sent me," Maddox said without preamble. "I'm to teach you how to use a sword."

Oh . . . , Heath thought. That didn't sound too bad.

Unfortunately, it was. At fifteen, Heath was still small and slight of build. Earlier that year, Rochelle had grown taller than him. No matter how he tried, he couldn't swing a sword more than three or four times before he nearly dropped it in exhaustion.

Embarrassed, he expected harsh criticism from the captain, but Maddox sat him down and said, "I was worried about this. Don't fret. Most boys from families like yours start at least basic training and learning how to use a dagger much earlier, and they've built up some strength by now. But boys . . . men can keep growing until they're twenty. You'll grow into yourself. I promise. I'll teach you the sword later, maybe next year."

"Yes, but I think Mother wants me to learn how to fight now."

"I know, and I have an idea about that. Be ready to go out riding with me tomorrow after lunch."

Although Heath had planned to spend tomorrow playing among the trees with Rochelle and Lizbeth, acting out a new story he'd thought up, he was curious to see where Maddox would take him. So the following afternoon, he had his horse saddled, and he was ready.

Maddox joined him, and they rode out the manor gates, heading south.

They took a forest path and went all the way to the edge of Quillette land. Up ahead, Heath heard a rushing creek, and he saw an unusual encampment, a collection of wagons with small houses built on top—like rolling homes. There were horses grazing at the outskirts of the camp and chickens pecking the ground around the wagons. Perhaps twenty people milled about the camp. Some of the women were putting vegetables in a large pot hanging on a hook over a fire pit built in the center of camp. Everyone was dressed in bright colors of scarlet or royal blue or purple, and most wore bracelets or rings in their ears, even some of the men.

Heads turned as Heath and Maddox approached, but then smiles broke out and some people called, "Captain, come and have lunch."

In his studies with his tutors, Heath had learned a little about the history of the Móndyalítko, but what he'd read had not prepared him for this sight. He felt as if he were riding into a larger-scale version of one of the plays that he and his sisters performed together.

Before entering the camp, though, he pulled up his horse. He didn't quite follow the situation. "These people are on my father's land."

Maddox stopped beside him. "I know. They come every summer and stay through autumn. They have your father's permission to camp and to fish in the creek. I rode out here the first week I arrived . . . just to make certain these people presented no danger, but I've no concerns. I've made friends with a few of them, and there's one I wish you to meet."

Heath marveled at this news. All this time, every summer and autumn, there had been a group of gypsies camping on Quillette lands, and he'd never known.

Maddox dismounted his horse, and Heath followed suit.

A woman with dark hair greeted them, smiling at Maddox and then assessing Heath. She appeared pleased and interested at the same time. "Captain, have you brought us a pretty young man?"

Maddox smiled back, "Leave off, Neda. He's not for you." He looked around. "Is Jace about?"

"In here," a low voice called. The door to one of the wagons opened, and a man emerged, coming down a set of makeshift steps. He yawned and stretched as if he'd been asleep in the middle of the day.

"You need me?" he asked Maddox as he approached.

The man was about thirty, with dusky skin and dark wavy hair pulled back into a ponytail. He wore a loose orange shirt and faded brown pants. His feet were bare.

"Yes," Maddox answered. "I was hoping to hire you."

The man raised an eyebrow, but Maddox continued.

Motioning to the man, he said, "Heath, this is Jace. He's very . . . skilled with a dagger, much better than me. Jace, this is my mistress's son. She wanted him trained with a sword, but he's not ready. He's got speed and balance. I thought learning the dagger could help get him started."

Though Heath was still puzzled, he flushed under the compliment. He had no idea he was possessed of speed or balance.

The man called Jace tilted his head and studied Heath. "You ever held a dagger before, lad?"

"No," Heath answered. He did wonder how Maddox had learned Jace was so skilled with a small blade, but he didn't ask.

"We'll pay you two silver pennies per lesson if the boy comes out here, and three if you come to the manor," Maddox said.

"Quite generous," Jace answered.

"Then you'll do it?"

"Why not?"

And with that, Heath found himself exposed to a new world, both inside and outside himself. Sometimes Jace came to the manor, and they practiced out in the front area of the stable, and sometimes Heath rode to the camp. He liked it there. For the most part, the gypsies lived as they pleased, just as Heath wished to continue doing. They all seemed to accept him, and none of the men found him off-putting.

It also soon surprised him how much he came to enjoy the lessons themselves. Like Maddox, Jace was a patient teacher, and he never pressed too hard. He taught Heath how to hold a small blade correctly, how to dodge, how to slash, and when to thrust. Heath came to understand that he indeed was possessed of speed and balance.

Even better, he impressed his sisters with his growing skills when they played their games in the forest—while he was the hero rescuing Rochelle. Of course he was careful, and he never got his blade anywhere near Lizbeth. He just brandished it and showed his sisters what he could do.

One day, Jace brought him a leather sheath to fasten to his wrist. Heath loved this idea. The next day, he made up a story about a forest brigand with a good heart, and Lizbeth played an evil nobleman who abducted Rochelle. Heath was able to pull the dagger from inside his sleeve and surprise both his sisters. They laughed and clapped.

And so . . . Heath's fifteenth year was the happiest of his life. He had his freedom, his sisters, his father, the quiet support of Captain Maddox, and a camp full of gypsies who accepted him for who he was.

Then, not far into his sixteenth year, the world began to change.

The first change wasn't bad. He had a growth spurt, and he grew taller than Rochelle. He could feel the strength increasing in his arms when he practiced with Jace, and Jace stepped up the training regime.

But in late autumn, the Móndyalítko packed up and rolled away, going to their winter destination and promising to see Heath the following summer.

Another change soon followed, and this one hurt.

One morning, Heath and Lizbeth waited impatiently downstairs for Rochelle. She didn't come. Finally, he went up to get her, and he found her in their mother's room—with their mother. His sister Carlotta was there, too, along with several women who were draping silk around Rochelle, and chattering about "the neckline."

Heath stood in the doorway, wanting to pull Rochelle away.

"Heath!" his mother said, spotting him. "What are you doing there? We're fitting your sister for gowns. Get out and close the door behind you."

"Yes, Mother."

Bereft, he went back downstairs and told Lizbeth what he'd seen. Rochelle didn't come down all day. Lunch was even carried up to Mother's room. Normally, Rochelle's muslin dresses were fitted from previous ones, and even if she'd needed to be fitted, it had never taken long and she'd never been called to Mother's room.

Heath and Lizbeth tried to create a story and play out the characters by themselves, but it didn't work without Rochelle.

Shortly before dinner, he caught her alone. "Why did it take all day to fit you for a gown?"

"Gowns," she corrected. "Mother is planning a visit to Enêmûsk, and I'm to go. I think she wants to present Carlotta to a few suitors, but she also wants it to appear as a family visit so we aren't too obvious."

"Oh . . ." Heath's discomfort grew. Mother was taking Rochelle to Enêmûsk? "Still, did you have to be up there all day?"

"I need gowns, Heath. We'll be attending formal dinners."

This was the beginning of a change in Rochelle that he could not seem to stop. A few days later, her first silk gown was finished, and when she walked into the dining room that evening, she looked . . . different. Her body was beginning to change, as his had, and her slender form was developing soft curves. The silk gown fit her snugly and the neckline was low. Her delicate face seemed more defined, her hair more lustrous, and her skin more creamy.

He didn't like it.

Weeks passed, and she took to walking to the stable in her new silk gowns—to visit her horse. Every guard in the courtyard or near the gates would stop whatever he was doing to stare at her.

She never had time for games of make-believe in the forest anymore, and she seemed to spend most of her hours in front of her mirror. She collected perfumes and earrings and small jeweled clips for her hair.

He grew desperate, missing the games they'd played out in the forest so much that the inside of his chest hurt. One morning, he cornered her. "Lizbeth and I have made up a story. Come outside today."

"I can't."

"You can't? Not even for one day?"

"Heath," she said sweetly. She always spoke to him sweetly. "Those days are gone. Mother, Carlotta, and I are packing for our visit to Enêmûsk. I am becoming a young lady now ... and you are becoming a young man."

A white-hot anger flooded through him. Turning on his heel, he walked away.

But she left the following day, and she was gone for two weeks. Every day was torture just for him to make it to darkness as he counted the time passing. When she returned, he fell to his knees and begged her forgiveness, which she gave.

The next morning, she came up to the attic with him and Lizbeth, and they acted out a game of make-believe in which Rochelle was a princess sold into slavery, and Heath rescued her. He was dizzy with relief afterward, like a starving man who'd been fed.

Both his mother and Carlotta seemed more animated for a few days. Carlotta had been presented to several eligible noblemen, and she was expecting a written offer soon.

A messenger came just before dinner. He carried two letters.

Rochelle was a vision that night in a white satin gown. Even Maddox looked startled when she walked into the dining room. Father stood up to greet her.

"Come and sit, my dear. We may have good news for your sister."

Everyone else in the family had arrived for dinner. Father enjoyed a little drama, and he'd waited to open the letters. Carlotta sat expectantly, watching him.

She was only in her twenties, but her hair was already streaked with gray, and her mouth was lined. Heath had often tried to feel pity for her, but she never had a kind word for anyone and couldn't seem to look at another person without finding fault.

Father opened the first letter and began to read. "Yes." He smiled. "It is an offer . . ." His smile faded. "For Rochelle."

Carlotta stiffened in her chair.

The second letter also contained an offer for Rochelle.

Mother looked stricken. "I am sorry, my dear," she said to Carlotta. "The next offer will be for you. I'm sure of it."

Heath felt sick and didn't know why. "What of those two offers?" He rarely spoke at the table, and everyone turned to him.

"Well," his father began, "I'll write back and refuse them. Rochelle is only sixteen. In my mind, she is too young for marriage."

Relief flooded Heath's stomach. He loved his father more than ever at that moment.

But the pattern was set, and over that winter and spring, every man with whom Father began negotiations for Carlotta would either vanish after meeting her ... or make an offer for Rochelle if he'd been allowed to meet her.

Father and Mother tried to make light of this. Carlotta did not. Lizbeth was often forgotten during this time period, even by Heath, as their games didn't work without Rochelle.

Sometimes Heath couldn't stop himself from begging his twin to come into the forest or the attic with him. She was always sweet, but she always had something else to do.

He began to have trouble sleeping. In his mind at night, he made up stories and he acted them out with Rochelle.

Summer came, and Jace returned. Taking up the dagger lessons again helped a bit. No one mentioned him learning the sword again. Mother was too busy trying to find a husband for Carlotta.

Heath gained permission from his father to miss dinner once or twice a week, and he spent those evenings in the Móndyalítko camp. The people there had little interest in the "adult" world, and they lived as they pleased. He knew they earned money by visiting neighboring towns and villages and putting on musical shows and telling fortunes. But otherwise, their time was their own, and at night, they entertained one another with songs and stories. A part of Heath's earlier education had involved music, and he sometimes brought his lute so he could take part in the songs, but he most enjoyed listening to the darker stories, with magic and curses and revenge.

One night, he noticed the gypsies drinking from a small, familiar-looking cask ... from his own family's outer storage sheds.

"Is that ours?" he asked.

Startled, Jace glanced at the cask and then looked chagrined. "I fear it is. There were so many that I didn't think anyone would notice if I liberated one."

Heath smiled. He didn't begrudge them a cask of wine, and neither would his father.

But then, toward the end of that summer, Heath noticed a change in his father. Alexis grew pale, and then he lost his appetite. A physician was called, who used the word "consumption." It never occurred to Heath that father might not recover. But halfway through that autumn, his father died.

Within a week, Uncle Hamish, his mother's brother, came to live with them.

The world had shifted again.

Heath was named baron of Quillette.

Since he knew nothing of the wine business, Uncle Hamish took it over, and he became master of the house.

Any and all love and kindness vanished from Heath's life—except for Rochelle. Lizbeth did love him, but she couldn't express it. Only Rochelle gave him love in the form of kind words. She began letting him come into her room at night to brush her long hair before bed. No one else knew they did this, but he relished the time she gave him.

The two of them celebrated their seventeenth birthday.

Carlotta was not yet married.

A week later, at dinner, Uncle Hamish pronounced Rochelle was of age to consider marriage proposals.

Heath politely excused himself from the table. He went outside and threw up.

After that, Rochelle had even less time to spare.

Noble families with unmarried sons would come to the manor for short "visits," and every man who walked through the door—married or not—followed Rochelle with his eyes. Offers were made, but somehow Rochelle always found a way to get Uncle Hamish to turn·them down. She smiled sometimes and teased, "Let's wait for an offer from a prince."

This seemed to have the desired effect, and polite refusals were sent.

However, Rochelle's string of refusals frustrated their mother.

Worse, with each new offer, Carlotta's mouth became more and more downturned.

Still, Heath lived in fear that Rochelle would be married off and taken away from him. One afternoon, he begged her to go riding with him, just for a few hours, but she touched his face and told him she had other things to do.

Angry, he strode out of the house and went out to the stable, climbing into the loft and lying alone up there. If he couldn't spend time with her, he wanted to be alone.

The stable was quiet and peaceful this time of day, and he'd almost dozed off when he heard hushed voices below.

"Samuel, stop. We can't. Not here."

"No one will see. Come on. There's a good girl."

Heath rolled onto his side and looked down over the edge of the loft to see one of the house guards, Samuel, and a pretty kitchen maid directly below him. Heath didn't know the girl's name.

Samuel dropped to his knees, pulling the girl down with him, and then pushing her onto the floor.

Although she pushed back at him, she didn't fight or

scream. "Let me up. We'll be caught, and I'll be dismissed."

"No one will catch us. I'll be quick."

After opening the top of the girl's white blouse, he tugged at it. Then he ran his hands over her bare breasts. Dipping his head, he began doing the same thing with his mouth.

Heath froze, appalled at the indignity, but he couldn't look away.

"Samuel, stop."

She wasn't fighting or crying out, and although Heath had no intention of revealing himself up here, he wanted the guard to stop what he was doing. It was so crude and raw . . . and it must be awful for the girl.

Then it got worse. Samuel grasped at the girl's skirts, pulling them up, exposing the rest of her body, and he pushed himself inside her, breathing hard as he did so. Heath's dismay grew as he lay there silently, just watching.

It went on for a while.

Heath knew the principle of such things . . . and they happened between men and women. Intellectually, he knew that his father and mother had acted out something of this nature to conceive their children, but he'd never realized what the woman had to endure. The sheer animal nature of it continued to fill him with horror.

Below, Samuel gasped, and a moment later, he rolled off the girl, leaving her lying there with most of her skirt up around her stomach.

"We'd best get out of here now," he said.

She began to cover herself, and when she was ready, they left.

Heath took shallow breaths. To date, his fear . . . his

terror had been that Rochelle would be married off and taken away from Quillette. That fear paled next to what he felt now. If Uncle Hamish married her to one of these men who followed her with their eyes, she would have to endure what the servant girl had just endured.

Rochelle was no serving girl.

She was fragile and innocent, and she would not be able to withstand such treatment.

Somehow he had to save her.

As Heath and Rochelle's seventeenth year wound to a close, she'd still managed to avoid her uncle accepting any offers. This brought Heath great relief, but he was troubled by the way a few of the manor guards never stopped watching Rochelle with their eyes.

One of them was particularly troubling. He was a new man Maddox had hired, and his name was Keenan. He was tall and muscular, with a handsome, weathered face. Rochelle took to riding more often, and she would ask him to saddle her horse.

Heath accompanied her when she allowed him, but he hated the way Keenan watched Rochelle's every move. A few weeks passed, and she stopped riding, but she often could not be found in the middle of the afternoon.

One day, Heath was so lonely for her that he went searching in the back of the manor, and as he walked toward a corner, he heard Keenan's voice . . . inside the house.

"You must let me speak to your mother or your uncle," Keenan said heatedly. "I cannot wait much longer. I love you, but this isn't right."

"No, not yet. Let go of me."

Heath stopped. The second voice was Rochelle's. He

bolted, skidding around the corner, and then stopped again.

Keenan had Rochelle pressed against a wall. Her hair was disheveled and the top of her gown was partly unlaced.

The whole world went white. Heath roared and charged, shoving with both hands so hard that Keenan went spinning. Heath jerked the dagger from the sheath on his wrist and brought his hand in front of his chest instinctively, ready to strike.

Keenan's eyes widened.

"Heath, no!" Rochelle cried, grabbing his arm. "Don't." She turned her head and called, "Captain Maddox!" Heath looked down at her hand, and he almost threw her off. He wanted to cut Keenan's throat.

"Captain Maddox!" Rochelle shouted again.

Booted footsteps sounded, and Maddox came half running around the corner. At the sight before him, he stalled. "What in the—?"

"This new guard you hired had his hands on Rochelle!" Heath spat, still wanting to spring. "Look at her!"

When Maddox glanced at Rochelle's hair and dress, his expression turned mortified. "Oh . . . my lady."

Something about this calmed Heath slightly. A house guard laying hands on one of the noblewomen was a serious matter.

Maddox turned in a rage on Keenan. "You are dismissed without a reference. I want you out of the barracks within the hour."

"Sir . . . ," Keenan stammered. "You don't understand. She—"

"She what?" Maddox snarled. "And you'd best be careful. If you slander this lady, you'll have more to deal with than a dismissal."

Keenan stared at Rochelle for a long moment, and then he closed his mouth.

Maddox turned to Heath. "I'll take care of this matter. You take your sister to her room and then get your mother. Rochelle will need the comfort of other women."

Heath nodded and felt a wave of gratitude for Maddox. The captain had stepped in and kept Heath from doing murder—which was probably a good thing now that he had time to think. Then Maddox had dismissed the offending Keenan from service, and now he had turned Rochelle over into Heath's care.

Carefully, Heath reached up to guide his sister down the hall. Poor Rochelle. She had no idea how close she'd come to real shock and suffering.

But she had been saved.

In the days that followed Heath and Rochelle's eighteenth birthday, much in the manor remained the same—only more pronounced.

Heath's mother pressed Lord Hamish harder to accept an offer for Rochelle's hand.

Carlotta grew more and more sour until the servants began to avoid her.

Lord Hamish began to drink more of the wine stores, and a few of the serving girls put in their notice with complaints about him.

Lizbeth grew lonelier, but Heath was too wrapped up in his own concerns to do much about that.

Winter and spring crawled by.

Finally, Jace and the Móndyalítko returned in the summer, and Jace told Heath, "You're getting so good with that dagger, there's little more I can teach you." Still, Heath found some comfort in visiting the encampment.

Then . . . as that summer drew to a close, Heath noticed an oddity at home that began to bother him more and more.

Maddox was not acting like himself.

Since his arrival at the manor, he'd been the one man Heath could count on to view Rochelle with the respect she deserved. He never watched her walk across the courtyard to the stables, following her every move with his eyes—like one of the house guards. He protected her and treated her as one of his sacred charges.

In the past few weeks, that had changed. Now . . . whenever she entered a room, he, too, followed her with his eyes. He was distracted and on edge, and on a few occasions, he couldn't be found when he was needed.

This disappointed Heath, and it made him feel even more alone.

One night, Maddox was late for dinner, and everyone had been seated before he arrived. He looked troubled as he took his seat.

"Pour some wine for Captain Maddox," Lord Hamish called to a servant.

Then Heath was caught off guard when his uncle stood and raised his goblet to Rochelle. "My dear niece. Your mother and I have such news for you . . . news for the entire family. We've been in quiet talks with the house of Pählen. Your sister Carlotta received a letter this morning from Castle Kimovesk, and have now entered formal marriage negotiations between you and Prince Damek . . .

who we all know will be the next grand prince of Dro-evinka. My dearest girl . . . you will be the grand princess of our nation."

Heath sat still in his chair. Prince Damek of Ki-movesk? He couldn't have heard correctly.

Rochelle stared at her uncle and then looked down at her plate.

"Are you not happy, my sweet?" Lady Helena asked. "Is this not the best news?"

"Yes, Mother," Rochelle answered. "I am overwhelmed."

"You cannot be serious?" Heath asked, rising to his feet and looking at his mother. "Damek? Prince Damek? You know his reputation."

Lady Helena was stunned speechless at first. Then she found her voice.

"*Sit* down," she ordered, "and conduct yourself as is proper at this table. We have great cause for celebration, and you will drink to your sister's impending marriage."

Heath sat and took a sip from his goblet, but panic filled him until he wondered how long he could remain at the table.

How could Rochelle find a way out of *this*?

After dinner, Rochelle went to the stables with Captain Maddox so he could check her mare—as the mare had been limping. Heath didn't care for this, as he no longer trusted Maddox, but he used the time to seek out Carlotta in her room.

He knocked on the door.

"Yes," she called from inside.

He opened the door to see her sitting at a desk. She didn't bother to hide her surprise. In the eighteen years of his life, he'd never once come to her room. As she looked at him, he tried to push down his revulsion. Her dry hair was coming loose from its tight bun, and her entire body seemed to exude the stench of bitterness. He knew she believed men spurned her because she lacked beauty, but Heath knew better. They spurned her because she lacked the ability to laugh or to love.

"What?" she asked him.

He went inside and closed the door. "You must find a way to stop these negotiations."

Looking back down at the letter she was writing, she said, "I'll do nothing of the sort. Rochelle will marry Prince Damek."

"But surely even you have heard the rumors about him, about the harsh treatment of his people. I know you feel Rochelle has wronged you, but you cannot help tie her to such a man. She's too delicate. Imagine the indignities she will suffer."

She looked up. The conversation felt odd because the two of them had never actually spoken more than a few words to each other.

"Indignities?" Carlotta echoed, and she gave a short laugh. Apparently, she did know how to laugh, but the sound was ugly. "Why don't you try slipping into the guest quarters in the early afternoon and listen at a few doors? You'll hear some sounds that will show you how *delicate* she is. Trust me, Rochelle will do quite well for that perverse prince. Now get out. I have work to do. I'm negotiating her dowry."

The hatred in her voice was clear when she spoke Rochelle's name. Heath had known Carlotta was bitter, but he hadn't known the depth of her hatred until now.

Leaning down, he put his hands on her desk. "If you

wish to spend your time listening at keyholes and inventing poisonous fancies, that is up to you. But I will stop this marriage."

"You can't. You're nothing here. You don't have the power to order fish instead of beef for dinner. Father set you on that path, but you let him. You're a child, Heath. Now I mean it. Get out."

Stung, he turned and left the room.

She was wrong. He would stop this marriage.

However, as the days passed, he could think of nothing he could do that would cut off negotiations. Rochelle spent much of her time in fittings for gowns, and he barely saw her.

Then he overheard his mother mention an upcoming family journey, and he stopped her.

"I'm sorry, Mother, what did you say? We're taking a journey?"

She was impatient. "Yes, all of us, to Kimovesk. Carlotta is not doing as well as your uncle and I hoped, and we thought it would be a good idea for everyone to . . . meet and spend some time with him."

Heath breathed out through his nose. "You mean you want Damek to see Rochelle." For the first time, he wanted to strike his own mother.

"Don't take that tone with me! And don't worry about packing. I'll have it done for you."

She swept down the passage away from him.

He stood there, trying to think. What if this wasn't all bad? What if his mother, uncle, and Carlotta met Damek and realized they couldn't sacrifice Rochelle to him like so much chattel? But . . . what if no matter how savage he was, they would not be deterred?

In that event, Heath needed a weapon. He needed
something to use against them.

Later that night, he wasn't sure quite when the answer
came to him . . . but it was sometime in the night.

The Móndyalítko.

The next morning, he prepared himself, saddled his horse,
and rode south to the encampment. Jace was crouched by
the fire and saw him coming.

"Is everything all right?" Jace asked as Heath dismounted.

Heath never visited at this time of day. "No," he answered. "I need to speak to you alone."

Jace walked beside him down toward the creek, and
as soon as they were out of earshot of anyone else, Heath
said, "I need help."

"With what?"

"Protecting Rochelle."

Jace shook his head. "Your pretty sister? Go to Maddox."

"No, he can't help." Heath paused, wondering how to
say this. For some time, he had suspected that a number
of the stories of spells and curses that Jace's people told
around the campfire might be true. "I need a spell. Something that will kill, that cannot be traced back to me . . .
but will still look like murder. I need it to look like murder."

Jace halted in his tracks. "No."

"No, you don't have such a spell or no, you won't
help me?"

"Just no."

Heath braced himself. He hadn't wanted to do this,
but nothing was going to stop him. "My father has been

gone nearly two years, and I don't think my uncle Hamish knows of your existence. If you don't help me, I will bring you to his attention, and I'll tell him that you've been stealing wine from our stores."

The sudden look of betrayal in Jace's eyes was painful to see.

"You wouldn't do that," Jace said.

"I don't want to! I don't have a choice." Over his last few visits, Heath had noticed the gypsies' food supplies seemed low and the horses were a tad thin. He wondered if they'd had a difficult winter and spring, but he hadn't asked. Reaching into the pocket of his pants, he withdrew a large, jeweled cloak pin. "Jace, look at this. This was my father's, passed down to me. See how large the jewels are? They can be removed and sold separately. If you help me, I will pay you with this."

Jace's eyes flickered when he looked down. The cloak pin was a family heirloom, covered in rubies and emeralds. It would feed his people for years. "And if I don't help you, you'll sell us out to your uncle and have us banished?"

Heath closed his eyes. "I don't want to have to do that. Please don't force me."

"Who do you want to kill?"

"No one yet, but we're leaving for Kimovesk soon, and I need a weapon."

Jace glanced down at the cloak pin again, and then he looked away in defeat. "Come back tonight. Come to my wagon."

When Heath returned that night, he expected to find an old crone of some kind waiting with Jace inside the wagon. Instead, Jace was alone.

Confused, even worried, Heath asked, "Who's going to show me how to use the spell?"

"I am." Jace sounded tense, even angry, but he motioned Heath inside and closed the door. "You'll need a fire for when you actually cast. But we have to keep this to ourselves, so I'm just going to show you what to do."

The inside of the wagon was fairly tidy, with a bunk built into one wall. Jace had cleared a space on the floor, and he'd assembled a small collection of objects. There was an iron hook, a small cauldron, a bottle, a sharp-looking dagger, and a piece of black chalk.

"The components aren't complicated, but one of them can be difficult to obtain."

Heath felt his excitement rising. When he first thought of this, it had seemed like one of the stories he made up and acted out in his mind every night. But Jace was in earnest. He wanted the jeweled cloak pin, and he wanted to keep a place on this land for his people.

"What do I do?" Heath asked.

"First, you build a fire and get it hot. Then you draw a triangle with this black chalk, large enough to sit in cross-legged."

Without being asked, Heath drew the triangle and sat inside it.

"You'll place the hook over the flames and the cauldron on the hook," Jace instructed. He picked up the bottle. "Pour this in first. It's purified water. You just need a little to help bind the other components."

Acting out the part, even without the fire, Heath pulled the hook closer, hung the cauldron, and poured in a small amount of the water. "Is that enough?"

"Yes." Jace hesitated. "The next component is your own blood. Don't cut yourself now, but you'll need to.

The forearm is best. Then bandage it and wear a long-sleeved shirt until it heals."

Fascinated, Heath looked at the dagger, imagining himself cutting into his own arm.

Jace crouched down beside him. There was just enough room on the floor for them both. "The words are simple, too, and you say them before adding the last component."

"Which is what?"

"Hair from the head of your target . . . and that is not always easy to get."

Heath wasn't concerned. "What are the words?" Something about this still almost seemed like the games he had played with Rochelle and Lizbeth, as if he and Jace were acting out a play.

Again, Jace hesitated. "Before speaking you'll need to choose a time . . . say one hour ahead for the spell to take effect. But the words mean nothing without intent . . . and intent is everything here. As you speak them, you need to focus all of your will, as deep as you can reach, upon the image of your target and the meaning of the words. Do you understand?"

"Yes."

Turning to the cauldron, Jace sat cross-legged and closed his eyes. Heath sat in anticipation as Jace began to whisper.

"Breath that is breath will be no more. One hour's time is all you have. Breath of life that is breath of life will be no more. In one hour's time all breath is gone."

Heath repeated the words softly to himself.

"Then you drop in the strands of hair," Jace finished. "But, Heath . . . once you've done this, if your intent was strong and focused, there is no way to stop it. There is no going back."

Heath nodded. He picked up the bottle of purified water. "May I take this? I can gather everything else myself."

Glancing away, Jace nodded. Heath took out the jeweled pin and set it on the floor. Then he stood up and walked toward the door.

"Heath," Jace said from behind. "Don't come back here again."

On the journey to Kimovesk, Heath began wearing a long-sleeved black wool shirt beneath his tunic. His mother didn't care for it, but he complained of being cold. He wanted everyone to grow accustomed to seeing him in the shirt.

After a two-day journey, they rode into the courtyard of Castle Kimovesk, and their host was not even there to greet them. Instead, they were met by a repulsive captain with a long mustache and a strange, small man with a birthmark who introduced himself as Master Lionel.

The castle was dark and depressing and forbidding, and Heath couldn't imagine Rochelle spending a single night here, much less being forced into slavery as its mistress.

They were taken to their guest rooms. Heath, his uncle, his mother, and Carlotta all had their own rooms. Rochelle and Lizbeth were to share, but this was a common practice for young, unmarried women. Perhaps Carlotta's unmarried state didn't count.

When the dinner gong rang, Heath braced himself for the worst as he entered the great hall, but nothing could have prepared him for meeting Damek . . . a cruel, corrupt, selfish man with the scent of violence running just beneath the surface of his pale skin.

Damek didn't hide his disdain for Carlotta, nor did he

hide his lust for Rochelle. His manners were no better than a peasant's. Heath took in Damek's long, dark hair and feral features and felt a good deal of relief. His mother would never give Rochelle to such a creature.

But then dinner began, and with the exception of Lizbeth, everyone behaved as if this were a pleasant dinner between nobles, speaking of taxes and the weather. By the time it was over, all his relief had vanished and his fear had doubled.

Could his mother and uncle still be considering this travesty of a marriage?

That night, he realized the truth when Carlotta went to Damek's private chambers to conduct dowry negotiations. Heath wanted to explode. He grabbed his cloak, put it on, and went out into the courtyard, walking alone, preparing himself, knowing what he had to do.

While Carlotta was still engaged with Damek, he went up to the east tower and slipped into her room. Her brush was on a small dressing table. Picking it up, he pulled out an entire handful of coarse, dark, streaked hair, and he put it in the pocket of his cloak.

Then he retired for the night to his own room.

The next day, Damek had planned nothing for his guests, and he never appeared. Rochelle tried to make the best of things, and she worked on some embroidery while talking to Mother, Uncle Hamish, Carlotta, and Lizbeth.

Heath announced he was going exploring, and no one questioned this. It was something he might do. Lizbeth asked to go along, but he kindly told her to stay. Then he began to search. It took him two hours to find a door leading down, and he emerged into the guardroom of an old prison.

There was a hearth.

A little over an hour before dinner, he quietly brought down a box he'd packed himself, with an iron hook, a small cauldron, the bottle of purified water, and the chalk. He also brought bandages.

After building a fire, he set up the cauldron and drew the black triangle. He took off his tunic and shirt so he wouldn't get blood on his clothes. He poured the water and didn't flinch at holding his bare forearm over the cauldron and cutting it with his own dagger, letting blood drip.

He'd brought down a few strands of Carlotta's hair, and he laid those beside him.

Closing his eyes, he focused all his intent, all his will, onto Carlotta and whispered, *"Breath that is breath will be no more. One hour's time is all you have. Breath of life that is breath of life will be no more. In one hour's time all breath is gone."*

Opening his eyes, he dropped the strands of her hair into the cauldron. It sizzled and meshed with the blood and water.

Then he bandaged his arm tightly and put on his black wool shirt in case any spots leaked through, so they wouldn't show. He pulled his tunic over the top. He wiped away the triangle and hid the bottle, hook, and cauldron behind an old desk.

Then he went upstairs to dinner, and he watched Carlotta die. It looked as if she'd been poisoned. He even accused Damek of poisoning her to plant the idea.

After that, he waited for his mother to tell him they were leaving, that they would not stay in this castle of murder.

The announcement never came. To his disbelief, the

next day passed very much like the previous one. Several nights later, he saw his uncle Hamish go up into one of the west towers to resume negotiations with Damek.

Heath went cold.

It seemed his mother needed more incentive. Then this madness would stop, and they would take Rochelle home.

Late in the night, after Hamish had returned to his own room, Heath walked quietly to his uncle's room, slipped inside the door, and found Hamish asleep . . . or rather passed out with a half-empty pitcher of wine on the floor beside him.

Pulling his dagger, Heath leaned down and cut a lock of his uncle's hair.

The mists closed in. . . .

CHAPTER FIFTEEN

As Amelie came out of the memories, she found herself looking into Heath's face, but his expression was far away, and at some point he'd taken his left hand from her arm and now had it pressed against the wall beside her head. He still gripped the dagger in his right.

She didn't hesitate.

Pushing as hard as she could against his chest, she shoved him down the few stairs and back into the guardroom, hoping he was so disoriented he might fall. As he stumbled backward, she drew the razor-sharp dagger from her right wrist and readied herself.

She wasn't going to be able to outrun him up these stairs, and she knew it.

As his feet hit the floor of the guardroom, he managed to catch himself and keep from falling. His eyes cleared, and he looked up.

"Did you . . . you see all that?" he asked.

She knew she should act quickly, that she would only survive if she relied on the element of surprise, but there were still pieces missing from his story.

"What about Maddox?" she nearly cried. "Did you kill him?"

Heath's entire body was still. "Yes."

"Why?"

"I had to." His light brown eyes drifted. "I found him searching my room, and I knew he'd begun to wonder about me ... or perhaps about Rochelle, and he'd gone up to search our rooms. He started in mine, but he found nothing. I keep the things that I ... require down here. But I could see he'd begun to wonder. When I found him, I was kind, and I told him that I understood why he'd taken Rochelle. I told him that if he'd come with me, I'd hide him in Mother's room and then I'd go to get her and let her listen to his side of the story."

"And he agreed?"

"He seemed grateful ... beyond grateful. By that point, he must have been lost for anything else to do. I motioned him toward the door. When his back was turned, I drew my dagger, and as soon as we stepped outside together, I struck ... just as Jace taught me, through the hollow of Maddox's throat. I don't think he felt much." A flicker of regret crossed his features. "I went downstairs without knowing Lizbeth was asleep in her room. I never meant for her to find him like that."

From her position a few steps up the stairwell, Amelie looked toward the cauldron and the long strands of red-gold hair. "But why didn't you kill Damek in the onset? That would have stopped the marriage."

"And where exactly would I get strands of Damek's hair?" he asked, sounding more bold now, more in control. Then he, too, glanced at the cauldron. "I didn't want to kill him. I wanted him to suffer from our family's breaking off the betrothal. I wanted everyone to know that he was so undeserving, so filth-ridden that even a lesser family wouldn't let a daughter marry him."

Amelie pointed to the red-blond hair. "But you'd kill Rochelle?"

"I'm saving Rochelle! After all you saw, you still don't understand? Even if I stopped this marriage, Mother will only arrange another. I'm sure of it now. Over the past days, I've become more and more sure. I have to save Rochelle. I can't allow her to suffer in the bed of a man like Damek." He took a step closer. "I'm sorry, Amelie, but I have to save her."

He was mad. She'd not seen it before reading his past, and it was possible he hadn't even been attempting to hide his madness . . . but that it only came out in certain moments.

Gripping her dagger, she allowed fear into her voice. "Please, Heath. Let me go and I won't tell anyone."

The tightness in his body eased, and he shook his head. "I am sorry. But you should not have come down here." He saw her life or her death as his decision.

She launched straight at him.

Céline strode toward Saorise with a javelin gripped in her hand. Saorise stood before the cauldron lost in a trance with her eyes closed. Her lips were moving, and she raised her left hand over the cauldron.

"*Prosterno . . . eroado . . .* Anton."

At the last moment, Céline saw what Saorise held in that hand: three stands of brown hair. Anton's hair. She must have pulled them when she touched the side of his face.

Saorise let them go, and they began to fall.

With no chance to catch them, Céline kicked out from where she stood, knocking the cauldron and the iron hook into the hearth. The three strands fell harmlessly into the flames and burned instantly.

Saorise opened her eyes.

Gripping the top of the javelin with both hands, Céline swung it, catching Saorise across the face with the shaft.

At the impact, Saorise fell backward, hitting the floor and dropping the dagger. Still conscious, she grabbed the side of her face and looked up wildly. Céline shifted the spear so that she held it point down.

"It was you!" she accused. "You murdered Carlotta and Hamish. Why?"

A part of her almost didn't believe this, even though the evidence was here before her. And what of Maddox? Who killed him?

"No . . . ," Saorise tried to say, holding the side of her face, which was turning purple beneath her fingers.

"I heard you! You were about to do the same thing to Anton!"

Saorise struggled to sit up. "I did not murder Carlotta or Lord Hamish," she said more clearly now.

"Then what was this about?" Céline demanded, jerking the butt of the javelin toward the fallen cauldron. "You tell me right now, or I swear I'll go to the base of those stairs, and I'll scream until the kitchen maids come running. I'll send them for Damek, Anton, and Lady Helena, and we'll see what they have to say when they see what you've been doing."

Saorise closed her eyes briefly and then opened them again. "If I tell you, you'll have me exposed anyway."

Céline gripped the javelin tighter. "I won't, not if you haven't killed anyone yet. But I need the truth. You were casting a spell on Anton, weren't you? Something to shut off his breath?"

Saorise looked up her. "Yes," she said finally. "I don't know who killed the others, and I don't know what was used. I simply called upon a spell that would appear close enough to what happened to Carlotta and Lord Hamish that Anton would be seen as a third victim."

"Why? Why target Anton?"

"Why do you think? You saw him with his father. You saw his father with Damek. I knew Lieven somewhat favored Anton . . . but I had no idea." Her expression tinged with fear again, the same fear she'd shown upstairs. "Lieven . . . loves Anton, and he can barely bring himself to speak to Damek. I did not know that."

Realization washed over Céline. "And Damek's rise to power is your rise to power."

Saorise said nothing.

Céline's mind raced for what to do. Exposing the scene down here would only make things worse. While she believed Saorise, there were others who would not. If Damek's counselor was accused of murdering several members of the bride's family, a wedding taking place tomorrow afternoon would seem bizarre to the other nobles. Prince Lieven would not want this.

Anton's role here was to help the marriage take place.

But if Céline didn't have Saorise held accountable and stopped, Anton would be in danger.

Taking a step closer to the woman on the floor, Céline lowered her voice. "I will not expose you so long as nothing happens to Anton. But if you try this again"—she pointed to the cauldron—"and he dies, I will go to Prince Lieven, and I will tell him everything I saw here. I'll be punished for not having spoken up earlier, but I don't care. You'll be lucky if he only has you hanged. He might sentence you to a traitor's death and have your entrails cut out."

Saorise stared up in silence.

Céline half turned away. "More, I will quietly tell several people in my circle, so that I'm not the only one who knows, in case you decide I'm your main threat. If Anton dies under any suspicious means, either I or someone else who knows about your attempt here will go to Prince Lieven, and you will be sentenced to death. One way or another, I'll make certain of it." She paused, thinking on what Anton had said to Damek that night when he held his brother against the wall. "Do you believe me? Nod if you believe me."

With cold eyes, Saorise nodded.

Amelie caught Heath off guard as she rushed, and she hoped to launch straight into him and drive her dagger between his ribs.

Somehow he pivoted at the last second, and she stumbled past him, whirling and slashing down to keep him from grabbing hold of her. As he dodged to avoid her slash, she ran past him and around the back of the desk for cover.

He spun to face her.

She considered herself skilled with a dagger, but she could see from the way he moved and the way he held his blade, and from all the memories she'd seen of him in training, that she would not best him in a knife fight.

"Heath, wait," she said, lowering her blade and both her hands behind the desk so he couldn't see them.

He hesitated. She set the dagger on the desk chair and silently pulled the poisoned stiletto.

"Stop running," he said. "Stop fighting me, and I promise to make it quick."

She said nothing and remained where she stood. Slowly, he began moving again, and he came around the side of the desk.

"I promise," he repeated.

She slashed, slicing across his bare chest.

He gasped and leaped backward, his face shifting to a mask of rage. Amelie dashed from the desk toward the door at the back of the guardroom. She heard him coming after, but somehow she made it and ran through, pulling the door closed behind her and holding the handle.

"Amelie!" he shouted from the other side, and she felt the door jerk in her hands. She held on with all her strength.

He roared something inaudible and jerked again from his side . . . but it was easier for Amelie to hold on this time. The third time, she barely had to hold on at all.

"Amelie?"

Now he sounded as if he was well away from the door, and after a moment, she cracked it, peering out. He was in the center of the guardroom, weaving on his feet, and he seemed to be struggling to breathe.

When he fell to his knees, she stepped out, still gripping the stiletto. Heath fought to take in air and failed. He collapsed backward onto the floor. Whatever poison Jaromir had used on the stiletto, it was fast.

As she walked toward Heath, he seemed so young, like the boy playing a make-believe hero with his sisters.

He looked up at her in astonishment, and then he stopped breathing.

In the great hall, after a somewhat lengthy discussion of harvests and taxes, Anton excused himself from the conversation with his father when he realized he couldn't see either Céline or Amelie.

The hall was crowded, and he began to search. He didn't see Céline sitting at the tables as she'd told him.

Or had she told him she was going to the tables? Perhaps she'd meant to take her rest upstairs in her room. But that didn't seem likely, not now that they were so pressed by his father's decision to move the wedding up to tomorrow.

Still . . . she might have gone upstairs for something.

Turning, he was about to head for the east archway when he saw her coming through it, into the hall. She looked around and then came to him.

"Is everything all right?" he asked.

She smiled. "Yes, I only needed to step out for a short while." She scanned the hall. "Where's Amelie?"

"I don't know. The last time I saw her, she was still sitting with Heath, but that was some time ago. I've been caught up talking with my father."

Céline's expression grew concerned as she continued her scan. "I don't see Heath, either."

"Could they have gone for a walk in the courtyard?"

As he finished speaking, Amelie came through the east archway, but he could see something was wrong. Her hair was coming down from its pins, and her gown was disheveled. The hem was torn.

He made his way to her, and she met him with bleak eyes. "You'd better come," she said quietly. "Get Damek, Lady Helena, and Rochelle, but don't bring anyone else. Have Céline go up to Lizbeth's room and stay with her there."

Not long after, Anton found himself below the castle in the old prison of Kimovesk. He'd not been down here since he was a boy.

Now he looked down at Heath's half-naked, dead

body, and he listened as Amelie's voice went on and on, telling the story of what she'd seen in Heath's past.

Lady Helena stood stricken.

Damek examined the contents of the cauldron.

Rochelle was on the floor, kneeling beside her brother, gripping his dead arm. No one tried to stop her.

When the five of them first entered the guardroom, both Rochelle and Helena had called Amelie a liar.

But then Amelie began to speak.

She was no storyteller, not like Céline, but in a way that made these situations better. Amelie did not embellish or add color or alter her voice. She began a tale when Heath was fifteen years old. As she described a few of the games he'd played in the attic or in the forest with Rochelle and Lizbeth, Anton could see Rochelle's accusing expression begin to change.

By the time Amelie had reached Maddox attempting sword lessons, Lady Helena had gone pale.

Both women knew Amelie spoke the truth. She knew details, private details that no one could know without having seen them herself in Heath's past.

Still, the story went on, and Damek turned from the cauldron when she told of Heath going to Jace for a spell that would kill from a distance and look like murder. Amelie finished with the death of Maddox, and then she pointed down to the strands of red-gold hair still on the floor.

"He was going to kill Rochelle tonight. He thought he was saving her."

Rochelle put her face in her hands.

No one argued with Amelie or accused her of anything now.

Anton could see everyone believed her, but her eyes

were still bleak. He couldn't imagine what she'd been through this night, first having seen the warped nature of Heath's past, and then being forced to kill him herself.

For some reason, Anton's mind went back to the story Céline had told to the small crowd at the inn. He thought of all the different forms of jealousy and the tragedies that might follow as a result. Céline had been right in what she'd said that night. Between siblings, jealousy was the most dangerous emotion of all, more than hate, more than fear.

Damek walked over and looked down at the body. Then he raised his eyes to Anton. "So it's over?"

Anton was numb. "Yes. You go and tell Father."

CHAPTER SIXTEEN

The following morning, after a nearly sleepless night, Céline crawled out of bed quietly. Amelie was still asleep.

Helga raised her head from her palette on the floor, but Céline put a finger to her lips. There was a silk dressing gown with a cord hanging in the wardrobe. She'd not had a reason to use it yet, but it seemed the most expedient garment, so she pulled it on over her shift and tied it. Then she hefted her box of medical supplies

Without speaking, Helga got up, came to the door, and opened it.

Céline left the room, went up to the third floor of the tower, and found the door to Lady Helena's room.

After setting down her box, she knocked.

Almost immediately, the door opened and Lizbeth stood on the other side.

"Oh, Lizbeth," Céline whispered. "I came to check on your mother."

The previous night, Céline had ended up giving Lady Helena another spoonful of poppy syrup to help her sleep.

Lizbeth stepped back. "She's still asleep, but you can check on her."

For having lost a much-loved brother, the girl appeared remarkably well possessed, but perhaps she was still in shock.

Céline checked Lady Helena's breathing, but decided not to wake her. Instead, she turned to Lizbeth, wondering how to broach a difficult offer. "Lizbeth . . . if you ever find yourself in need of help, you know you can come to Anton, don't you? You only need to send word or come to Sèone yourself."

Lizbeth sat on the edge of the bed. "Thank you. That is good of you to say." She sounded so adult. "But I think Mother will need me now. Last night, before you came to give her the poppy syrup, she tried speaking to Rochelle. She asked Rochelle if the two of us might come to live here at Kimovesk." Lizbeth winced. "I hated that idea, but I didn't expect Rochelle to be so cold. She told Mother no, and then said that Mother would be expected to leave for Quillette the day after the wedding. It was awful. I think she blames Mother for Heath, but I also think Mother doesn't want to go home now that it will be just her and me."

Céline had no idea what to say. In such a short time, this family had lost three members to death, and now they were losing a fourth member to marriage. They had lost a valued captain who'd lived with them for the past three years. Indeed, Helena and Lizbeth would be alone in a large manor.

"I'll take care of her," Lizbeth said, touching her mother's hand.

"You were always the best of them," Céline said, "of your brother and sisters. I hope you know that."

Lizbeth's face was so serious. "Does Rochelle still have to marry Damek? I mean . . . if she said no, after all that's happened, could she still go home with us?"

"I think that's out of our hands," Céline answered, but the question made her wonder. She stood and touched Lizbeth's shoulder. "I'll come back in a little while."

Slipping from the room, she stood in the passage for a few moments, and then she walked to Rochelle's door and knocked.

"Come in."

When she opened the door, she found Rochelle sitting at the dressing table, brushing out her hair.

Their eyes met in the mirror, and Rochelle turned. "Yes?" she asked.

Céline went in. She had no idea what to say, but in spite of their purpose in coming here, in spite of their duty to help seal this marriage, she couldn't remain silent.

"After all that's happened," she said, "if you wish to escape this wedding today, no one would blame you for calling it off. You could cite distress over the death of your brother, and you could leave with Lady Helena and Lizbeth, and then later, you could quietly end things. Your mother would not object."

Rochelle assessed her carefully. "*Miss* Céline, please let me make two things clear. First, I am marrying Prince Damek this afternoon, and nothing is going to stop me. Second, I loved my brother. I am fond of Lizbeth, but Heath was the only thing in this world that I loved. I'm going to be grand princess of Droevinka, and I would have kept him at my side and given him power." Her eyes narrowed. "No matter what your sister says, he would never have done me any harm, and she killed him. I will never forget that. Never." She turned back to the mirror. "Now leave my room."

With nothing else to say, Céline left.

Later that morning, after a brief talk with his father, Anton went up to the sisters' room and knocked on the door.

Helga opened it.

Anton was relieved to see both Amelie and Céline inside. Both of them wore simple wool dresses and had not yet begun to prepare themselves for the wedding.

He hung in the doorway as all three women watched him curiously.

"What is it?" Helga asked, and then she belatedly added, "My lord."

He took a deep breath. "I've just spoken with my father, and he told me that as a reward for our success here, we'll be allowed to skip the ceremony, and we can leave as soon as we're packed. Father says he'll act as Damek's witness, and I'm excused if I wish to be."

"What?" Amelie asked. "Won't that seem ... odd? Your brother is getting married this afternoon. How will it look if we won't stay even a few hours to attend?"

"I think Damek and I are long past false displays of brotherly support."

"What do you want to do?" Céline asked.

"I thought I'd ask you."

"Truly? You truly won't mind if we leave now?" she asked.

"I'll do whatever you prefer."

She sank down onto the bed. "Oh, Anton, take us home."

CHAPTER SEVENTEEN

A day and a half later, the small contingent crossed an open field, and Céline could see Castle Sèone in the distance.

Sitting on the bench of the wagon, Helga had been criticizing Sergeant Bazin's driving for much of the journey, so Amelie trotted her little black gelding up beside the wagon, pulling Helga's attention and trying to give poor Bazin some relief.

Before leaving Kimovesk, Anton had procured Johanna a horse, and she now rode beside Rurik. Anton hadn't even questioned Céline when she told him the young woman needed a new home and position.

The weather was cool, but it wasn't raining and a break in the clouds overhead let a stream of sunlight through.

Along the journey home, Céline had had a good deal of time to think, and she was troubled by growing concerns that she didn't have as much control over her ability to see the future as she'd previously believed. During this investigation, the mists had shown her snippets of the futures of Lizbeth and Maddox and not enough to have allowed her to change the course of events.

Worse, when she read Lady Saorise, the mists had shown her scenes from two years in the future and had not shown her the scene of Saorise attempting to murder Anton. After some consideration, Céline thought she now understood why. At the reading, she'd focused all her energy on learning of Saorise's possible involvement with the deaths of Carlotta and Lord Hamish. The mists had shown her scenes to answer that question ... scenes that depicted Saorise's investment in the marriage and thus making it unlikely she was the killer.

Céline had asked a specific question, and the question had been answered. How could she learn to make the mists show her what she most needed to see? This was something she would need to explore in the coming days.

Thankfully, they were almost home.

Anton's horse drew up beside Céline's, and Anton looked down at her. Right away, she knew something was wrong.

"Céline," he began, "we're almost to Sèone, and we've all let some of our manner toward each other ... slip. I've been the worst offender, but once home again, we'll need to go back to how things were before."

"You mean I'll need to call you 'my lord' every time I address you in front of someone else?" She tried to sound light but knew she hadn't fully succeeded. They'd been through a good deal together this past week.

Some of the haunted loneliness came back into his eyes. "Yes." He looked straight ahead. "I value all that you do for me, and I wish I didn't need to ask so much of you. I wish ... I wish ..." He didn't finish the sentence.

"I have wishes, too," she said. "Have you thought about how either of us might attain them?"

"I've yet to come up with any answers." He paused. "Have you?"

"No, but perhaps we'll figure it out."

Looking down again, he nodded. "Perhaps we will."

There was about an hour of daylight remaining when Amelie and Céline finally walked through the door of their home, the Betony and Beech.

Amelie took in the sight of their familiar surroundings.

Oliver greeted them with a yawn, and then he began rubbing on Céline's legs. There was a bowl of fresh milk inside the front door.

"I'll need to send Erin a gift for looking after him," Céline said.

"Yes," Amelie answered.

Although she'd been managing to behave like herself for the most part, she had not been able to put Kimovesk behind her, no matter how hard she tried. She still smelled the dank air of Damek's castle. Whenever she closed her eyes, she saw Heath lying dead on the floor or she remembered the things she'd seen in his past.

She'd been hoping that walking through the door of her home might help, but it didn't, or at least not yet.

Céline was watching her.

"Why don't you go for a walk in the village?" Céline said. "It will do you good to be outside among the market stalls of Sèone again."

Although Amelie wasn't sure that would help, at the moment it sounded better than staying here. She didn't even want to bother changing from this wool dress into her pants—and that was saying something. "Are you sure you don't mind?"

"No, of course not. Go and take a walk."

Turning, Amélie headed back out the door. The weather was fine for autumn, and she turned toward the market.

Then she stopped.

A tall man with a goatee, wearing a tan tabard, was coming down the road toward her. He halted a few paces away.

"Jaromir," she said.

"I know you just got home, but it's been the longest week of my life. I've seen the prince is safe, and I had to come see you."

She had no response. He was so open. So honest. She'd missed him.

"I've an invitation," he went on. "A group of minstrels arrived, and they're performing this evening in the market. The village is all a-twitter. Master Earnshaw at the sweet shop has been making candied apples all day."

"Candied apples?"

Jaromir tossed a coin in the air and flashed her a grin. "I'll buy you two."

Something inside her melted. She knew she had to be cautious around him and she had no intention of becoming another in a long line of his mistresses, but at this moment, there was nothing in the world she'd rather do than go to the Sèone market with him and hear music and eat candied apples.

He held out his arm.

She took it.

ALSO AVAILABLE FROM
NATIONAL BESTSELLING AUTHOR

Barb Hendee

WITCHES IN RED
A Novel of the Mist-Torn Witches

Far to the north, the men of an isolated silver mining
community are turning into vicious "beasts" that slaughter
anyone in sight. The mines belong to the noble family of
Prince Anton—ruler of Castle Sèone and Céline and
Amelie's patron—and Anton's tyrannical father has
ordered his son to solve the mystery as a test of his
leadership. He has no choice but to send the witches into
the perilous north to use their abilities to discover the
cause of the transformations. Given how much they owe
the prince, the sisters have no choice but to go.

Together with the overprotective Lieutenant Jaromir,
Célene and Amelie enter the dark world of a far-off
mining camp tainted by fear, mistrust, and enslavement.
Now the two must draw upon strength and cunning they
never thought they possessed not only to solve the
mystery, but to survive....

Available wherever books are sold or at
penguin.com
facebook.com/acerocbooks

R0200